A Day in Summer

First published in Great Britain in 1964
This edition published 2026
Copyright © The Estate of J.L.Carr

ISBN 9781904016076

THE QUINCE TREE PRESS
www.quincetreepress.co.uk

A Day in Summer

Typeset by The Quince Tree Press. Cover design by R.D.Carr. 'Sunburst' and 'House' colophons drawn by J.L.Carr. The songbirds below are Joan Hassall's and the feather on the next page is by Thomas Bewick.

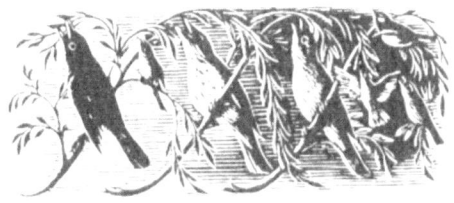

James Lloyd Carr was born in 1912, attended the village school at Carlton Miniott in the North Riding and Castleford Secondary He died in Northamptonshire in 1994.

this book is sold subject to the condition
that it shall not by way of trade or otherwise,
be lent, re-sold, hired out, or otherwise circulated
without the publisher's prior consent in any form of
binding or cover other than that in which it is
published and without a similar condition
including this condition being imposed
on the subsequent purchaser.

Printed in Great Britain

By the same author

Novels

A Day in Summer
A Season in Sinji
The Harpole Report
How Steeple Sinderby won the FA Cup
A Month in the Country
The Battle of Pollocks Crossing
What Hetty Did
Harpole & Foxberrow General Publishers

Social History

The Old Timers of Beadle County

For Children

The Red Windcheater
The Garage Mechanic
The Dustman
The Old Farm Cart
Red Foal's Coat
An Ear-ring for Anna Beer
The Green Children of the Woods
Gone with the Whirlwind

This is a Printing Office,
Cross-roads of Civilization,
Refuge of all the Arts against the Ravages of Time.
From this place Words may fly abroad
Not to perish as Waves of Sound but fix'd in Time,
Not corrupted by the hurrying Hand but verified in Proof.
Friend, you are on Safe Ground:
This is a Printing Office.

What is this world, what asketh man to have?
Now with his love, now in his colde grave
Alone, with-outen any companye.

The Knight's Tale

Morning

THE ENGINE, pulling its three coaches, steams over the plain.

Far behind it now is the city and its people, multitudinous, anonymous, stirring in patternless activities; and this train moving fussily through the early morning darkness is bringing a man from out there. He is a quite ordinary man. All his life he has stood back from things; but what he does today will make it memorable and himself suddenly extraordinary, so that it will be many years before he will be forgotten in the little town to which he is travelling.

But now it is very early and vague shapes are only beginning to appear from the darkness and May mist: hedges, stacks, dark shapes of bullocks mooching under a chestnut tree, a blurred farmhouse, chimneys and roofs, a stone horseman prancing across a stone square and a church in its yard on the farther hillside, everything grey, indistinct. In the yet wide valley of the narrowing plain, a stream draws a darker line through banks of reed and willow by a decaying mill. A wood rises like a sea-creature, shaking the darkness from its shape: a bell begins to toll.

And far off, one can hear this train approaching.

Huddled in his corner seat, alone in the compartment, Peplow raised his head and shrugged off the doze into which he had forced himself. He was stiff and cold: everything was cold.

For a moment, he tried to make out the picture on the opposite wall, half-shadowed by the luggage rack.

Felixstowe... Folkestone? Some place with a blue rug of sea spread at its doorstep with a name beginning with F. It was too flat for Folkestone. Felixstowe? What was Falmouth like? Folkestone, Felixstowe, Falmouth, Fernandez Po,

Fairyland… Great Minden. Concentrate on Great Minden: it couldn't be too far ahead now.

Great Minden. A name, nothing else! A place to meet with the other man! How odd; a town, a big village of strangers to whom neither he nor I have a single obligation…

I've never taken a day off like this before, he thought, even at school, even on the squadron. Perhaps I should have had a chit from the Manager.

["I wonder if you'd mind very much if I take Friday off?"

"I suppose not. Is someone ill? Is it urgent?"

"No - well, it is and it isn't. As a matter of fact I have to go off to a place in the country and shoot a man. Yes, that's right, a man. They call it Great Minden. Perhaps you know it?"

"Really! Great Minden! I had an aunt living near there. If you wouldn't consider it an impertinence, may I ask who - whom?"

"It's the man who ran down my boy last summer. He's with a fairground outfit, and on Friday he'll be at the Fair there I understand. So it would be very convenient."

"Naturally! Shall we see you again on Saturday? Monday?"

"Well, no. I've more or less decided it would be better for me to finish myself off too. In comfort, on the way back, all being well. It would by-pass the embarrassing formalities that usually follow. I'm sure you understand."]

He felt the now familiar giddy throbbing at his temples again and drew up sharply. This was how he had felt when he first had noticed the Manager's covert glances, when morning-coffee conversation had dwindled; when his wife had suddenly burst into tears as they sat in the garden.

He rose stiffly and stamped uncertainly up and down between the seats, pausing after a while to stare into the mirror. The face grinned mirthlessly back. He examined with interest the neatly parted hair, cut short to hide advancing greyness, the neat collar, the cricket club tie.

"Mr. Blot, the bank clerk! *Snap!*" he said quite loudly and sat down again.

Hilda didn't really believe my story about working late Thursday and finding it convenient to stay overnight in town. She didn't believe it and she didn't care. I suppose it's fair enough. Why should she? We've been scraping along on good manners. And yet before Tom was killed…

He groped into the inside pocket of his business suit, past the clumsy shape of the service revolver, and found his watch. Five forty-five; Great Minden in twenty minutes. It was almost dawn.

He rubbed away mist and dirt from the pane and peered incuriously out, at a solitary house by a big tree, a chestnut, its flower-spikes glimmering in the half-light. A farmhouse half lost in the fields, a faint light in an upper window; on his way back at the end of the day he would use it as a marker. It could as well be here as anywhere else.

His lips set stubbornly. At school, in business, on the squadron, he had hung back, uncommitted, on the fringe of things, suspicious of taking sides, becoming involved. Now they had forced him out, made him stand up and be counted one way or the other. It had taken him quite a long time, ever since the acquittal. Very well!

He looked again at his watch and taking his brief-case from the rack, moved over to the other door.

Then, suddenly, he went back to examine the picture. Felixstowe! It looks nice, he thought. We should have given it a try as a change from Cornwall.

The train began to brake. Great Minden.

Already seated at his upstairs window overlooking the little Square, Herbert Ruskin stubbed his first cigarette of the day and nudged his wheelchair so that he could prop his gross bulk on the sill. He looked down at the stone horseman and across the roofs to the hillside beyond.

Summertime! Warm mornings such as this one, before the brightness was muddied with clatter and petrol fumes! Long days, long calm days of sun, open doors, salads, strawberries, fields of green, unstirring barley, the great limestone wall of King's Chapel dim at first light, and those wonderfully still woods skirting the runway behind Dover seen from the air in the early morning, coming in from the Gravelines-Cherbourg night patrol. These were the sort of days he best remembered. He lit another cigarette and thought of past summers.

Along the passage behind him he heard water whining up the pipes; his landlady was just up. Across the Square he glimpsed a curtain twitched back to give just enough light for the butcher to dress by, fiddling about with his solid truss, pulling on long patched pants, palming in horrible false teeth. In the room above, the springs of Croser's bed grated as he grovelled and twisted deeper into it.

"Just remembering last night's bout in the hedge-bottom, you randy young tup!" Ruskin muttered. "Which one was it? Baby Doll or pussy from the parsonage?"

He remembered the long, hot summers of 1940 and 1944. Particularly 1944, a vintage year if ever there was one.

"Nineteen-hundred-and-forty-four," he said softly, giving each syllable exaggerated value. "My Last Summer!"

He repeated it.

"Nineteen-hundred-and-forty-four!"

A last summer and a last supper, when the cup had been

forced to his lips and his body broken in a crucifixion of pain. That summer of brilliant moons with no hiding place for his ridiculous Albacore lurching above the sea! That summer of long days lolling in the unmown grass and poppies by the squadron's tents, drowning in the sun! That last summer of apprehensive nights above the continental coast peering down for the tell-tale wake of E-boat, or coaster, with Mullett fretting about the tank between them, a fat bathroom cistern full of octane, and the tracer floating up all around - and wanting to stay alive.

Day after idle day, night after night of fear - until the last hour of the last summer, the dive at an unsuspected spherr-brekker and suddenly cannon fire everywhere, tearing through wires and wings! He remembered the explosion, the flames, the terrifying, hopeless fall, branches wrenching out the roots of a collapsing fuselage, the final flash, Mullett's shrieks; and then pain, like the fire itself, a prodigal blaze of terror and humiliation and, afterwards, something gone, something as well as his legs. And his last summer merging into a new season of pain.

He tossed a second half-smoked cigarette from the window.

He had heard the morning train draw into the station so that he was not surprised to see its only passenger, turning into the Square, pause and look around him. Like a Weights and Measures Inspector, he thought, *very* respectable. He was only a little surprised to see then that it was someone he had not seen for more than ten years and had never expected to see again.

That's the odd thing about all this, he thought, nothing surprises me. It's like a tunnel with people running up and down, uninvited. Croser, that ghastly tradesman opposite,

Bellenger, the parson and pussy parson, and now this one. It's all crazy, meaningless.

He leaned forward.

"Peplow!" he called softly, "Peplow!"

The man turned, not sure where to look, then seeing Ruskin, mechanically raised his hand, utterly incredulous.

"Come up." Ruskin pointed down at the door. "Come up, Peplow."

He pulled his wheelchair back from the window.

Not enthusiastic, he thought. Very definitely not too enthusiastic but more than considerably shaken. But what is he doing in Minden?

He was breathing hard and his heavy cheeks trembled. He heard uncertain footsteps on the landing.

"Here," he called. "I'm in here, in the end room, the door straight in front of you."

"Ruskin! Whatever are you doing here?"

"Live here - what's left of me. It's got to live somewhere. Even in this over-governed country they don't shut us up just because we give some people the willies and others a sharp attack of conscience. Oh, go on for God's sake, have a good look at me: I'm used to it."

"I wrote to you."

"And I didn't answer. I didn't answer anybody. Bloody considerate of me. I let you all off. You had permission to forget me. And you did. You don't need to tell me I was well at the back of the Peplow box-room. 'Ruskin R.L.H., D.F.C., pranged, said to have got the chopper, now known to be only half right. Very sad. Dossier closed. Strike him off.'"

"I wrote to your navigator's people. I remember doing that."

"Well, he couldn't write himself, poor sod, could he? Weepy-nosed Mullett! He was a damned sight too clever; it killed him. His trouble started when he passed for the grammar school and they taught him trig. He should have stayed swede-bashing; I used to tell him so. His young lady liked him in his officer's uniform, he kept saying. That's what he used to call her, 'my young lady'. He used to keep a picture frame jammed with about fifty snapshots of her and he used to stare at it to inspire him, I suppose, to bind on and on about the right-coloured stair carpet for the little semi he never had. Reams of it! My, you should have heard him scream when the fire got at him."

Peplow grimaced.

"Mullett," he said softly. "I'd forgotten. He was some sort of a clerk, a railway clerk. His father was a farm labourer."

"Well, he's a hero now. A stone in a War Cemetery somewhere says so; it's Official. And didn't he sire the Welfare State? That's better than festering away forty years in a branchline booking office isn't it? Anyway, he's safely tidied away, not left lying around to make people nervous, like me. Lucky Mullett!"

Peplow nervously rubbed his palm up and down his thigh, his pale eyes flickering across the room, anywhere to avoid the swollen torso, the quivering face, wondering how he could divert the conversation.

His anxiety was unnecessary.

"Quite a reunion, isn't it?" said Ruskin. "*Peplow*... present. *Ruskin*... half present. *Mullett*... absent (no apology received). *Bellenger*... present but has to leave early for another engagement."

Peplow stared, startled.

"Bellenger! The Old Man? He can't be."

"He can and he is."

Ruskin swivelled his chair.

"Look in the mirror. See that ridiculous statue? Well, look beyond it. It's the big house, the one with the parapet, over in the far corner, rather nice job, Queen Anne isn't it? *Chez* Bellenger!"

"Incredible!"

"Ah, my boy, life is full of incredibilities. I practically picked this place with a pin; it was just a case of anywhere to get away from my mother fussing, Dad twitching whenever he looked in my direction and both of 'em decoying like mad to distract guests who, very naturally, wanted to have a good stare at me. Especially kids; I fascinate them. Then this woman had an advert in *The Church Gazette*. ('Comfortable Home for Young Gent. Invalid not Objected to,' I think she'd put. Anyway, I had wonderful qualifications.) So I came here.

Just like that. And Bingo! Bellenger was sitting where you're sitting. 'Welcome to Great Minden!' [He even brought me a bunch of flowers.] 'I'm the Welcome Wagon Lady,' he said."

He broke into a high-pitched laugh.

"Bellenger!"

"Bellenger."

"And you came here quite by accident? It seems so odd, you two of all people."

"Why?"

"Well..."

Peplow drew up sharply. Herbert Ruskin was watching him. For a moment he saw the remembered, young, eager face peering from the grossness.

"Why?"

"Well, it is rather a coincidence, isn't it?"

[That's not what you meant. So you knew and you haven't forgotten, have you, you poker-faced bastard? No wonder they made you adjutant: seeing everything, remembering everything, saying nothing. You remember all right. How much did you know about that fortnight? And how much did Bellenger know? Well, he's past saying and, unless you've changed, you never will.]

Peplow had risen and stood, disturbed, by the window looking across the Square at the stone house. He had scarcely thought of the squadron for some years now, even when Tom was alive and, after that, everything had been pushed deeper. Involuntarily, his agitation increased.

"Wasn't he a solicitor?"

"Well, he was I suppose; he had some sort of an office in one of the downstairs rooms but the only people who went to him were too poor to go anywhere else; he didn't send bills. His wife died before the War and left him with a couple of girls who've turned out to be the godawfullest harridans you ever saw. All the same, he must have shaken the natives badly when he came back home with a gong and a baby."

He looked quizzically at Peplow.

"The baby really knocked them for six," he added. "So he hung on to it. Good for The Old Man!"

"Any family yourself, Peplow?"

"I had a boy."

"Had?"

"Killed outside the house - on the pavement. Run down by a lorry."

"Hell!"

"He was ten." Peplow turned away. "Ted Bellenger living

here!" he said.

"Dying here, so the landlady says. She says someone told her he won't last the day through. You're just in time to pick up his identity disc, Peplow."

"Dying! But I used to classify him as indestructible, more or less immortal, the oldest man who ever stayed forty. I used to think he ate bee stings or whatever one does to slow down virility seepage. Remember how women used to go for him in a big way, when we had those E.N.S.A. concert-parties and afterwards in the Mess? Some of them young enough to be his daughters. Remember that girl..."

There was a knock and the landlady shuffled in carrying a tray of toast and tea.

"We do it by telepathy, don't we?" said Ruskin. "This is Mr. Peplow; he's a private detective come to whip up some divorce business. He knows what these country towns are like when one scrapes off the surface. He's come early to catch 'em at it before they get up. Has Croser got anyone in bed with him?"

"Oh, Mr. Ruskin!" she giggled.

"Never mind," he called after her. "Tell me later, when Mr. Peplow's gone. He'll be back for lunch though."

"But isn't it inconvenient? After all it's the Fair."

"Oh, so you know that it's Feast Day?" Ruskin cocked his head but Peplow did not reply.

"You were in a bank or something weren't you? Come to check before you foreclose on some poor devil's mortgage?"

"That's about it... one way of putting it, I suppose."

"Expect to be staying a day or two?"

"No, I should be finished in time to catch the night train back."

Ruskin laughed. "You're a dry devil, Peplow. You've not

changed, have you, since 'forty-four? Still wearing the same old gag."

"Changed? Me? But we all change, don't we? We change whether we want or whether we don't. Things happen and we alter. Not much at one time maybe, but we change all right."

There was an overtone of anger in his voice.

"Things push in at you. Remember Mullett, Morrison, Brightwell, even Bellenger. Did they want it served up the way they got it? Look at yourself. Is this what you expected? Is it? Did you want things this way? Did they? Did I? Hell, we change all right."

Ruskin's fingers, clenched on the wheels of his chair, were white. Startled by this outburst, he stared into Peplow's face, at the lost, miserable eyes.

"God knows all I wanted was to be left alone, perhaps one day to land a manager's job in some backwater like Minden and then sit back and watch my boy grow up. You wouldn't say that was asking too much?"

He suddenly stopped, struggling to regain composure.

"I'm sorry," he said, going to the door. "Forget all that. I'll try to call and see Ted Bellenger."

"I don't think he'll know you; he was unconscious most of yesterday. But you ought to look in, I expect, and I'd like to know what the form is. After all it was the adj.'s job to keep us genned up, wasn't it? Lunch is at one. See you then."

[Changed! You've changed all right. Who's pushing you? Your boy; you miss him don't you? But you didn't mention your wife. Just for a minute you took down the shutters but you had 'em up again pretty quickly, too quick for me to find out why we've had the honour of a visit, you secretive bastard.]

Above, Croser turned heavily on his bed.

The sound roused Ruskin. He took a pad of cheap lined paper and a ball-point.

"Dear Rector," he wrote in round, backward-sloping hand.

"Last night your wife broke the Seventh Commandment with that school-teacher again. Croser's his name. Everybody says why don't you divorce the bitch?

"Yours truly, A parishioner who only wants to Help."

In his back kitchen, the butcher growled over his breakfast.

"Got ought special on today, love?" his wife asked anxiously.

"Ought special! Nought but them blasted Feast riff-raff from up North trying it on wangling meat on tick all day! Nought but that damned hurdy-gurdy dinning in my ears till midnight! Nought but usual haggling and arguing at P.C.C. meeting tonight! Is that ought special?"

His wife lifted the frying-pan lid and hurried to put two more rashers and another egg on his plate.

"I was just thinking," she said, and waited.

"You was thinking what?"

"I was thinking what do I have to say if Rector comes up about Churchyard and you're not in? You said you'd give him an answer one way or another by now. They say he's getting ever so worked up about it."

Her husband brought knife and fork down with an immense clatter on to his plate. For a few moments it was hard to tell if speech was prevented by an overfull heart or mouth.

"It's because you're People's Warden," she went on. "You're that essential in the town." Her superior intelligence permitted her to indulge this one retaliation for thirty humiliating years.

"No," he eventually shouted. "It's a *No*. I've made up my Mind and it's a No. Money money, it's all he's after. Money's his God. Pay, pay, pay! If he had his way, he'd take everything we addled. Now I'm telling you straight, if he wants Churchyard fettled up, he fettles it up hisself."

He repeated this with great emphasis and solemnity.

"He does it hisself. He gets his back down and he does it. And I'd tell him that to his face if he walked in here this minute and, when I'd finished telling him, then I'd ask him for that £4 16s. 4d. his trollop of a wife owes me. He must think people like me are made of money. Is there any wonder he's only preaching to pews?"

His wife put a round of bread soggy with dripping on his plate and from behind it, darted in another thrust.

"Well, that's what they say," she said sententiously, "I've heard them say it; he's getting worked up about that graveyard. I mean I'm only repeating what they say. What's it matter where you are or what it looks like on top when you're underneath, I say. I mean - think of you and your family, love. Think of all the Lambs that's buried there, your dad and mam and your grandad and his dad, what's it matter to them if they're covered with nettles or not? It's not a public park is it? Folks don't go there to sit. I mean, take last Sunday when I went to put a few flowers on your mam's grave, all that was in was a couple of dogs chasing each other and doing things."

"What would the old dad say if he could see it!" the butcher cried. "Aye, what would he say! I tell you what he'd say. He'd say it was a Disgrace, a right Disgrace, that's what he'd say. He'd say it was an Insult to them that had passed on."

"He would, he would," lamented his wife, playing on him like an instrument but not quite sure what the tune would be.

"Well then, this is what I say. Let him put his own house in order and then he can go on about us. Let him straighten up that great wife of his and then he can preach that we ought to do this and ought to do that. Aye, and until he does, us churchwardens, the pair of us, 'll see P.C.C. doesn't vote him a ha'penny for the yard. Nay, not one brass farthing!"

He brought down the flat of his hand on the table. His voice had risen, his appetite had gone.

"That's right, dear, that's right," his wife said. "But remember what the doctor told you. You haven't to let yourself get upset. Not with your arteries as they are. That and not eating too much fat."

Memory of what the doctor had said came sharply back, the churchyard turning another and more sombre face towards him.

He began anxiously to read the county cricket scores.

But his wife had still not punished him enough.

"And that man Ruskin," she said, "I only pulled back the curtains an inch or two, no more, as you were putting on your things. And there he was, glued to that window, fascinated, when you had your pants half on, fattening hisself on other people's pleasures because he can't have none hisself. They should ha' shut him away in a hospital."

Her husband shoved back his chair and rushed furiously into the shop. She poured herself a cup of tea and began a leisurely breakfast.

In the best bedroom of his house overlooking Sheep Street, Edward Bellenger, roused from semi-consciousness by a fierce spasm of pain, knew that it was morning again.

This will be my last day, he thought. I can scarcely see any more even though it's broad daylight. I can't control my urine any more. I can't even turn in my bed. I'm as helpless as a baby again. I could tell it two weeks ago. That young doctor was too jolly; he knew I was finished.

This is the last day. I can scarcely see. My eyes must look like my father's did the day he went: they were faded like the eyes of an old collie-dog. I wonder where she is; I wonder...

["He wants his bottle again. Here, Dad, here's the bottle. I'll fit it for you. You see... it's not worthwhile. Look, he's done nothing again. And the smell! We shall have to change the sheets again. Is it always like this when they're going? Wet his lips with the brandy, just a sip in the teaspoon. Look, he loves it. Look at him lick his lips. Queer, isn't it?

"Listen, that's Nicholas back from the church, send him off for the milk. Tell him he's not to come up.

"He wants the bottle again. I'll fit it. I know he won't do anything. That awful smell! When they get like this it's the best thing for them to go."]

They're crude, thought Edward Bellenger, and yet they're my own daughters. Who do they both take after? Their mother wasn't like that. Where's Nick? Why doesn't he come to see me? Does Ruskin know I'm like this? Has anyone told him? Does she remember? Where is she? And if she knew, would she come?

He struggled against rising pain as the darkness closed in again.

["Look, he's gone off again. Let's go down now. You see, I was right; it wasn't worth while telling him about that man who called. 'Peplow,' that's what he said, wasn't it? Did you notice that awful twitch under one eye? Nerves definitely."]

The squat church stood on the hill's brow. Looking back, Peplow could see Minden's plan: roofs, streets, the bronze horseman above the Square, the road to the station, the stream and the broken mill, the featureless plain. He casually wondered when the first lorries bringing in the paraphernalia of the fairground would arrive, He thought of the appalling disaster of Herbert Ruskin propped in his wheelchair, of Ted Bellenger beginning his last day, this day that, already, was scarcely going as he had planned it.

Turning away from both view and thoughts, his trouser leg was caught by a bramble runner and bending to loosen it, he became aware of the appalling state of the churchyard, a wilderness of self-sown elderberries, leaning stones, broken jam jars, matted grass and nettles. Then he heard the low murmur of voices and turned back towards the open door of the church.

It seemed empty, an arcade of thick pillars rising from the stone-flagged floor, a stunted chancel arch and, above it, Dives writhing in faded vermilion flames, stretching agonised arms to a half-obliterated Lazarus cradled in a heaven of peeling paint. Entering quietly, he knelt behind the only other communicants, two elderly women. A small boy, the acolyte, knelt in the sanctuary; the Priest faced the east window.

Listening intently, he followed the murmuring voice "'This is my blood of the New Testament... which is shed for you and for many... for the remission of sins... Do this as oft as ye shall drink it... in remembrance of Me.'"

[Ruskin; how could he have become That? What had done it? The amputation? Or what came after? That ridiculous piping voice, that mountain of fat! They had salvaged someone but it wasn't Ruskin.]

The Priest raised the chalice and drank.

Following the women, he too rose and knelt at the rail. The wafer was put into his hands and, afterwards, the cup to his lips. He involuntarily shuddered, the hair rising on his neck - was this an absolution?

The insistent murmur went on: "'Drink this in remembrance... that Christ's blood was shed for thee... and be thankful.'"

Head bent, the taste of wine in his mouth, it suddenly seemed quite natural that tomorrow, at this time, someone else would be kneeling in his place and that he would be dead.

A few moments later they parted on the flagged path. The women, much older than he had supposed, limped off towards the road and the Priest, a slightly built youngish man with an indeterminate look about him, his hands pushed up his sleeves, went slowly off into what appeared to be a wood.

The last incumbent's wife had been a pantheist, believing trees should stand and grow without restriction until they died naturally, so that the couple of acres of glebe had returned to a sort of primeval formlessness of gloom and scuffling wings. The rectory itself was in a clearing, facing a grassed-over carriage drive, its yellow bricks giving it a cold and vulgar look. On the north side, almost all its windows were permanently shuttered and, to the south, blinded by gigantic creepers. When first they had come to live here, it had seemed romantic and he had teased his newly married wife, Georgina, calling her his "*belle au bois dormant*". But now, it was just one more depressing inconvenience which he lacked the money to put right.

After the morning sun, the stone-paved passage between the locked, empty rooms chilled him. In the huge, half-furnished living-room a depressing smell of stale cigarette smoke and liquor still hung around. A tin-opener and an empty tin, a fork, a plate on which rejected sardine tails stuck in their own grease, littered the dusty table. For a few minutes he sat in one of the two prim utility armchairs, feeling the silence of his immense house settling around him - twenty-eight rooms, twenty-two of them shuttered and empty, locked, dark and still, the staircases and corridors uncarpeted and cold, four cellars each leading into the next, damp, musty, cob-webbed, utterly silent.

He took off his glasses and polished them, then rising wearily he went upstairs. Here was the room they had set aside as a private chapel, and this the study, its narrow utility bookcase half-filled with paper-backs, here the immense bathroom with its tangle of pipes, then his own bedroom… on to the end of a long passage to his wife's door. He tapped gently and went in.

Once again, the second-hand smell of tobacco and neglect.

On the muddled bed his wife sprawled face downwards, her black hair tangled across the pillow.

"Georgie!"

The sheets had slipped from her naked shoulders and back. One hand dangled over a bedside ashtray heaped with fagends and spent matches. A pile of society illustrated and physical culture magazines was scattered over the rug.

"Georgie!"

She stirred slightly, one hand groping to pull a sheet over her back.

"Go away, clear off," she muttered.

He stood irresolutely, then turned towards the door. Something caught in his feet and he stooped to disentangle her dressing gown, letting the heavy cream satin run slowly through his fingers. Then he stepped back into the corridor and quietly closed the door.

Ten minutes later, sitting alone at the table breakfasting on a plate of toast and a pot of tea, he wondered how the day would turn out. His wife's infidelity was now so open and frequent that they must be close to the final break; the congregation of his church had shrunk to a handful; he was at loggerheads with his Churchwardens and Council and in debt to tradesmen. Life seemed planless and hostile and he saw no comfort anywhere.

How had things come to this pass? Was it too late to unravel the mess, to make a new beginning with Georgie, to establish a reasonable relationship once again with the parish? He suddenly struck the table with the flat of his hand.

This was how the day must turn out. This way - he would face up to his wardens and insist that the churchyard be cleared up. This way - he would demand that the Diocese provide them with a smaller, modern house. This way - he would confront his wife's lover and tell him that the affair must end. This way - he would ask Georgie to make a new beginning with him.

A New Beginning!

It can be that, he thought with growing excitement. Now today - this Feast Day - A New Beginning!

"I saw you in Church," Peplow said to the boy who had caught up with him as he went down the hill, "Do you get up as early as this every morning?"

"Oh, no, it's Feast Day: that's why we had a mid-week Communion. We don't usually have one."

"Keen churchman, eh?" said Peplow.

"Well, I suppose I am. In a way. But I don't really like getting up early, though once you're up it's all right isn't it?"

He grinned, his big dark eyes flickering sideways.

"My father says anybody can do things he likes doing, but doing your duty is doing the things you don't like doing. He says there's too many dodgers already without any new recruits. He says we should always make a point of 'having a go'. He says it develops Character better than Cricket does."

"Hm-m-m-m-m," commented Peplow, enjoying the conversation. "Well, one's dad always knows best. Mine did too. I remember him buying me a little plaque one day when we were in Beverley, half-a-crown I think it cost him.

'The Man who Wins is the Man who Works,
The Man who Toils whilst the Next Man Shirks.'

He said that I ought to hang it over my bed and I did. He said it would make me successful and it didn't." He laughed quietly.

"Have you any children yourself and do you give them good advice?"

Peplow did not answer and the boy looked up curiously.

"Yes, I have a boy. And I *do* give him advice. Why I even kept that plaque and he hangs it over his bed too. Do you go to school here in Minden?"

"Yes, I do, but I was going away to my father's old school in September. Now I don't know whether or not I shall."

"Oh."

"He's quite ill…, my father. He hasn't been able to talk since Wednesday. That's a bad sign, isn't it?" He looked anxiously at Peplow.

"Perhaps it's only a throat complaint."

"He's quite old."

"Older than me?"

"Oh, much older than *you*. He was a navigator in the last war and a pilot in the one before that. So he must be quite old, mustn't he?"

"He must indeed."

"Yes. He says that's the only real lie he ever told, about his age when he went to join again. He says it isn't too bad to tell a lie if it isn't to avoid punishment or if it doesn't harm anyone except yourself, but one has to think a lot about it first, and weigh it up."

"Your mother?"

The boy looked quickly away.

"My father says she went away before I really knew her."

Peplow was suddenly ill at ease and they walked on in silence between hedges heavily overhung with may. A light breeze stirred the scent of the flowers: honeysuckle, fool's parsley.

"Have you come to live in Minden?"

"Me? Oh no. I just came for the day."

"For the Feast?"

"The Feast! Well, in a way I suppose. How long does it go on for?"

"Only today. Tomorrow they pack up and go. It's always this date each year - unless it falls on a Sunday, then it's held on Saturday. It's to do with the statue. Did you notice it? It's a man on a horse."

"Yes, I wondered about him. Who is he?"

"It's Sir Theodore Firbank. He led the charge of the dragoons at the great Battle of Minden and he was struck down at the Hour of Victory."

"He was, was he. I suppose he was a Cavalier."

"No, nearly everyone makes that error, my father says. The Battle of Minden wasn't here in Minden: it was in Germany. But Sir Theodore lived here, in the Hall, when he was home from his regiment, only they didn't call it Minden then. They called it Little Oatley. But when Sir Ephraim Firbank, Sir Theodore's father, heard that his son had fallen he was stricken with grief and when he came to, he had the name changed to Great Minden and the statue erected."

"How confusing!" remarked Peplow, adding hastily: "but you have explained it excellently: like a history book, in fact." They had reached the Square.

"After that he died."

"Who?"

"Sir Ephraim."

"Oh!"

"Well, I turn this way," said the boy.

"I hope you find your father better, and I hope that I'll see you again so that you can tell me some more about Minden. And, about that other thing... things often turn out all right in the end."

"Goodbye, and I hope you enjoy the Feast."

Peplow turned away. Suddenly he halted, hesitated for a moment and then called out, "Hi! You didn't tell me your name."

He stood waiting, half reluctant to hear an answer of which he already was quite sure. The years gathered in the brief interval. "It's Nicholas. I'm Nicholas Bellenger."

❀ ❀ ❀

The knocking kept on.

"It's time. It really is time, Mr. Croser. You'll be late for school. I'm not going to knock any more. This is definitely the last time. Definitely! Get up, Mr. Croser."

Mr. Croser, hearing the peevish wailing through a fog of sleep, groaned irritably.

"I'm getting up. All right, I'm getting up. I'm awake," he called in a strangled voice. "I'm awake now."

"Your bacon's done. It's been done five minutes. It's under the grill. It's spoiling. It's using up electricity. Definitely! I'm going to turn it off. It'll be cold. Unless you get up!"

She beat on the door with the flat of her hand.

Mr. Croser rolled over with a cumbrous heave and, twitching the soiled pillow over his head, muffled the accumulating cries. When he removed it, he could hear the slap-slap of his landlady's oriental slippers on the linoleum-covered landing and then the shuffle-slap as she went down the stairs.

He pushed his legs out of bed and, still not opening his eyes, fished the plate of three false teeth from a tumbler and jammed it into the front of his mouth. Then, dragging up his trousers and pushing in his shirt, he shambled off to the awful bathroom, hating the day.

I must get there early before Prosser. There's those compositions still to mark: she'll want to see them. God stop Thickness's mother coming up today. Oh, why did I hit him? I needn't have hit him. Why did I have to hit him on the head? Why did I have to do that? I could have hit him anywhere else and it would have been all right. And I'm not in the Union either. As if I wasn't bogged down enough already! Maybe Thickness didn't tell his mother...

His mind raced dangerously on like a telephone exchange with all the wires fouled.

I can't go on like this. I'll go off my rocker. One of them will have to go. I can't keep it up. It's Georgie that's doing it. I was all right just with Effie till I started up with Georgie. She's too intense; she takes it out of me. It's Prosser and her, they're running me into the ground.

He dwelt pleasurably on the picture of himself, absurdly young, irresistibly attractive, bewildered, cornered by three rapacious women bent on his corruption, on the snatching of that jewel in his bosom - his fleeting youth.

That lucky swine Ruskin, sitting on his bottom all day with sweet fanny adams to worry about, he thought sourly; the Vision had faded.

"Mr. Croser, your bacon's out. I've put it on the table. It's cold now. You're late. You'll have to hurry. Mr. Croser! Mr. Croser!"

"I'm coming down, I'm coming down," he shouted back, stifling a gust of rage, glaring fiercely into the mildewed mirror at the long sallow face, wondering for the ten thousandth time if his nose really was slightly too long.

These digs are awful, but they're cheap, he thought savagely, combing out little spurts of scurf before settling it with brilliantine. It's Ruskin who gets all the service here. Anybody'd think he was her private god on the mantelpiece the way the old binder fusses after him.

He slid his college tie until the knot covered the frayed part.

Effie, I'll stick to Effie. I'll take her away from here. I'll tell Georgie we're all washed up. Then I'll settle down with Effie. Then I'll try to suck up to Prosser and hope she'll pass my probationary teaching year. Then I'll get another job and take Effie away from this squalid dump to some place where we can live.

He began to trudge down the stairs.

Keep in with Prosser, he thought savagely... Who could?

He bolted his breakfast, brooding. Then, pushing back the teapot, he glared with distaste at the pile of unmarked composition books and wished that he had stayed behind on Thursday evening to clear them. *The Life Story of a Penny.* Blast! In what reckless moment had he chosen that title! How drab a theme it seemed this bright morning, and yet how persistently and painstakingly each child had categorised the vicissitudes of the coinage: "I was born in a big workhouse called The Mint..." "My mother was a Machine. She had a lot of other children..." "I was one of a family of brown-faced brothers..." and so on and on until unscrupulously intelligent children brought their subject to a melting end, and stupid children, crushed by the seeming indestructibility of money, dwindled into speechlessness in the middle of an incoherent sentence on the third page.

As his red pencil, circling a forgotten capital or halting a runaway sentence, stabbed mechanically across the pages, he thought of Effie and last night among the bushes by the mill pool. He considered her plump thighs and the odd smell of perspiration she carried around with her, the way she sagged when the hot encounter became too fierce, and many an indifferent author received the accolade of "Good" who only merited "Very Fair". He wondered if he had been stupid to delay the wedding until they could put down a lump sum on a semi-detached.

After all, they could join the queue for a house on the council estate; one of the bank clerks had taken one (though one had to admit that he was Welsh). He saw Effie in a *crêpe-de-Chine* nightie in a Hollywood-sized bed, a circular one, surmounted by a bulbous artificial silk eiderdown, while he undressed leisurely before a gas fire and did a few boxing lunges and feints into the mirror-panelled walls.

["I was born in a big machine with a lot of other pennies rattling in a tub, and the man said take this tubful to the bank..."]

How miraculous, stupendous, colossal it would be to go to bed early on a Saturday and to wake up very late on Sunday with her bending over him with a cup of tea and the *News of the World,* waiting obediently to snuggle in and light a fag for him and say, "And what else can I do for you, lovebird?"

She had an untidy mend in her nylons last night. When they were married he would forbid her to wear mended stockings except for housework. No sagging either - she would have to wear tighter garters so that they stayed up smooth. And she must buy much higher stiletto heels too. He desultorily circled a small "c" in "Constantinople" and crossed out "pasha" and wrote "passion" above it and indulgently awarded "Excellent".

The hot May sun shining on his head had inflamed his imagination to a more unworthy conflagration. And the other one? Georgie? His earlier depression had sloughed off, succeeded by a victorious optimism. Couldn't he enjoy the double delight: carry off Eff to the best bedroom of his council house and still drive away with Georgie in her car, say once a week? His varied personality needed variety. But could he keep up with the demands of two exciting women? Perhaps he could, if he sucked yolks of raw eggs and lay utterly relaxed for twenty minutes after lunch or disobeyed Prosser's orders about not sitting when teaching. The challenge excited him.

He ran a finger along the inside of one thigh and vigorously nodded. "I can do it," he muttered confidently. "I'm sure I can do it."

He heard Herbert Ruskin's wheels slur across the floor and, for once, felt sorry for him.

Miss Adela Prosser, Head Mistress of Minden C.E. School (All-Age-Unreorganised), pulled on her lisle stockings and then began to make the bed. Although there was only a hint of the tunnel in which, all night, still as a medieval effigy, she had lain, she began to strip blankets and sheets and to pummel and smack the feather mattress with hard, double-handed slaps, edging methodically around the bed to do it. Her nerves were on edge this morning.

When the bed was trussed down tightly, she peeped down into the street and across at the house in the trees opposite and when she was quite sure that none of the Bellengers was watching, drew back the heavy plush curtains. If she was aware of the splendour of the day she showed no sign of it.

Her elder sister was seated already in the high-ceilinged dining-room, waiting with ostentatious patience to give her cup a sharp blow with a teaspoon to show her displeasure. She had pulled her skirt above her fat knees, unloosing its lowest button so as to absorb ultimate comfort from the one-kilowatt electric fire.

"Lydia, dear, I do keep asking you not to wait for me," Miss Prosser said. "I don't mind in the least the toast being cold. In fact, I prefer my toast cold. I really do. You know I do. Please don't wait for me - ever again."

Her sister did not reply. Instead she lifted off the outer

and inner cosies from the metal pot and poured out two cups.

"One spoonful; no, one-and-a-little! Your nerves are edgy; I can hear it in your voice. I'll give you one-and-a-little."

"My nerves are perfectly settled, Lydia, and I shall only have one spoonful as usual, thank you."

The elder sister smiled deliberately at her, put in one spoonful and added a little.

"So you didn't sleep well again?" she asked, her tone mocking her words.

"I slept perfectly well. Why shouldn't I sleep well?"

"Feast Day, it worries you. Notice it every year. Nerves edgy. Always the same on Feast Day. Though I must say I'm surprised you don't grow out of it."

Miss Prosser did not reply.

"How the years go by," her sister went on. "I am fifty-five and you are fifty-two. Why, you have been Head Mistress here for twenty-two years. Fancy! Twenty-two years! You shouldn't have. Not with your brains. You ought to have gone on and become an inspector or whatever it is you have above you.

"You know perfectly well why I remained here - for Mother and Dad's sake."

"Good gracious, why? Wasn't I here? I could have looked after them well enough."

Miss Prosser stirred.

"Lydia, we've been over all this before. Dad begged me to stay. You know that as well as I do. Why do you have to keep reaping it all up?"

"Little Miss Duty! Listen to her. 'For Mother and Dad's Sake!' Little Miss Big-Heart! We all know why you stopped. I wasn't born yesterday, miss."

Miss Prosser ignored this.

"We were very fond of each other. I liked to please him. I think he grew lonely as he grew older and then, after Mother died... But must we go over all this? Can't we ever talk about anything else but what has gone? Need we live on the past? We're not young and the future is diminishing. What has gone has gone. We can't bring it back."

Her voice rose wildly and neither heard the other.

"If we can't talk about our own parents, then what can we talk about, pray? Well then, you tell me what? Talk about what?"

[The red-rimmed eyes, the pale face, the thin grey hair, the room and its users still as an old photograph: sideboard, pricked rug, coal-scuttle, the ponderous tick-tocking of the marble clock...

What can we talk about? What *can* we talk about? Indeed, yes, what? We live here together, imprisoned in this cold house by the memories of the past. We live here together because we were girls here together. We live here and we hate each other and we hate the past. And the present. And we fear the future.

This is not what we were told Life would be like. We didn't expect this. What is happening to us? What must we do? What *can* we do?

We are dying here together as our parents did. And what can we talk about? Not our thoughts, not our thoughts!]

Down by the stream, at the inner bank of a bend where the water was sluggish and meadow-sweet and rushes grew, Nick Bellenger stood. He was loitering on his way home, carrying the milk, waiting to watch the Feast go by, listening for hoofbeats, hearing the cry of other horses fenced in fields as they strained against the hawthorn hedges to watch their own kind pass down the dusty road. The lorries bringing the heavy machines and the stalls would come later.

The leading caravan was driven by the Proprietor of the Feast. The boy noted the tall bowler and that all four buttons of his corded jacket were fastened, that he had no collar or tie, only a dark green, silk handkerchief crossing at the throat with the two ends tightly drawn down under his armpits.

The old man saw the boy. The skin wrinkled at his eyes. He gravely nodded. The boy watched and smiled. His large dark eyes widened with delight. This was the Feast and this was the Proprietor of the Feast. He forgot his ill father and the now unfriendly house, his secret formless fears.

This was the Feast and he was the first to see it.

Why has he come, thought Herbert Ruskin. Why here? Not to see Bellenger or me, not just for a day off. He must know someone here. The Feast? There's some connection. But what?

But for that tic under his eye, he's scarcely changed. He looked like a bank clerk then, he looks like an orderly-room wallah now. Something's eating him. He used to be such a calm devil. You can't shake Peplow, the bods used to say. But he's shaken now all right. Calm on top - most of the time - but there's plenty bubbling below. He used to bind on about details; everything had to be just so. Now he doesn't care.

Maybe we didn't know him. He was just there. Maybe that was the important thing about him. Stone's heavy, water's wet, Peplow was there. New types coming in from training stations, the rest of us either buying it or finishing a tour of ops - but the general view was that he'd been around from when the whistle went. "Ask Peplow, he has all the gen." "Ask the adj., he knows." "Ask him, he'll even lend you his bicycle."

He never disagreed with bods.

"I'd like to string up every last one with a hook through his throat."

"That's right, old chap."

"Jerry's just like us, human, he doesn't like this any more than we do."

"That's right, old chap."

No wonder no one disliked him; no wonder no one was very fond of him. You could knock it back all night with him and you knew no more about him than before the first canfull. He must have been close before they made him adj.; afterwards, it hurt him to admit it was raining.

But he didn't miss a trick: he saw it all.

He knew about Bellenger. He knew about her. He knew about me. He's the only one who really did know what happened. The Old Man may have guessed - but Peplow knew. He knew the lot and kept quiet.

Why has he come? He belongs to the lumber room, he's out of context, he should have stayed where I put him - in my Last Summer. If he'd told me what he wanted here I could have helped him. Here, it's "Ask Ruskin, he has the gen." "Ask Ruskin, he knows." "Ask Ruskin, but he hasn't a bicycle..."

He reached for the top drawer in the chest, felt for his binoculars and began to watch the butcher and the butcher's shop.

In their stone house - scullery and room down, two bedrooms up - condemned even pre-war but still pushing like a sore thumb into the low side of the Square, the Thickness family had just finished breakfasting on bread, dripping and fried potato. They were a semi-vagrant family from the North of England who had casually taken root in the place. The eldest of the six children was Edwin, aged eleven, and the youngest was two. Despite continued child-bearing, poverty and domestic disorganisation, Mrs. Thickness, at twenty-eight, had managed to retain a great deal of the comeliness of the sixteen year-old girl who had made the bitterly repented mistake of saddling herself with an idle husband. There was a sort of ample promise about her, life bulging and pushing voluptuously out of her blouse and skirt, a slovenly Venus.

"Edwin," she said, "get down yard, lad, and pump a bucketful before thee goes off to school."

"Why can't he do it?" replied Edwin glaring at his father. "He's got nowt else to do. He hasn't a job and he's too old for school."

"Don't thee gi' me any lip," cried the man, starting up.

"Touch me. Just thee touch me," replied Edwin, thrusting out his neck. "Thee touch me. What'll tha do?"

"He'll do nought," said Mrs. Thickness, "because that's what he's best at, doing nought. Now Edwin, be a good lad and fetch me that bucketful."

"He's useless, he is," said Edwin bitterly. "All the other lads' dads got a job to go to. Why doesn't he?"

"It's the War that did it," the man said earnestly. "Ever since then..."

His wife laughed scornfully. "That War o' thine! It seems to have put the stopper on everything except eating, sleeping and thee knows what. Th'art a prince o' that. Tha never tires of it. If that War did what tha says it did, it should have clipped thee off proper and made a right tidy job of it."

"Are you going to take us to Feast tonight, Mam?" asked the boy.

"And where's brass coming from?"

"There's some in tin. You said there was half-a-crown in it kept special for Feast."

"Aye, and so there was till yesterday. Then His Lordship had to have his fags and then there was nought in t' tin."

"Thee had half o' them," her husband said resentfully.

The only reply to this was the crashing slam of the back door and a bucket. Edwin, heir to the Thickness misfortunes, had gone to school.

"Not that blouse, Effie," said her mother, "it doesn't suit your complexion, dear. That tangerine isn't for you. It's a dark person's colour. That dark sea-blue's your colour: it shows up your blondeness, if you follow me. It's a Mysterious Colour. That tangerine isn't you. I can't understand why Mr. Croser likes it as much as you say."

"Oh, don't keep on calling him Mr. Croser, Mum. You'll only go and offend him, and he says tangerine gives me Dash. He says the sure and certain sign of a provincial is to match everything, gloves to match, hat to match, till you look as if you're on your way to a chapel anniversary. You should hear him go on about it. He says this tangerine lights me up like champagne. He says tangerine's a passionate colour. He says it sort of ripens me. He's very good at expressing things."

"A passionate colour," her mother repeated doubtfully.

"Oh, Mum, not the 'passion' in magazines. It's a way of describing things like black being a 'sad' colour and green being a 'cool' colour. It's the contemporary way of saying things."

"Well, if Sidney likes it… Men are queer that way: even your dad used to like one thing better than another."

She paused, blushed faintly but went boldly on.

"When we first were married he used to beg of me to wear a black flannel nightgown."

"Black flannel! Well that's a scream. You'd have looked like an undertaker. Mum, you didn't?"

"Of course I didn't. But, all the same, he was cut up. He never asked me again, but I could see he was cut up. That's what I mean, men are queer about some things. You'll find out."

She simulated an air of mystery, but Effie was not to be diverted.

"Well, a tangerine blouse isn't a black flannel nightgown. You've got to admit that. I mean, black flannel! What a scream! Why, even when you're dead they dress you in white…"

"You needn't keep on about it. I've told you I didn't give in to him. If he'd have asked me before we were married, I don't know what I'd have said. But you know what your dad is: he's not the sort to mention nightgowns in ordinary conversation, is he?"

The two women looked at the littered breakfast table. They knew that the topic was exhausted and each hoped the other would change it.

"If Sidney likes it then I suppose you ought to wear it," her mother said eventually. "But, all the same, tangerine isn't you. You were in early last night, weren't you, dear?"

"Sidney had some compositions to mark. He's always at it: it's his Schemes-of-Work, he says. It's that Miss Prosser. She keeps on at him. That's why he looks so pale sometimes. She's got her knife into him. He says that if he isn't very careful, she can get him the sack because it's only his probationary year. He says it's nothing to do with his work; try as she might, she can't find any fault with that. It's because he's male and because she was left on the shelf that she's against him."

"We should feel sorry for her," her mother said complacently. "That tangerine blouse, dear... why don't you ask him if you could have it more rose-tangerine... darker, you see, to show up your blondeness. Put it to him like that flatter him - 'to show up your blondeness'..."

The clatter of the school bell made both glance hurriedly at the clock. Effie brushed her mother's cheek with unsmudgable lipstick.

"Oh, Mum," she said. "Sometimes on days like this when its warm and I think of things, I could burst. Do you think I'm in love... really?"

Out over on the other side of the Square from Herbert Ruskin's window, the butcher had spread-eagled a sheep's carcass upon the lintel hooks of his open door and was briskly splitting it with a cleaver. Newsboys were returning from their rounds, a postman trudged in from an expedition into the country, the seedy photographer slouched towards his failing business, shopkeepers swept their frontages and put up sunblinds. There was an air of warmth and promise and cheerful activity in the village. Somewhere behind the tree-submerged rectory a cuckoo called monotonously, insistently.

The last flurries of children rushed through the playground gates and, behind them, looking neither to right nor left, Miss Prosser, stiff like a clockwork doll, costumed for a healthy climbing holiday near Bridlington, chest out, stomach in, marched to her daily battle-front where, hovering on the last redoubts of Middle-Age, she launched forays among the rumbustious, invincible children who grew so quiet and warily defensive whenever she approached.

"Ah!" said Herbert Ruskin, "Onward, Christian Soldier!"

The County Extra-Mural tutor had told him that she was writing a memoir of her late father, her predecessor as head of this same school.

["A memoir!" he had exclaimed.

"Well, it's a long composition, but she calls it a memoir!"

"Will it be published?"

"If she can pay the printer."

"But whoever will buy it?"

"The County Library will have to buy one for its local history shelf, half a dozen more will be taken by old pupils who are prepared to believe that any material success they've had was because of his teaching instead of their inbred greed, duplicity or luck, and she will have to give the rest away to relatives at Christmas. Even half-cousins-by-marriage will get one. But it will have been worth it. Gives her purpose, nourishes her ego, delays the process of mental decay. Of course it will be quite unreadable. She writes in counting-house English as favoured by ambitious clerks at the turn of the century.

"Besides, think of the subject: Prosser *Père*, Pillar of Minden Society, never putting a foot wrong, censorious, pompous, prodigiously righteous. If a man leads too virtuous a life he has some right to exact grudging admiration from frailer flesh, but it's too much to expect us to be deliriously excited by a detailed catalogue of his excellences. And she'll entitle it *Dear Footsteps* - certain to."]

Miss Prosser, biographer, crossed her school's silent threshold and was lost in the cloakroom jungle of racks and numbered pegs, like a savage creature taking on the colour of its hunting grounds, and, at a shambling run, Mr. Croser appeared in the Square, panting and blown with too much love. Ruskin grinned. "'As pants the hart for cooling streams'," he murmured, "and Prosser hasn't even sunk her teeth into him yet for her first love-nip of the day."

He would liked to have been present.

Resembling a cockerel unexpectedly reprieved from the poultryman's hand, returning ruffled but unrepentant and rampant to his familiar midden, Miss Prosser had seated herself at the big desk in the assembly hall. Behind it she became a much more formidable character than a younger sister at the breakfast table or the devoted daughter magnified by Herbert Ruskin's binoculars. All the classrooms were grouped about this rostrum - it lay at her school's crossroads - and through the glass partitions she presided over everything that went on, a conductor detecting the faintest false note in the din of learning.

First she unlocked, opened and closed a battery of drawers in a salvo of officious bangs. Then, taking the Daily Timekeeping Book and irritably checking that one signature was missing, she glanced at her watch and drew a thick denunciatory line below the last name. She was just in time: Mr. Croser, almost running, appeared before her.

"Good morning, Miss Prosser... a fine day for the Feast once more," he said breathlessly, at the same time unclipping his propelling pencil and nudging away the blotting paper which hid the Time Book.

The inexorable red line!

"The clock must be wrong," he said in a ridiculously shrill voice.

"Nonsense, you are late. Please sign your name below the line so that I can draw the attention of the Managers to yet another unsatisfactory feature of your work - that you are incapable of being in your classroom at 8.50 a.m."

His eyes, flickering up from her blouse and across her face, noted that the high flush of her cheeks had deepened and that her grey eyes were moist.

"Oh, Lord," he groaned. "One of her Days... and I'm It."

His heart began to pound and his lips trembled.

"Very well, Miss Prosser," he managed to say, turning to escape to his room.

"And it was little else than a gross impertinence to suggest that my watch was wrong, a gross, unpardonable impertinence, especially from a teacher in his probationary year."

"Yes, Miss Prosser," he replied hopelessly. "I can't imagine what made me say it. I'm very sorry."

He noticed that two or three teachers had busied themselves near their classroom doors so as to savour tasty morsels of his humiliation.

"I have checked your lesson notes: you will find two spelling errors – 'develop' has only two 'e's' and 'grammar' ends 'ar'."

He blindly took the book and turned away.

"And call at my desk at the end of afternoon school to sign my report to the Managers - if you please," she called after him. "And send me yesterday's Composition books so that I can check your marking."

Then she hit a little desk bell several peremptory blows.

Edwin Thickness, the Big-Bell monitor, waiting in the hall corner, and, despite the previous day's affray, oddly dismayed by the discomfiture of his teacher, began to heave on the rope, sending the teachers bustling out into the playground to piece together the jumbled portents of the day and to prophesy darkly as they marshalled in their classes.

That's the bell for morning school, thought Edward Bellenger, and Nick's gone off again without seeing me. He ought to have come today. There is an Arrangement for him when I've gone. What? It will come back to me in a moment when things clear a bit. Now, I can't remember. If she knew, would she come and take him away? Was I really nothing to her? And the child too? An episode? Where is she? Will she know?

His breath came and went in short harsh gasps, his fingers twisting and picking at the hem of his sheets.

Not like this, I shouldn't go out like this. Ten years ago that was my time. I should have gone then on one of those nights, one of those frighteningly brilliant nights - God knows, I tried hard enough then - after she left me. Ostend... Gravelines... the night that Engineer's crate caught it... Heavens, how she burned in the air! Poor devils! In a great curve till she hit the sea! Dixon - was he the navigator? Hobson? Dying alone as they came back, the floor half gone. Was Peplow with him, wounded too, the other fellow dying in his arms? Was it Mullett? No, he was with Ruskin.

Among the leaves and flowers of the chestnut outside his window, a thrush began to sing and a mirror sent glances of sun darting across the bed.

What made her come to me? I was too old. Was it seeing the kids who joined the squadron and died before they knew what life was all about? "Why not have a last fling before your turn comes up too"...was it that made her come?

And it was spring.

All madness! But she got over it and I didn't. Gone without a word - why?

And Nick, the child of my dotage, and my only link with her! It baffled people. Ella and Margie, shocked or pretending to be... crazy with curiosity but wouldn't ask me, only discussed it bitterly, endlessly, behind my back: 'Who *was* the mother? Was she young? Pretty? Married? Why did she leave him? Will she come back?'

And Herbert Ruskin could have told them all they needed to know. Almost all!

A fierce, wringing pain crumpled his inside, forcing out a low, gasping moan. This was death, mean, degrading, unjust, and this was his last day. The school bell gave one final, spasmodic pulse - and stopped.

With the bell's last jangle, Herbert Ruskin saw the knot of mothers gathered at the playground's gates had stopped chattering and were looking expectantly at the school doors. It opened and small girls, mostly in white, appeared sedately, singing. Their soft voices drifted across to his window. It was the Feast Song:

> "*Mother of Christ, hear us we pray.*
> *This is Thy Day, This is Thy Day...*"

It was always the same. Child after child, in pairs, streamed out, their teachers clucking and pecking and pushing them into a wavering ring around the jaunty young general riding above their heads. And here was this man Croser, the ruffled lover, compelled to drag out a ladder like a window-cleaner.

She's riding him, decided Ruskin. She's given him the caretaker's job; a couple of big lads ought to be doing it. She's got his face in the mud and now she's grinding her heel on it. After the sweaty triumphs of last night, a *very* cold dawn!

The ladder was wrestled up against the charger's haunches. Miss Prosser's little flat figure was vibrating irritably. No, that was the wrong place, quite the wrong place.

The assistant, looking apprehensively over his shoulder, nudged it along.

Here - would this do?

No, no, no, no!

He went on, inching the ladder, still looking wretchedly for confirmation from his Head Mistress.

Her gloved hand went up imperiously... Stop!

Ruskin adjusted his field-glasses and examined Mr. Croser more closely.

Had a rough night down by the old mill-stream, he thought. And who had been Nellie Dean - his pneumatic blonde or long-legged Georgie? Could have been both by the way he's sagging. Women'll kill him before he's forty.

The shrill tune of recorders caught his attention and a group of little girls advanced from the ring, each alternate child holding up a garland of red and white may. One by one, they climbed the ladder, then placing one hand firmly round the hero's neck, manoeuvred a wreath over his tricorn and long, tapering nose, showering petals upon his epaulettes. Their school-mates began to clap.

How ridiculous! thought Ruskin, turning his binoculars

on to the bronze face. That long nose, it looks just like poor little Mullett's and I've never noticed the likeness before. I don't suppose he wanted much to die either, Mullett crouched behind the octane cistern, Sir Thomas crash-landing that charger! Men with long noses never have any luck; maybe they don't deserve any.

A moment later the procession moved reluctantly back again into the building, the shopkeepers left their doorways, fairground women loitering on caravan steps turned heavily back to their babies. Mrs. Thickness returned brooding to her vile scullery.

The inconclusive blood-bath at Minden in 1759 had once more been celebrated and Herbert Ruskin's landlady, tapping on the door, came in for his breakfast tray.

"Your friend gone?" she asked, flopping on the sofa and accepting a cigarette. "Oo, that Croser, Mr. Ruskin, he's definitely the limit. You should see the mess he's left that room of his, ashes and butt-ends all over the place. And his pillows! You should definitely see his pillows, daubed up with his hair grease. And his bed smells something awful. Stinks, some people would say. I used to think schoolteachers were respectable before he came here. And did you hear him come in last night?"

"Half-past one."

"That parson's wife again. I heard her car drive off. [Well, it isn't her car. Somebody is supposed to have lent it to her husband so he can get round to see people. That's what they say.] She lets him out in Station Street but she doesn't deceive any of us. And look here at what I found in one of his drawers."

She giggled.

Herbert Ruskin examined the photographer's group

posed in the road outside a terrace house.

"It's his folks all right," she laughed. "Look - there's his Dad. He's the image of him but for the moustache he's got extra. And his Mam. Look, his Dad's not even wearing a collar. You can see what he's used to. Working Class - definitely!"

Peplow had seen the wreathing too.

These country places are the only places for children, he thought. There's room to breathe. People know each other. Tom would have liked it here. We could have gone for bike rides on Saturdays. We could have gone fishing. I could have shown him how to rub brasses. We could have gone church-crawling: he liked learning. They all said he was a good scholar.

["What did you learn today, Tom?"

"We had about Richard the Lionheart and The Crusades and about the man who went singing round the castles till he found the King."

"…'And ye shall find the King in all his beauty.'…"

"And then we had the Rule of Three."

"It sounds like magic… Three, Three, the Rule of Three; two, two, the Lilywhite Boys! Magic."

"No, it's Arithmetic. They're If, Then and Therefores… If three pigs cost £12, then…"

"If, Then and Therefore! That's life itself, Tom - or what it ought to be. If we do this, Then this will happen and Therefore… but there's a malign Fate, older and darker than Reason! One is one and one alone but now shall never be so…"

"You're not listening to me, Daddy - you're not listening."

The voice had a hint of terror in it.

"I am, oh I am... Keep on talking, Tom. I *am* listening, I am..."]

He started and turned away. A heavy blonde girl was staring curiously at him from the open door of a hairdresser's shop; his lips must have been moving. He began to saunter unconcernedly away, tears pricking at his eyes.

"That's queer," Effie said, "talking to himself! Never seen him before. He's not a local; he must have come for the Feast. He looked ever so sad. And that twitch on his face!"

She caught a glint in a window and turned quickly.

"Ooo," she said furiously. "That awful Mr. Ruskin. It's right then what people say: he *does* spy on everybody through his binoculars. Well then!"

She turned back, took a deep breath and tightened her blouse. "So what!" she mouthed in the window's direction. "Have a good eye-full."

"Fight the good fight with all thy might," Mr. Croser sang without passion.

[My damned back; it's breaking. Isn't she going to let us sit down this morning? My mouth tastes awful. It wouldn't be so bad if I was in Prosser's position, if I could shut myself in a quiet little office and add up milk bottles or look for mistakes in other people's registers. But Teaching! Fastened in with forty-five little stinkers! "Please, sir, this, Please, sir, that..." I should have gone straight to bed after taking Effie home. My trouble is that I never know when to leave off. I must be going off my rocker. Two women! It'll kill me.]

"Run the straight race,

Through God's good grace," he mouthed.

[She doesn't care about me really - not like Eff. She doesn't love me. She's just using me to pass the time. I bet she goes off and sniggers when it's over.

Last night, up at the Mill. Boy! She must be a bit off her rocker. Maybe she's Queer - The way she lets herself go: it's frightening.]

"Lay hold on Life and it shall be
Thy joy and crown eternally."

[But what a woman! She certainly knows her Stuff O.K. Does she carry on like that with her Old Man? What a weekend with her must be like! Friday night, Saturday morning, Saturday night, Sunday morning, Sunday night, early Monday morning...]

The idea made him feel faint.

[I can't keep it up. Effie's beginning to twig something's wrong and I can't keep on telling her I've strained myself in a P.T. lesson.

But last night! A world of swirling darkness and bitter scent, a conflagration of desire! I'm not me. I don't use words like that. It's not Me. Something comes over me when she's on my mind.]

The reeling mill loft swung dizzily around him again and, for a moment, he thought he was going to collapse among the singing children. The Chief Assistant was looking curiously at him.

"Are you all right, old man?" he whispered.

[I can't marry her. How could I take her home? She's not my sort. She'd laugh her head off at Dad and Mam and our Freda. And all the aunties.

What does she see in me? She's a clever devil all right. She knows I'm not her sort. I wonder what her husband thinks about it all? It's all very nice for her - she can sleep it off while Prosser kicks me around like an old football. I bet she's still pigging it in bed...

He thought drowningly of her long limbs stretched under the sheet.]

"Quietly - crosslegged - sit," ordered Miss Prosser.

Mr. Croser collapsed on to the needlework basket. It creaked.

"Are you all right, old man?" the Chief Assistant whispered again. "You look terrible. Feeling sick?"

The children too flopped gratefully down to the hall floor; everyone was very still. From his place crushed in the middle of the multitude, the boy, Nick Bellenger, intently watched Miss Prosser. He noticed her flushed face and moist eyes. During the hymn he had heard her shrill voice half a tone sharp, dominating the singing, and he felt anxious.

The staff could have put his apprehension into words... the woman below the rostrum, pounding away at the walnut piano, had thought, Ah, she's singing sharp; it's going to be a bad day for someone.

"Someone has scratched *a Word* in the Boys' Toilets," Miss Prosser began ominously. *"An Evil Word.* It has *Four Letters.* And he wrote it not once, not twice, but three times. Three times!"

Mr. Croser, brooding on his wrongs, was jolted back into the present and began to make panic-stricken calculations of the sum of his lateness, plus an Evil Word written three times in the Toilets, plus the high flush now spreading along Miss Prosser's neck. He shuddered at his reckoning... her Report on his probationary year would sear the paper. And she hadn't mentioned God yet!

Nick, his gaze still fixed on the angry eyes, imperceptibly

moved his bottom and tried to take his mind off a tickle in his nose, too afraid to wonder what Word it was. Beside him, even the redoubtable Edwin Thickness, scratching a wart on his left hand, had become quite pale.

"Some sinful boy... some dirty-minded boy... this Evil Word... Jesus, our Blessed Saviour... sins... filth... He died that we might be forgiven... lavatory..." Their childish courage ducked as the words hissed and banged above their heads.

The piano player, looking dully at the yellow keys, thought, She's talking about Jesus. That settles it. Someone's in for it before the day's out. Croser. It *has* to be Croser; he was late. I must keep well out of her way. It ought to be Croser. Oh, please let my class behave nicely today. Please let it be somebody else. Please God, let it be Croser.

By now, the Square had filled up with lorries, trailers, caravans, all the paraphernalia of a fair and its people, busy as ants, throwing up their one-day town. Everything was happening at once and sounded so. First, the bare ribs of stalls and booths, like a winter undergrowth of red willows skirting the deeper thicket of helter-skelters, flying-boats and the roundabout. The hub of all this contrivance, the huge steam-organ in all its brassy opulence, incongruously rubbed shoulders with the garlanded Victor of Minden prancing above the din and confusion.

The butcher, turning from hanging a welcoming sign to the newcomers: *Cash Only - No Credit* above his threshold, looked again for the strapping tawny girl with whom he had made a very satisfactory barter arrangement last year.

Effie came to the door of her boutique.

"Well, it's only once a year, thank goodness," she said to the photographer's mate. That was the thing one should say. If one wanted to have a footing in local society, one had to say things like that. But in her heart a vague childish excitement stirred - The Feast, the Roundabouts. The Organ! Just then, she heard someone exclaim scornfully "Botike! What's a botike? Why don't she call the bloody place a barber's shop for tarts?"

Effie drew in her breath sharply. It was the Proprietor's elder son. He turned and looked sourly at her. "Botike!" he repeated.

This was a new view of her trade and she refused to consider it.

"Thank Heaven, it's only once a year," she repeated with convincing emphasis. "Scum! Vulgar scum!" And she was only partly mollified when a little girl, bright eyed, dark-skinned, told an even smaller companion to look at that lady with the beautiful golden hair like a princess's.

Inside the school, the children, turning impassive faces at their teachers, shut out the irritable or earnest instructions and listened ecstatically to the exciting banging and squeaking going on behind the frosted panes, hurrying away from the dusty plains of arithmetic to the magic forests of the Feast. Mr. Croser, flicking the pages of The Old Testament, heard it and wondered how cheaply he could spend the evening. Miss Prosser heard it and bitterly remembered a Feast of ten years ago.

Looking down over the hither and thither, Herbert Ruskin momentarily forgot Peplow and Bellenger in the pleasant expectation of a day out of line and the hope of a little craziness before the end of it. He watched the skilful putting together of everything by men who seemed to have contracted out of cramping social obligations, men with the brazen look of freedom about them! He particularly watched one across by the hairdressing establishment, a man of about thirty, tall and handsome, purposeful as a wild animal in his movements, who as he watched, nonchalantly strolled off to a waiting woman. He saw how provocatively close he stood without quite touching her body, so that the woman had to bend back her head, taking in every word, every movement of his face.

She was a local woman - a Mrs. Thickness. Ah, so you are taking bookings early then? Ruskin thought sardonically. An organiser! An early bird. Can it be that Mr. Thickness is not furnishing his quiver with as potent arrows as of yore! Or is it desire that faileth? Poor Mrs. Thickness! Poor Mr. Thickness! And the Feast cometh but once a year. My! Love! Music! Heat! Why do people pay to be flea-bitten on the Costa Brava when Minden's just round the corner? We should call it La Fiesta and all wear masks.

From the window of the Post Office, Peplow too was watching the couple and his body shuddered with a sudden spasm of blazing anger so that he grasped the edge of the desk. When last he had seen this man he had been grinning with relief, slapping his oafish brother's back, half dancing to the pub opposite the Assize Court to celebrate his acquittal. Above, a timber cross-piece reared into the sky, it's very purposelessness suggesting purpose. Somewhere tonight, Peplow thought, there will be a quiet spot, away from the lights. And that will be the place.

Mr. Croser herded his immense class back into its huddle of desks and battened it down until playtime. He hurriedly scanned his Record Book under the heading *Scripture,* and found that he was not due out of Chronicles I until the following week. He wondered if he dared skip ahead into Chronicles II and get his teeth into the Queen of Sheba... the Queen of Sheba was something one put some Life into, whereas Chronicles I was a mere Hebrew Debrett and Stud Book.

"Not with Prosser in her present mood," he decided prudently. "She'd be certain to come in and find me in the wrong Book."

The waiting class was becoming restless.

"Quiet!" he shouted, flicking the pages, praying for inspiration.

"'Sibbecai the Hushattite, Maharai the Nepothathite, Azmareth the Baharmarite,'" he read scornfully. No meat in them. If this was the Scholarship Class, I could make a reading test out of it, but half of this shower can scarcely read *Old Dog Tom.*

"So-and-So begat So-and-So," he muttered. "It's sex disguised as Biography, but then, that's what Life boils down to... So-and-So begat So-and-So... its a revelation."

He wondered if he had time for a quiet read, with the desklid up, at the Song of Solomon. It's this heat, he thought desperately, I'm randy.

"Please, sir," called Thickness boldly. "Can we take out crayons and draw something while you're finding the place?"

"Stay in at playtime and write out Psalm twenty-three," Mr. Croser answered mechanically. "Here, what's this... 'Benaiah, the son of Jehoida; he went down and slew a lion in a pit on a snowy day.'"

He hurriedly sought other information. There was none. Only these bare bones of the story stuck up, still exposed in a desert of genealogy, after ten thousand years... "and slew a lion in a pit on a snowy day."

Mr. Croser braced himself, took a deep breath and let the wind of inspiration blow where it listed.

"Now," he began, "I will tell you, as a Special Treat, about the great Prophet Benaiah, one of the best known warriors of The Old Testament..."

He carefully wrote a time-consuming copy of "B-e-n-a-i-a-h" in Marion Richardson script on the board.

"When this Benaiah was at school, he could fight all the other boys in the playground. He also was top of his class and a Monitor. He had everything ready for his teacher at nine o'clock and frequently brought him sacrifices such as flowers and fruits. What a Boy! I could do with a Benaiah or two in this class."

He wondered if he dared add, "and an occasional packet of cigarettes," but once more decided on prudence. The class was listening intently. To be Monitor was an honour more to be desired than to be a Judge of Israel.

"In the evenings he delivered newspapers and mowed lawns so that he could buy coal for his aged mother and tobacco for his aged father. Of course he passed the Scholarship."

"What was his favourite lesson?" asked Thickness.

"Naturally, arithmetic," snapped Mr. Croser. "Problems!"

"Oh!" Thickness said dispiritedly and sagged back into his desk.

"When he left the grammar school (where he had been a prefect) he worked for the king. He was a Civil Servant. One day this king was in real trouble. He sent for his counsellors... 'Find me a real tough man for a real tough job,' he said... 'One who doesn't smoke, drink, swear or sap his strength in any other unseemly way.'"

"What does 'sap his strength' mean?" Thickness's hand was up again.

"Ask your dad; he knows," Mr. Croser shot back, regretting it almost immediately. "And they all with one accord, cried, 'Benaiah! Benaiah, long live Benaiah' (And also his grandad, the great Obadiah)" he added gratuitously, eloquence going to his head.

"'Now Benaiah,' said the king, 'there's a great big lion roaming around that has devoured fourteen people so far this Hungry Season, and he's on the job again and I want it stopped. Now sally forth and get thee thy sharpest spear and go thou and slay it,' and Benaiah said Yea, that he would.

"Now outside it was snowing hard but Benaiah didn't give it a thought. He turned his back on the Christmas Party which was raging all around, the free bar and buffet and dancing girls, and he got out his skis and..."

The bell rang.

"I'll finish it tomorrow," said Mr. Croser. "Get out your arithmetic books - and look sharp. We'll start with some Mental... 'If one car has four wheels, how many wheels will twenty-eight cars have?' No, the steering wheel doesn't count."

They all thought hard about cars and Mr. Croser thought about one car... She would be up by now, and just lolling about... resting.

A high wall of crumbling stone trapped and held the heat in the garden, tangled, neglected, untilled, a wild place of broken glass-houses, brambles, choked trees and knee-deep weeds. To the rector, it was yet another mirror to his inadequacy and he avoided visiting it. It was weeks since he had been here, longer than weeks, an autumn ago and, now, the brown stalks of the Michaelmas daisies and golden rod still stood up among the new growth. Bindweed straggled across the peony and rose bushes, the blackcurrants were almost lost among nettles, the raspberry canes had broken order and deteriorated into a green mob.

Soon, he thought, the paths too will disappear and the birds and small creatures will own it completely once more.

He walked slowly along the alleyways matted with last year's and the year before's decaying leaves. Then he stopped. Only another pace away, his wife was kneeling. At once she turned and saw him.

"Georgie... my dear... what are you doing here?" he exclaimed.

She rose, flicking the corded knees of her slacks, and threw down a trowel.

"Why, you've a little garden here."

[How can I get away? I shouldn't have found her here. She will never come again. It will be still another link gone. How little I really know her. And now it is almost too late.]

"Georgie, what a delightful little spot you have made! Those foxgloves, wild ones! You must have brought them back from one of your drives in the country. May I peep?"

She pushed past him.

[Be quiet. Leave it alone before it's too late. You're just chattering. If you must talk, say what is in your heart. Tell her it is breaking, that you want to make a new beginning, that you love her...]

"Don't just ignore me, Georgie," he said bitterly, turning quickly to hold her arm. "I can't bear it."

As his fingers touched the dark silk of her shirt, she

stopped as if he had burnt her and stood quite still. His hand fell.

"Georgie, listen. We can make a New Beginning. Please let's try again. Please. Let's fight back. Let's not have Minden beat us. We weren't like this when we came here. Remember? I'll start a club for the teenagers; perhaps you could get a dramatic society going for the young married couples - something simple to begin with like The *Cat and the Canary* and then, you know, work up to things like *The Farmer's Wife*, Galsworthy, maybe *Candida*. You could play the lead to give them a standard. And the Teenagers' Club could make the sets. They could have one of our empty rooms; I read about it in *The Spectator*, they call it a Theatre Workshop.

"We could do it. I'm sure we could do it..."

He had begun speaking hurriedly but, gradually, his voice lost confidence and he ended lamely, "And we could bring new life to this awful place and maybe to ourselves... begin all over again as it used to be. Remember?"

For a moment it seemed that she would go without answering, but she turned.

"You really believe that? Really? That there is a place in this sink for us? Don't you understand that they loathe you almost as much as they despise me. You're finished; you've had it. They don't want you. They're waiting for you to go. So far, they've only been trying to freeze you out but if you don't go soon, they'll throw you out... petition the bishop or whatever one does to be rid of a failed priest. Have you no pride left at all? This everlasting wrangling with the wardens over this or that! What's the latest feud? The graveyard? Start a dramatic society! At least I know when I'm a washout."

"You had that year in rep."

"Yes - I had that year in rep," she mimicked - "doing what? Walking on and walking off. That's all. And I wouldn't even have got that far if I hadn't bulged in all the right places so they could sell a half-row nightly to aged incapables. The only thing I ever did well in my life was to ride and I was stupid enough to marry a man who could scarcely afford to buy me a bicycle. We're both washouts. For God's Sake, let's face it, then perhaps you'll come out of dreamland."

"I'll look for a better living - with a modern house - perhaps a school chaplaincy…"

"It's past that now. Money or lack of it can't alter things. We can't begin again. Something's happened and nothing you or I can do will change it…" Her voice was dull and without emphasis. "I could scream when you come near me."

All at once her voice rose hysterically.

"Now do you understand?" she cried.

His face turned very pale, his lips trembled and he remained quite motionless as she turned away.

"Georgie, our marriage! It mustn't break up. We made our vows…"

A wood pigeon answered another across the silence: a cat, half-wild, appeared from the raspberries and slipped away.

"I need you. I don't think I can go on here without you. I've been thinking. Bellenger is dying, his daughters don't want to keep Nicholas. They might let us have him here with us: we could adopt him… It might help us to go on. A child! He needs us: perhaps we need him."

When he raised his eyes she had gone.

When I'm married, thought Effie, I'll not stick this for long. If he won't let me give up the Business, I'll have a baby whether he wants one or not. It's not that I want a baby, feeling sick for weeks and weeks and always having to trail around with prams and pushers and wet squares. But it can't be worse than this.

Her next client sidled in.

"Good morning!" she said to the floor. "I hope you don't mind me being so late."

Effie smiled as brightly as Madam Lucille's Salon had laboriously taught her.

"I know how difficult it is for you country people," she answered. "What with the buses... it must be very difficult."

"Oh, but I wouldn't want to live in the town," said the Client, "I just couldn't bring myself to live here."

"You like the quiet and the birds singing, I expect. Yes, sit here."

"Oh, it's not that. There's always such Things going on in a town like Minden, isn't there? It would make me nervous."

[You ought to have your head examined, you stupid creature, thought Effie. Nothing's "went on" here since the Year Dot, which was a long time ago.]

"Yes, all sorts of things go on in Minden," she answered enigmatically.

"I'd be frightened," said the Client.

[I wonder what she's fishing for, wondered Effie.]

"Did that Mr. Loatley ever turn up again?" asked the Client in uninterested tones.

[Oh, so that's it - the Great Loatley Mystery!]

"Mr. Loatley?" Effie said. "I don't think I've ever heard of him. You did say '*Loatley*' didn't you? Was there something about him? There's a Mrs. Loatley but not a Mr. Loatley as I've heard of. Just turn your head... that's beautiful."

"It was funny how he just disappeared, wasn't it," said the

Client. "I remember him ever so well. He had a big fair moustache and a red face. He used to sing at our Chapel Socials - 'Jerusalem' and 'Watchman, what of the Night?' We used to like him: he was ever so jolly."

"I shall have to ask my mother about it," replied Effie, knowing the answer to that one… "I expect he went off to Australia or lost his Memory or something. There's usually an explanation, isn't there?"

"Oh, but nobody saw him go, did they," said the Client, "at least, so I've heard. He didn't go on the trains and you know what it's like in the country: somebody's bound to see you on the road or in the fields. Poor Mrs. Loatley! It must worry her a lot wondering what became of him. She must wonder if he's alive; there's never been any talk of her marrying again, has there?"

[Who'd marry that old bag of bones? thought Effie.]

"Well, she's not so young as she was," she said.

There was a long pause. The Client's furtive eyes wandered around the floor, seeing nothing in particular except hair shorn from her predecessor's head which Effie slothfully had left lying. After a time she said in a hard, decisive tone: "The Police ought to do something about it."

There was another long pause.

"My husband says so," she added.

[I'll wear my barathea sheath tonight for the Feast, even though it constricts me, thought Effie, Sidney likes it and I'll wear my new red silk duster too; he hasn't seen that.]

"Why am I here?" wondered Mr. Croser, looking over the bowed heads and the cramped arms scratching at the twelve-times table; but he meant it in a geographical and not a metaphysical sense.

"Do it neat," he said flatly. "If you don't do it neat, you'll do it again, and don't forget what Miss Prosser said about flat-topped threes from now on. Everybody puts flat-tops on their threes - it's a New Rule."

A little girl in the front row, who had been working industriously, jerked up her head and began to say that she had finished. Without a glance at her work, Mr. Croser swiftly interrupted.

"It's not neat enough," he said. "Do it again, and when you've done that, do your Nine and Eight Times and then your Pence Table."

The class, learning the folly of too much zeal, changed down into bottom gear.

I shouldn't have let them talk me into going to college, he thought. I should have gone to sea like I wanted. I wish I hadn't passed my School Certificate. That's where the trouble started... when They kept on telling me, "Pass your School Certificate and you'll always have Security." Ah, he thought bitterly, That's the point I went wrong at and look where it's landed me - with a load of whining kids in my lap and a psychopath on my back. And even the job isn't secure...

I could have been in the East now, the Orient. There's Opportunities there. I could have jumped my ship and set up in Trade. In Moulmein Pagoda or Angkor Vat! I could have traded with the Natives. There's Hard Cash in it. Buying and Selling, that's where the Hard Cash is. A Trader! I would have been a Big Man out there. The Natives would have looked up to me. The White Master! Tuan Croser! They would have brought me presents to keep in with me. Those Chinese girls in the last month's *National Geographic* weren't half bad...

He ruminated pleasurably on almond eyes, black hair, high, tight silk dresses swaying, the long slit to the thigh. I could have stayed a Bachelor, he thought. I could have had two or three, maybe half a dozen concubines. At eighteen, when they started to go over, I'd give them a fiver for a dowry and pack them back to their village and take on another batch. Labour's cheap out there; I'd make it clear their only job was to keep Tuan Croser happy and content.

Thoughts of the cool, dusky room smelling of sandalwood, the ample divan, the compliant twittering shapes, all dimly resembling voluptuous Effie's, were too much for him, He felt suddenly breathless as though his legs would buckle under him.

"Stop now, children," he called. "Now write down these answers. Don't write till I tell you. All heads up. Ready! Five add five, take away four, multiply that by itself, divide that by six, add two, add four, multiply by twelve, take away forty and put down your answer. Quickly!

"Next - if six cows can eat a pasture in twelve days, how long will it take eighteen cows to eat the same pasture?

"Next - if an Eastern trader bought some bales of silk for £10 and sold them for £100, what was his profit in rupees if eight rupees make £1.

"Next..."

Minden is small enough to understand, thought Peplow. There's the Square, the road down the valley to the Station, the road past the church going off into the hills. One road in, one road out! Very convenient. Just the right number of roads for one's reasonable needs, one in, one out.

He looked around the Square.

Butcher, baker, no candlestick-maker but there's a photographer, fish-and-chips [No frying Mondays and Sundays], jeweller, undertaker, chemist, either a Buddhist temple or a Baptist chapel [can't tell at this distance], paper-shop, graveyard turn sharp left uphill. Everything that one needs for a civilized living except a picture-house. Everybody guaranteed to see everybody else twice daily and if you don't, either you're dead or he's dead. Splendid!

And this Fair - a village inside a village! Minden *en fête!*

The sun was very hot; the cold railway carriage, the dark house by the chestnut tree, even early breakfast with Herbert Ruskin already seemed remote. I should have taken a day off more frequently, he thought ironically, turning his attention to a bill tacked to a gate post.

MILLIONS NOW LIVING WILL NEVER DIE
Speaker - Mrs. Corley of Gornard
Subject - FOR THE TRUMPET SHALL SOUND
Tonight at 7.30. All Welcome.

Not too apt, he thought, and it's a definite contradiction of what I was told by the rival firm up the hill earlier on...

"Are you interested, friend?" He had not noticed the elderly woman, rather plain and tallish, standing behind the sagging iron gate.

"Why not join us tonight? There may be a message for you."

No one, as far as Peplow could remember, had interested himself in his spiritual welfare since Sunday School and inexperience thus prevented him from a prompt refusal of so abrupt an invitation.

"Have you a burden that you wish to shed?" she asked.

"Probably," he replied foolishly.

"Then you'll come?"

"Maybe I will - shall," he muttered, making to move off.

"And afterwards, we have a cup of tea together, like the brethren of old did. And it's free." Her rimless spectacles glinted as she nodded.

"Maybe I shall," he repeated.

"You look tired. Won't you come in for a moment and sit down? There's a cup of tea in the pot."

"Advance publicity?" he said.

"Publicity?"

"You know - a sort of taster. If I like it then I can have some more - after the Meeting."

She didn't smile and, half against his will, Peplow followed her to an old kitchen table standing among rough grass under an overhang of hawthorn and elderberries.

He sipped the hot, strong brew. "It's an odd title," he said. "I've not heard of it before." He pointed vaguely back to the gate. "That bill - *'Millions now living will never die'!*"

"Ah, that!" she said. "People laugh at us. Some people. It's the Second Coming when Christ will come to sit in judgement on the Nations, when the Dead will rise up and we shall all stand before the Great Seat. It's all in *Revelations*: I'll give you a book about it."

She smiled.

"You're a stranger here. Maybe you've come just for the day - for the Feast?"

"In a way," he replied. "I expect you might say I did come for the Feast - in a roundabout sort of way."

"You're not with it, then?"

"I shall be staying till the last train back, that's all. The Feast's a big thing here?"

"We count the time by it... People say 'before the Feast',

'after the Feast', 'It happened round about that Feast when it rained all day...'"

She looked up at the sky.

"It's bright enough now," she went on, "but it's building up. You watch, there'll be a storm before the day's out. It's going to be close and heavy. People will do odd things - they always do anyway on Feast Day. It's the noise and the lights. Only the electricity in the air'll make it worse. I've seen it happen times; I've lived here all my life."

Peplow looked across the dusty patch of poppies.

"It's a nice house," he said, depressed by the severe stone walls and the dreary paintwork.

"Not in this house. I haven't lived in this house all my life. This was my husband's father's house. The Loatleys lived here ever since I was a girl and before that. There's three floors."

Peplow stood up. "It was a good cup," he said, "and it was extraordinarily good of you to ask me to have one with you."

She looked at him, searching his face.

She wants to tell me something, he thought. Something's bothering her, something she's got bottled up and she can't get it out - even to a stranger who she'll never see again.

He vaguely wondered what it was.

I mustn't get involved with anyone, he decided stubbornly. Not even with Ruskin, nor Bellenger, let alone with this poor old creature. It's happening again - people just talk at me. Well those days are over. They've got to live with their troubles. We're all on our own.

"I saw you come this morning," she said. "I get up early. You're a friend of that Mr. Ruskin's, aren't you?" He nodded.

"They go on about him in Minden but he's not as bad as people say. What do they know what he has to put up with?

Only people with their own troubles understand."

She looked desperately at him. He nodded.

"You'll come back tonight?" she said. "I hope you'll come. Will you?"

His answer was lost in a rush of noise; it was playtime. The children gushed out on to the gravel like beer bursting from a bottle that has blown its cork.

"It's the toilets that make Trouble," Mr. Croser told Peplow through the fence of spears imprisoning the children. "You see, if an Accident happens, we're responsible. Especially now, in the Welfare State. You get a cut or a little bruise, even a graze, and off their parents troop up to County Hall with a great long complaint, half of it lies, and demand Damages. Damages! And then the Officials get back at us. Come down in swarms. It's all bound up with Money. Anything to do with Money brings them down from the County. It doesn't matter about Education, but Money, that's a very different matter… So one of us has to Circulate in the yard so the Head Mistress can say - well, so she can say what I've just said, that someone was Circulating in the yard at the time. Then They can fight it in the Courts."

"Well, what have the lavatories to do with it?" asked Peplow.

He had always been curious about the mechanism of schools. Besides, it still surprised him when teachers occasionally dropped their masks of infallibility to complain of tyranny.

"It's the Door," said Mr. Croser, who warmed to this one topic in the world of education which he really understood.

"Children don't have the distaste of toilets which we do.

They love to linger there. It's like a Club is to us. Their Club is the Toilets. But it's the Door really that fascinates them… just to hide behind it or push people through it or stop people going through it. If ever I rise to be a Head, do you know what I shall do, and the first thing, too?"

He paused impressively.

"I'll have a Door built in the middle of the playground."

"Really! A door! A door to where?"

"Nowhere!" Mr. Croser declared triumphantly. "Just a Door that opens and shuts with Nothing on each side of it. That's the nub of it. Then there'd be absolutely no excuse for playing in the Toilets. The Problem would be solved."

"Remarkable!" said Peplow, passing a cigarette through the railings. "Do you like teaching?"

Mr. Croser put the cigarette in his waistcoat pocket.

"I can't smoke on Duty," he said, "so I'll have it later. Oh, yes, it's a Vocation with me, I love it; it's in my blood. Why did you enquire, if I might ask?"

"You look tired."

"Do I really? Well, I was up late marking books and preparing lessons. And then I have Other Commitments. A teacher has to be a Leader in these rural communities. There are certain things they expect of us. We have Standards to maintain. Sometimes I feel quite worn out obliging people. You see, to these people we represent the Outside World. Sometimes I don't get to bed till early morning. Are you here for the Feast?"

"Yes. Do you live here?"

"Are you kidding! Me! I just lodge here. I come from a real town. Castleford! We have two rivers, the Aire and the Calder, and Canals as well. People who've been on the Continent say it's like Venice only cooler and less vermin.

We make bottles and medicines."

"How convenient!"

"There's no Life here. They're not Real People like they are up north. Here, they're all inter-bred. You don't dare open your mouth here; everybody's everybody else's half-cousin. You should try teaching their kids. It's murder. Because of the Inter-Breeding."

A middle-aged woman wearing a dust coloured linen blouse and tweed skirt came hurrying round a corner of the yard.

"The Bell, Mr. Croser!" she cried irritably, "the Bell. You're three minutes late. Ring it."

"My God!" he exclaimed in great consternation, and began to jerk a small brass bell up and down, like a mourner wringing his hands.

Mmmmm, thought Herbert Ruskin. There you go, you old witch. "Millions now living will never die!" Are you still hiding that husband of yours or is he feeding the raspberry canes? Why don't you snatch his feet up in the bath and have done with it; I'm all for efficiency.

Mrs. Loatley, making no concessions in her blue serge dress to the blazing sun, plodded along the pavement, straw bass in hand, and disappeared into the chemist's shop.

What a scorcher, he marvelled, and in May! The hillside beyond the roofs rippled in the glare and the woods on the ridge seemed to tread the air.

Ah, and here's Miss Blondie Bouncy-Busybody, prancing off for her eleven o'clock chit-chat and fag. You still haven't tumbled to what's afoot yet, have you? Perhaps I should drop you a line. But you'll get your Sid in the end: he's not really in Georgina's league. He's Third Division like you and Hartlepools United. He'll stray, rutting around but, in the end, he'll come creeping home for ego-therapy from his great big pink rubber doll.

Effie was moving disdainfully across the Square, through the half-assembled bits and pieces of the fair. She quivered as she walked and the dark, wiry man who, earlier, had been with Mrs. Thickness, straightened his back and grinned and whistled after her while his companions smirked at his forwardness.

Ruskin felt a tide of anger rising, then laughed it down. I'm behaving like an outraged ratepayer, he thought, and she isn't even on the council pay-roll.

Another series of eloquent wriggles and she was beyond his field of view and he pushed back on his wheels until he could reach a shiny set of Hollywood Annuals, thumbing his way through them to find a picture of Bridget Malabar in a foam bath... the two had exciting resemblances.

When a few minutes later he returned to his window, the rector's wife was crossing towards the butcher's shop. She was wearing a grey silk dress fitting tightly across her hips and breasts, and raising his binoculars, he examined her with pleasure.

"Hell!" he murmured, imagining the dark-skinned body beneath the rippling cloth. Priests shouldn't have wives like that. It's bad for them, gives them ideas below their station, leads them into temptation, drags them down to the bottomless pit that flameth evermore, or whatever it is. They should be forbidden by the bishop to marry anything except humble spirits with secretarial qualifications.

He watched her parley with the sour-faced butcher. Ah, no meat today! Only cutting you a thin slice off an old bill

That's bad. With a woman like you in his house, the poor man needs red, underdone bloody meat to fire his ignition. Tinned sardines won't charge his batteries, sweetie.

He remembered Croser, his cheap suit, oiled hair, hungry body. A jackal hanging about on the fringe, he thought, watching for what falls without a fight. Not like Bellenger in his hey-day, bold, predatory, wresting his quarry from the teeth of the pack. Well, every dog must have his day and this was Croser's.

The butcher had followed his customer to the door shading his eyes against the sun's blaze, and was staring after her. Ruskin focused on his face. A customer sidled past him into the darkness of the shop.

"Ah, *tu aussi,* you horrible old eunuch!" Ruskin muttered. "Back to your carcasses! What else do you want? Isn't having a little gold-mine enough?

"What a lovely thing to have, a private gold-mine! Butcher mining away and Butcher's wife and Butcher's pimply daughter, all industriously digging at it, shovelling our lumps of gold to cart off to the bank on Fridays.

"Butcher and Company. Gold-Miners.

Proprietor, ex-Home Guard corporal.

Served on his fanny holding the Minden-Gornard Sector.

(When not serving black-market chops to pals who could pay.)

Wears the Victory Medal day and night on his underclothes.

No known religion but is a churchwarden.

Keeps small gold god on slaughter house shelf.

Ambition - to dig enough gold to buy twenty Skegness chalets and live off their rents.

"What a ghastly fellow! But he has two legs."

Herbert Ruskin's knuckles whitened as he gripped the window sill and his torso shuddered. When he failed to control the trembling, his head sank into his hands, and he wept.

"It was quite an interesting little ceremony," said Peplow, stirring the coffee that the waitress had just put before him... "The crowning of the Statue, I mean."

The woman opposite him did not appear to have heard.

Then she raised her head. "I'm sorry," she said. "Did you say something? I'm afraid that I was wandering." He repeated his words.

"Oh, the Wreathing! I'm afraid that I didn't see it this morning. Did anything go wrong - it usually does?"

"Well, the young man with the ladder seemed to be having a bad time of it. He was in a bit of a flap. The woman in charge is a bit of a tyrant, I should imagine; she was handing him a good length of rod to kiss."

The woman laughed shortly.

"Are you in Minden for the Feast?"

"Yes. A sort of flying visit. I expect you live here?"

"My husband is the rector. We've lived here for five years."

"Well, it seems a pleasant enough place."

"You think so?"

"Not very exciting?"

"You should try it. Do you like whist and tennis tournaments? And being watched?"

"Not particularly."

"Stay away then."

"Well, I suppose being the rector's wife rather..., what

shall I say..."

"Say 'cramps my style'. It's true."

Peplow caught the overtones of bitterness in her voice and looked more closely at the slightly protruding eyes, the sombre look, the hint of perspiration on her upper lip.

"They watch you all the time," she said. "You can't move in the country without someone knowing about it - even at night. Country quiet! Push your ear well down and you scorch it. These people don't need television and a library. They have it all on tap - fiction and non-fiction, with a particularly strong line in pornographic biography. The pumps never close - Day and Night Lubricity Service!"

"Oh," Peplow said uncomfortably.

"Look over there, to your right. No, on the other side of the Square, a little to the left of the chemist's. There's a man in the upstairs window. Looks like a frog, no legs though. It sits there all day and half the night too, I imagine, and it watches everything, doesn't miss a trick. You know the conjuror at parties... 'Take any card from the pack - any card at all...' It's the same with him except it's, 'Take any name...' The Lady of Shalott was a novice..."

"I'm afraid that I know him," Peplow said hastily.

"Too bad," she said calmly, "I would pick him. But, anyway, there's a couple of hundred people here with almost as complete dossiers. After all, he can only see the front doors; they know what goes on in the back bedrooms."

She lit a cigarette and looked carefully at him through the smoke. She must have been thinking over her next words.

"You know, changing the sordid subject, you've not come here for any old reason, have you? You've come here for something; I'd like to know what? Oh yes, you have. I'm quite sure you have. You're on edge. That's an odd thing to say to a complete stranger, isn't it? Well, you began the conversation. Why should we always scrape about on the surface? If one can't talk to someone one will never see again, then who can one talk to? And I know that you're waiting for something to happen or you're going to make it happen."

"Do you usually jump in at the deep end like this?"

"No. But this could be an unusual day, couldn't it - for me, for you?"

"All right - I have a chore to do. But, except to me, it's not a terribly important one. It's so easy to imagine everything revolving around oneself, isn't it? I used to make a big point of taking a detached view... you know, keeping out of things, not becoming involved. I find I'm slipping, but I still think it's the right attitude. After all, who cares about one? Really cares I mean?"

"Maybe one or two," she answered. "No more than that."

"Well, why should anyone care? We're all in the same boat, we think we know one another, but we don't. We can't. It's like walking into the cinema in the middle of a picture: one has to guess what's gone before and, half the time, one's wrong. You mentioned Ruskin. Would you believe that he was one of the most handsome men - and one of the bravest I ever knew? Here, you all see him as he is: a torso, a cut-off body, with a damaged mind. Yet he remembers who he was. I know he does. And he hates what he has become."

For a moment or two each was occupied with private thoughts, Peplow already regretting his outburst.

"Perhaps you're right," she said - "but it's all terribly depressing isn't it?"

"I used to think so, and steered clear of it. Now, I feel I'm in the cesspool too."

She slowly pulled on her white gloves. All at once she leaned forward and touched the hard shape in his inside pocket.

"I learnt it at the cinema, you desperate man," she said, a slow smile suddenly giving charm to her dark face. "Don't miss. Whoever it is, he's sure to deserve it. Now I must go. I enjoyed our little talk."

Peplow stood up.

"It was nice meeting you," he replied. "Goodbye."

He followed her out, brushing against the heavily built blonde girl whom he had noticed standing outside her shop earlier in the day.

"Oh, I never thought I'd make it, dear," Effie exclaimed, puffing and placing both hands over her breasts as though to still them.

"I never thought I'd make it. That Bumby woman, she just kept yapping away... 'Do you think he'll notice it's dyed?... Do you think I ought to have it dyed?... I wouldn't for myself; it's him... He wouldn't like it grey, he'd think that I was getting *passée*... And, at the same time, he wouldn't like to think it was dyed...' The silly old basket; she looks about two hundred and one."

"I know, isn't it horrible!" replied the photographer's assistant. "It's just the same with us. Some of them just won't be their age. 'Don't make my nose too long,' they tell the Boss. 'Don't come too close... I won't smile because of my dentures... Don't put anything in your picture below the neck...' It makes you retch, doesn't it? Human beings!"

I wonder if I ought to tell her about that blackhead on her

chin, thought Effie.

They sipped genteelly at the grease-flecked coffee and blew big puffs on their cigarettes. No, she decided. She'd thank me to my face and then go away and take umbrage.

"I saw Sid outside Blatter's yesterday. Boy, was he looking those rings over! He stayed there all of ten minutes. Just staring! Every morning that comes just now, I expect you to be flashing a stone. I simply can't wait to see it. I wish I could settle down like you. It must be lovely to have a steady like Sid. And he's so handsome and distinguished! You can tell he wasn't brought up in Minden."

"He's going to take me home on his summer holidays," Effie said nonchalantly. "Castleford! He says there's two picture-houses *and* an indoor swimming bath and they have tea-dansants every day except Sunday and then, instead, you can go into the Memorial Garden or hear a Sacred Concert. I hope his family like me."

"I expect they're well-to-do. Ooooooh, I do envy you."

"Well, I suppose they are," Effie replied. "But he doesn't talk much about them. I think he had a lonely, unhappy childhood," she added romantically. "Sometimes, he looks ever so sad, a kind of haunted look in his eyes as though he wants to tell me something and can't put his feelings into words. You know!"

The photographer's assistant went to both weekly changes of the Gornard cinema's programmes and did know.

"Will he let you stay in Business when you're married?" Effie giggled and leaned forward.

"No... he says he won't share me with anybody. He says I needn't get dressed until he's gone to work," she whispered in an excess of confidence. "He says I can sit and eat breakfast in my negligee."

"It's like another world listening to you, Eff dear," the other exclaimed enviously. "None of my boyfriends ever say things like that. They're just crude. I could listen to you for hours, honest I could, hours and hours. But you know how my Boss goes on… wittling on if I'm a minute late. Well, cheerybye! Back to the dark-room. You should smell his breath today! Pickled herring! For breakfast! The peasant!"

They stubbed their fags in the saucers and went.

"I hear everything's not going too well up at the rectory," the Client said exploratively.

"Yes, it makes you think," Effie answered. "I'm not a churchgoer myself but you'd expect people like them to show a better example. But Mum says it's only a business with them, just like the rest of us. And it's a soft job, too," she added viciously, remembering her pinched toes.

"Well, I only go at Easter myself, though I was brought up Church," went on the Client. "He always seems a nice man. He doesn't try to shove Religion down your throat like the Baptists, and go on about Sin. But she's a queer one," she added slyly.

"She isn't one of my clients," said Effie. "They say she goes to Northampton to have it done. Some people are like that. They can't get it into their heads that they only pay more plus the bus-fare for exactly the same treatment. But you can't explain to some. The more they charge you, the better the hair styling, they seem to think."

"I'm sure that I'm always very satisfied here," said the Client.

[It's just what people say about her, she marvelled. She doesn't know about Sid Croser and that woman. Fancy, she's full of tittle-tattle and thinks she knows Everything, but she doesn't know That. It makes me hoot.]

"What are we going to do when you and that nice schoolteacher get married?" she probed.

"Well, I can't say. We haven't fixed on anything definite yet. Mr. Croser doesn't know whether he'll stay in Minden. He needs more scope. If you're ambitious, you need more scope, don't you? But he'll want me to give up the Business. He's laid that down."

[This was untrue. Mr. Croser several times had emphasised that having a family would drag him down the social ladder and that, unless he changed this view or Nature intervened, Effie was not expected to laze in the nest but to busy herself feathering it.]

"Do you think they'll keep together?" asked the Client, gnawing away. But Effie was lost in the ever-worrying speculation about what occupied the darker corners of Mr. Croser's fascinating mind.

"Beg pardon?" she said. "My thoughts were elsewhere." The Client repeated her question.

"Who?" asked Effie. "Oh, them two! Mum says you'd have expected him to have chosen someone more suitable. I saw her only this morning, with a man. He wasn't a Minden man neither. They were as thick as thieves. She even touched him in public."

"They say she has money of her own," the Client maliciously prodded, still closely watching Effie's face in the gilt framed mirror.

"Well, she puts plenty of it on her back. She never wears the same thing twice."

This reaction was more helpful.

"She looks her age though," pressed home the Client,

"and her hair's dyed. It has to be at her age. It's time she cut her capers. Some women can't get used to not being sweet-and-twenty anymore."

She had forgotten her original aim to pump Effie and was carried away by the recollection of her own marital disaster.

"Men!" she added bitterly. "They never grow up. They run round sniffing at every skirt like dogs, yes like slavering dogs..."

The Treatment was completed in a bleak silence and she left.

Easy to tell that what people say is right and that her husband's gone off, thought Effie, brushing away the shearings into a *Daily Mirror*. Embittered, definitely embittered! When a woman gets like that she deserves to be left. A man can only be expected to stand so much when he gets home from work. Fancy meeting that face!

And she was trying to pump me... Well, the cheek!

Effie disliked being pumped.

Mr. Croser turned to page 61 of *Teaching English to Our Children,* under the section '*Compositions... How to stimulate Children to them.*' I want something they can't go on about, he thought, something to keep the marking down. They all got too darned interested in the blasted Penny; something to pin them down to a half-page of marking and yet take up the time.

"My Life, by a Snail."... "A portrait of my Father."... "If I won a Thousand Pounds."... "When he awoke, he looked around him - Go on from there."... Just the job!

He wrote it on the blackboard.

"When he awoke, he looked around him." It's dead enough to

muzzle Shakespeare, he thought.

"And remember - no blood, no robberies, no space machines, no fairies, no battles, no cowboys or Indians, and no guns," he called out to make assurance doubly sure.

"Take up your pens. Make a deep dip, raise your faces twelve inches from the point of nib, and begin."

The class obediently bent and wrote laboriously, "When he awoke, he looked around him," then, baffled, they paused, staring like captives-at-the-oar at the ceiling, the sepia picture of Jack Cornwell V.C., each other's heads, their nibs. Then, one by one, they found a gap in the unpromising hedge of verbiage and crawled through into the delirious world of childhood dreams.

"And there was an orangey-red flower growing, nearly as big as he was. It was growing just above him in the sandpit," wrote Nick. "And there was a tree for climbing with juicy fruits on it. It was a pomegranate tree. There was a dog called Spot, too, because it had a brown spot on its left ear. This dog came up to me and rubbed its nose on my leg and climbed up the tree with me and we sat there eating the juicy fruits. And we looked through the leaves..."

[My father isn't going to get better, he thought. I think he is going to die. Fred Ellis was sent to a Home when his father died. I wonder if I could find my mother? If she knew about everything, maybe she'd come for me. I'd like that. I wish I hadn't asked Father that time if he was my grandfather really, because the other boys said he was. The aunties don't care for me but I'd rather stay with them, even so. I mustn't show anything. Father says it doesn't do any good to show it when you're frightened. Perhaps it won't be so bad...]

He vaguely wondered about the nature of death but only knew for certain that the two of them would never go camping again or go to the seaside or sit quietly together in his bedroom, content in each other's company.

Miss Prosser had entered the room very quietly, put on her spectacles, briefly surveyed the blackboard and then made a foray down the middle gangway. As she peered over shoulders, she cried peevishly, "Spelling!"... "Get your nose off your pen nib."... "Too much ink on this blotting."... "Writing's sloping backward."... "You're not to use commas till next year."... "Spelling!"...

It was the moment of disenchantment.

She reached Nick and snatched his book.

"Is this all? - no more than this? What have you been doing, Nicholas Bellenger? Lazy boy! Seven lines! And seven lines of nonsense! ['And the dog climbed up the tree with me...'] A dog up a tree! And this dog sat eating juicy fruit did it?" She slashed twice at the page with her thick red pencil. Nick, bewildered, looked at the long raking gashes. Tears pricked at his eyes.

"A dog in a tree! Balderdash! I'll write to your father and tell him how you waste your time in school. He'll be delighted. Won't he be delighted! You'll never pass the Eleven Plus." She passed victoriously on her way to the door, crying, "Spelling."... "Finger marks."... "Inky fingers!"

Thickness leaned daringly forward towards Nick.

"The bitch!" he hissed.

She's gone, thought Mr. Croser, who had followed her up and down like a sergeant at a kit inspection, his pencil ostentatiously poised to take incriminating evidence. She's gone and not one word of criticism at me. Optimism flooded his fears but, at the same time bringing, like scum to the surface, an uneasy feeling that he had let down his class and, to his consternation, this was succeeded by a foolhardy recklessness.

He bent over Nick and pretended to read the wrecked page.

"I think it's jolly good, Bellenger," he said. "Especially the adjectives and the part about the dog climbing the tree."

The recklessness, encouraged, swelled to madness. "I had a dog once that *could* climb trees," he added.

With Thickness he was on more familiar ground. He had lip-read his malediction and finding himself in utter agreement with this perspicacious assessment, he returned him what was left of the sweets confiscated the day before and gave him a Progress Star.

But back in her office, Miss Prosser pressed her buzzer and told the genie-like monitor to tell Mr. Croser he was wanted and must come immediately. It had been a feint before the body blow.

"I have found a mistake in your register," she said.

"Oh," he replied apprehensively, his newly-found courage ebbing, "I checked it over very carefully after what you said last time, Miss Prosser."

He twisted his head fearfully and tried to find the offending detail among the regiment of red lines and black noughts.

"You know what I am talking about, Mr. Croser. There's not much goes on in my school that I don't find out, is there?"

"Very little, Miss Prosser," Croser answered, trying to twist his features into a servile grimace.

"And what should I take that to mean? Yes, what do you mean by that? I take exception to that remark," she cried, and slapped her desk sharply. "You think that because I'm a mere woman you can speak to me as you like, don't you? You don't like working under women do you? That's what it boils down to, isn't it, Mr. Croser? You think mere women are made to be silly little playthings for men such as you, don't you? 'She's only a woman: I can treat her as I like' - I know that's what you think."

Mr. Croser wagged his head stupidly.

"I didn't mean anything, Miss Prosser, really I didn't. I just meant what I said. I mean you do know everything that goes on, don't you? I mean everybody knows it, don't they?"

Horrified, he saw the red blotches start up into his tormentor's cheeks and moisture gathering in her eyes.

"Oh, so you won't admit it. You won't admit the mistake. Very well, send Phyllis Hawkins to me. Go on, send her. Well, don't stand there, send her! Send her."

"She ran home," Mr. Croser muttered, "I can't send her."

"But you didn't change her mark to a nought, did you? You thought that I'd not notice. You didn't think I would find out, did you? You were trying to deceive me."

"I smacked her and she ran off. It was after I'd marked the register."

"You have attempted to deceive me and that I can never forgive. You supposed that it would not be noticed by me. Well, it will be brought to the notice of the School Managers. Let them draw their own conclusions? No - you may not go. There is another matter. There are several other matters. Your class defies you, you smack the opposite sex, you falsify your register, you arrive late, you are the disrupting element in my school…"

The words came tumbling out.

"Yes, I know that you talk about me behind my back to the other teachers. Oh no, you needn't shake your head. I have other ways. I have several other ways of finding out. I know what is going on. But we shall see who is Master in my school. We shall see..."

Her voice had risen and she was striking the desk hard slaps.

"Go back to your classroom. At once!"

Mr. Croser turned shakily and fumbled his way out, beating at the side of the glaze-bricked corridor as he passed, half blind with helpless rage.

"She's not fit to have charge of little children," said Effie, "I've heard stories that would make your hair curl."

"Tell me some," said her Client who had wit, "I'm sure that I'd find it a more pleasant way than having my head fastened in this contraption."

Effie brushed this aside.

Clever, she thought, she's being sarky.

"A Person I know told me that her Methods are all out-of-date. And I must say I never learnt nothing there. And this Person says she gets worse. She's just a great big bully; you should have seen her slap some of the girls. 'Just let her slap you just once,' my mother used to say, 'and you run home straight away, there and then, and I'll go up and see her.' But she never did; I suppose I was cleverer than some of the others, and she never did."

"Perhaps it's the Change," suggested her Client.

"Perhaps it is, but there's no need to make Everybody else's life a Misery, is there? And this Person I know says Everybody's life is a misery. She tries to mould everybody into her own pattern my friend says, and if they try to be themselves, she takes it as a personal insult. And she still has about ten years to go."

There was a pause.

"Poor woman!" said the Client.

"And the queer thing is, they say she used to be quite different; she used to be lively and in the Tennis Club and rode on the backs of men's motor-bikes. In fact, some people used to complain that she didn't act like a teacher should, my mother says."

"Life in a village must be very trying for teachers," commented the Client.

"She even used to slip into The Fusilier for a gin-and-tonic, they say. It takes a bit of imagining I must say, but that's what they say. But can you imagine it!"

"In Minden, no," the Client said briefly.

"And people were talking, Mum says. There was even talk of getting the County to have her removed. It was quite a scandal. Coming back on pillions in the middle of the night... she even used to go to away-matches with the Wanderers and scream up and down the touchline, and you know what disgusting things go on in those football buses when the men are boozed up on the way home."

"But, all the same, it must be very difficult to lose one's virginity with all those high-backed seats around, don't you think? It can't be the most convenient place for an orgy," said the Client.

"Then, all of a sudden, it stopped, Mum says. Just like that. Overnight, as you might say, and she changed. Now, nobody can have any fun. Gone from one extreme to the other! This Person says that just being young is excuse enough for her to stick her knife into you."

In an excess of feeling, she cut off a strand which should have been left on, and for the next five minutes had to make compensatory forays on other areas of the head. The Client bleakly watching this in the mirror, resolved that the extra fare to an out-of-town stylist would be money well spent in future.

"Ah, that's just how I wanted it," said Effie in well simulated ecstasy.

"Is it?" replied the Client drily. "I'm not sure that it's how *I* wanted it. Next time, we must talk about the weather... or the Rector. Look, he's on his rounds."

"Oh, Lord, lo here he comes, and he's seen me," Herbert Ruskin muttered savagely. "Any day but this! The only day in the blasted year when the place wakes up and there's anything to see outside this damned window; and he has to visit. The man's off his rocker. God knows he has enough to ram down his own throat without trying to help me swallow my lot."

He greeted the Rector with bare civility and nodded to the sofa.

"Just popped in while passing to see how you were, Herbert."

[Herbert! Who told him he could call me Herbert. I don't call him Ephraim or Uriah or whatever name his unfortunate father inflicted on him.]

"You look well."

"I'm always well; the top half of me." [All right - flinch. I didn't ask you to call.] "You lucky devils with all your legs. If I'd known what I know now, I'd have remustered to Padre, Chairborne, Mark One, or were you fellows classified in Lukes? I bet I could have sat on my fanny as well as the next man and briefed Lancaster crews on the Sermon of the Mount. [Version to be used in time of national peril.] 'Thou shalt love thy neighbour as thyself, unless instructed contrariwise by a superior officer and then thou shalt blow him sky-high, yea and his wife and his babies three, his ox and his ass and, for good measure, especially the stranger that is within his gate.'

"Rev. Ruskin! I'd have been very highly thought of at H.Q. Canterbury. Bags of promotion for Ruskin! Three rings for a canon, three and a half for an archdeacon! But no, not me. Glory boy! Bird Man! Knight of the Air! And a free National Health Service chair till death do it and my pension part! Look at me. The interesting part is what's below the chair seat. No gorgeous mate to share my bed like you have! How would your ravishing bride like you without a pair of legs?"

The Rector laughed nervously. "We must look on the bright side of things. I've brought you a few *Readers' Digests* to look at. There's a rather stimulating article I liked..."

"Look at me instead, half dead."

"Oh, come!"

"Half dead! Half of me in the grave already! And not even in holy ground. Just off the perimeter track at Knocke-le-Zout. Not even in England! Not even in a coffin!

No useless coffin enclosed his legs,
Not in sheet nor in shroud they wound them...

No, just thrown into a hole like a decayed dog. How would you like half of you thrown into a hole without a funeral service?

They carved not a line and they raised not a stone.
But they left them alone in their glory...

How am I going to rise in the Latter Days? Half in your rubbish dump and the other half at Knocke? Even Stanley Spencer would find that hard to handle."

"Oh really, you're going too far, Herbert."

"Listen, I'll repeat it; they dumped them in a hole. The Luftwaffe boys told me. They told me that only one bod even bothered to attend their funeral. Yes, *there* was a wonderful chance to help that you missed. You could have raised your hand and intoned, 'And ye shall die like men. And fall like princes.' Yes, this bod, the only mourner, they said his kite came down to nought feet through showers of you know what and fired a double-red over the blaze. And then did an encore and fired off another! Poetry! You can't deny it. Shakespeare couldn't have done better than that. Very dramatic! It impressed Jerry enormously.

"Now there was a countryman to be proud of. He didn't forget the proprieties. My legs' and Mullett's only mourner! And who do you suppose that Christian soul was? Bellenger, poor old Ted Bellenger! I bet he had to kick his pilot into doing it. They ought to have made him Poet Laureate [War substantive rank, of course] for it."

"I'm afraid Mr. Bellenger isn't at all well," said the Rector, taking his chance to change the embarrassing course of conversation. "He's very ill indeed, poor man."

"Poor man! Bellenger isn't poor. I'm poor, you're poor, but Bellenger had Everything in his time. He's had everything, done everything. The Lot! Life, armfuls, bucketfulls of it; he even had the North Sea all to himself once. Do you know why we called him The Old Man of the Sea? Because he ditched half way between Ostend and Bradwell Bay and drifted in a dinghy for five days. Can you imagine it? Five days, and five nights! Alone, after he'd pushed his pilot's corpse overboard when it began to smell."

He paused.

"Well," he said ruthlessly. "Can you imagine it, Rev.? You

can't and neither can I. The sea's a big place even when you go down to it in ships. All around you, nothing! You think, if this ship goes through a hole, who'd know? Then imagine what it's like in a raft, a thin sheet of rubber between you and It. Too cold to sleep at night, too damned afraid you might miss help to sleep in the day. Fighting off your thoughts will you die of thirst or hunger or cold? Will you die sane or mad, muttering or shrieking? We can't imagine it, it's beyond us. Yet Bellenger did it, and lived."

He dislikes me too, his visitor thought bitterly. He wants nothing from me. My ministry has no meaning for him. We can't touch each other. He doesn't care what he says to me because he doesn't care what I think. He dislikes me so much that he tells me the truth.

Ruskin's pendulous face had grown old as he talked. Behind his eyes, torture.

"Look at it, Rev.," he said softly. "I know it's there. Look at it. But you can't help me, can you? They don't teach this sort of thing at theological college, do they? Yet if you could do that one thing, all your years, your wasted years in this place would have been worthwhile, just for that."

Suddenly, he thrust forward his massive neck and pushed a forefinger at it; his eyes protruded.

"See it?" he whispered. "No? but it's there: 'Instead of the Cross, the albatross...'"

He broke off as suddenly as he had begun and straightened in his chair. For a moment they stared wide-eyed at each other. The Rector broke the frightening silence, trying to throw off his depressing feeling of inadequacy and confusion. He jumped up briskly.

"Must get on my way. Lots more to do this morning! Now, is there anything I can get for you?"

Herbert Ruskin shook his head, ignoring the proffered hand. He heard his visitor hurry down the staircase and, as the outside door closed, he turned his face to the wall and cried in anguish, "And while he was out there, struggling to live, I took her away from him."

The Rector always had to fight down apprehension as he crossed the school yard. He knew that he wasn't welcome, that his weekly visits were only received with the barest civility because he came there by right; it was a church school and he was chairman of its Managers. He stepped from sunlit playground into no-man's land of gloomy cloakrooms and then warily up to the front line of the grim battle-front of learning, with Miss Prosser directing the skirmishing.

"Good morning," he said nervously. "I've come on my weekly visit, as you see."

The Head Mistress was checking milk bottle totals and did not answer.

"But please don't bother to get up," he hurried on, "I've just popped in to have a quick look round and perhaps I can call on my way out, if you would care to show me that defective drain which you reported."

"Do, Rector, do," exclaimed Miss Prosser distractedly. "Do."

He passed on into the Hall and paused as though unsure which room to visit first. But his intention had been fixed since early morning.

"Please do not interrupt your lesson," he said rather officiously to Mr. Croser, "I'll just listen a while." Mr. Croser was doing *The Lady of Shalott*.

> *"Only reapers, reaping early*
> *In among the bearded barley*

...it's onomatopoeia," he said, groping into the lumber room of grammar school memories.

"Onomatopoeia," he repeated, and picking up a chalk stick, took a step towards the blackboard but thought better of it.

"It means repeating letters, like the 'b' in 'bearded barley' or the 'r' in 'reapers reaping'. Do you see?" he pleaded.

And this is the man who is taking my wife away from me, thought the Rector. This ridiculous parrot chattering away here!

What does Georgie see in him?

He stared hostilely at Mr. Croser's trousers, bagged at the knees, the over-tight waistcoat, the badly shaved chin, the cheap suit. This is my wife's lover, he thought incredulously. This is the man with whom I am sure that she has committed adultery.

"It's what a poet does - onomatopoeia," went on Mr. Croser, recovering his confidence.

"It seems silly to me," said Thickness, taking advantage of the visitor's presence to preserve him from harm. "Everybody knows what barley looks like."

"Well that's what poets do," answered Mr. Croser, injecting syrup into his tones to show he regarded Thickness's rudeness as a child's *naiveté*. "If they didn't do things like that, they wouldn't be poets.

> *Only reapers, reaping early*
> *In among the bearded barley.*

It's Beautiful. Maybe it isn't to you now, but it is. Some day, Thickness, you'll think it Beautiful too," he added desperately.

"This? This! This!" the Rector's brain hammered. He turned blindly to the door.

"Thank you," he said. "Thank you. That was very interesting." For a moment he stood irresolutely in the Hall: then, hands trembling and pale faced, he rushed back into the classroom.

"Onomatopoeia," he said in a low, fierce voice. "It doesn't mean what you said it does." Then he turned once more and hurried out.

There are thousands of places like this, thought Peplow, thousands of names on the map: Moreton-in-Marsh, Hinton-in-the-Hedges, Newbottle, Oldborough, Long Buckby, Shortcommon, Great Minden... ghastly little settlements. But wonderful places if you happen to live in them. And people hurry back to these places or never leave them, hate other people who live in them, consume their lives organising or tidying them or looting them, become hysterical at the thought of being buried out of them, jockey for the insignificant honours offered by them, look with hostility at the world outside them.

He thought of settlements buried in drab valleys, frozen on hillsides, perched at the sea's face, and of other places like them in the vast unknownness of China, in the steppes of Central Asia, ant-heaps in India, clearings in the great African rain-forests, Sandy Creek, Evansville, Jonesville, Rockerville, settlements at obscure crossings of tenth-class roads, where people met at tumbledown stores and were the world. He thought how odd, how frightening, that he would never see these people, that men were dying faster than his own footsteps in the street, men that he had never known and that each death was a personal epic.

These people here, here in Minden! Before this morning, I didn't know they existed. No, nor they me. And yet if I fell down dead, how alarmed they would be! "A man fell dead," they'd say, and never forget it. They would keep on telling people met at tumbledown stores and were the world. "He was gone before I reached him. And no one knew him…"

But, before I came here, I was dead already: they didn't know me. And when I leave here, I shall die again. Only maybe five hundred people are alive for any of us; the rest have no existence.

He was passing the open window of the school and, glimpsing the young toilet enthusiast, paused.

"And the people there call it Mother Ganges," Mr. Croser was booming. "They consider it to be a Holy River. Spell it, Bellenger… No, it has two g's… remember that, two g's. You spell it, Thickness. It is one of the Great Waterways of India. It flows into the Bay of Bengal. It is 1,654 miles from Source to Mouth."

It's a drug, thought Peplow. We are told these things to take our minds off the horror of our isolation. We stare wide-eyed at each other like drowning men washing away in the floods, a glimpse… then gone.

He turned out of the Square towards the hill going up to the church and saw Mrs. Thickness, slatternly, sullen, leaning from an open window in a row of slum cottages. Their eyes met, indifferent, unrecognising. In a moment, each had forgotten the other. Above, at the wall surrounding the churchyard, he saw a lonely figure looking down on the town; was it a man or a bush or a post?

It was a world of strangers, each engrossed with his own

tremendous problems, sometimes throwing out an arm as if to clutch another slipping away in the current, struggling ridiculously like a spider in bathwater racing towards the plug-hole. He turned back towards the Square and suddenly halted. The sullen woman's face was alight. She was leaning eagerly on the sill, her heavy breasts half-bared to the man he had come to meet in Minden and, for a moment, he felt an overpowering urge to touch the man's shoulder and to say, "Here I am. Do you remember me? I am his father. You are the man who killed my son."

The church clock began to beat out the hour. It was midday. A hot, blue midday casting hard black shadows below the thorn bushes on the hills where the sheep huddled, below the great chestnut tree by the lonely house, below the elderberry whose gross white blossoms disturbed the darkness in Mrs. Loatley's garden. In the street, people moved sluggishly, children going home for lunch dawdled, those left behind clung dispiritedly to the iron palings, the Feast Proprietor's two sons sat on their haunches in the cool back-yard of The Fusilier spat in the stream and drank deliberately.

The heat bounced back from the footpath along which Miss Prosser, making no concessions to it, marched briskly. The deserted railway platform drowsed and fish boxes, dumped from the midday train, sweated and stank. In his shop, the butcher, still depressed, emptied meat back into his refrigerator and put up shutters before going off to the backroom to reaffirm his belief that God disapproved of the Rector as much as he did.

The streets of Great Minden emptied and became still.

The last stroke of the clock died away. A postman moved slothfully along the doors, dropping letters from away, with deadpan faces, into halls and porches, like tabs fed into computing machines, jogging, edging, nudging, the courses of action.

Herbert Ruskin understood this.

Even on Feast Day they can't let you alone, he thought. Not even for a single day! Always elbowing! No peace! You work out a course for the day and no, one's scarcely airborne but it's Diversions. Utter confusion, no system!

He looked angrily at the three letters and opened the one addressed in unfamiliar handwriting. It was from the Minden Cricket Club thanking him for five guineas and telling him that he was gratefully re-elected a Vice-President. He grunted. Having both a pension and a private income, his difficulty was in dispensing rather than preserving his money. Feeling himself already exposed to a perpetual downpour, he felt no need to provide for a rainy day.

The second he threw into the basket and then picked out again. It was from his mother.

"Daddy and I will visit you next Saturday... L. is asked to Cowdray for polo next weekend.... R. made forty-three (run out) against Marlborough... they have asked me to open the fête at Oakshott... I suppose I must go..."

She would have written it at the bureau looking up occasionally at his picture - slim, confident, and gay in his uniform. Then the last sentences: the words which she must have turned over for days, until she felt sure that nothing there would hurt him:

"Oh do give up this idea of living alone. I'm so sure that it's so bad for you - Daddy and I want you so much to come back to us.

We call the Terrace Room 'Your Room'. You could wheel yourself out through the windows..."

"You could wheel yourself out..." The phrase grated across his nerves and he tore the pages into strips.

There remained one more. It was addressed in the all too familiar handwriting. What does she want? he thought irritably. I didn't reply to the last letter nor to the one before that. Can't she understand that it's over, finished? God knows, I've made it plain enough to her.

He pushed the square envelope back across the table and, all afternoon, it lay disturbingly across his consciousness, demanding attention.

There were letters for the Rectory too. The Rector read Ruskin's anonymous note, went white and squashed it into his pocket. The other was for Georgie from her mother.

"Pip called in yesterday on her way from Fair Oak Gymkhana with the children. Ann is growing so quickly now. She says the pony (the one Daddy gave her last autumn) is too low for her. And they'd scarcely gone when he had another visitor. You'll never believe it - Peter Jagger! Peter, after all these years! Do you remember how he used to haunt us during your school holidays? He's married some French girl he met in Algeria - he didn't let us see her - and he's looking very prosperous. Apparently his grandfather left him everything... He asked after you. A little private whisper - I don't think he's quite got over it, even yet..."

Letters from away, nudging, edging the course of the day. A word here, a glance there, a random touch! And that's how it happened to Peplow's wife. She pulled open a drawer, put in her hand and felt - as she had felt a hundred times before during the past year. But this time it wasn't there. *It wasn't there.* Her heart beat faster, began to race; she lifted the vests, underpants, collars, handkerchiefs. No. Then drawer after drawer was wrenched out and the contents rifled, thrown on the bed, on the floor, anywhere. The revolver had gone.

She ran wildly through the empty house to the hall and telephoned the bank. The reply struck her like a blow, and she slowly put down the receiver, knowing that the moment she feared had come, yet not knowing what to do.

When the daily woman called him for dinner, the Rector was turning the huge wheel which pumped water from well to house. He unhooked his jacket from a bough of the willow which thrived in the dampness and followed her in.

His wife had begun eating already, groping around her plate for the food, reading the *Daily Express* propped against the water jug. She did not look up as he came in and he scraped the remaining meat and fried potato on to his plate. The woman, entering with the milk pudding, looked curiously at them and the Rector, noticing her expression, flushed.

"It's here again, Mrs. Braithwaite," he said, "the usual Feast Weather. Just wait a month and we shall have the other side of the penny, the Church Garden Fete. The rain falleth on the just and not on the unjust. Will you be joining us at Evensong tonight?"

"I'd like to, but our George won't go to the Feast on his own, not by himself. He's crazy to see that Snake-Woman they're all talking about but he won't go unless I go with him."

"Perhaps you could come first and go later, and bring George too. Six-thirty; tonight I shall have the Short Form, only twenty minutes."

"Well, I'll see," she replied dubiously. "It's that hill. Our George doesn't like the climbing. If it wasn't for that hill you'd be surprised what a difference it would make. My husband says it's that hill that stops people from coming. Beats him, he says, how they could be so stupid in the old days as to build it up on a hill. What about the old folks? he says."

Honour satisfied, she put down the tray.

"I've brought the coffee now," she said, "so as not to disturb you again."

Georgie turned from the paper and looked with distaste at the fatty globules floating on the surface of her cup.

"Must you solicit the daily help for your Services?" she said irritably.

"She sometimes comes."

"But why try to drag her up here to Evensong, poor wretch, on Feast Day of all days, the one day a year when Minden less resembles a corpse than usual? Anyway she won't come and why should she?"

"But that's the whole point of it, dear. It's a Holy Feast, the Feast of St. John. The other things grew up around that. Oh, a quite extraordinary thing happened this morning. I had a complete stranger at Communion. Quite well dressed; I wonder who he could be? Has anyone moved into the town this last week, I wonder?"

"Well, it isn't one anymore," she said, ignoring his effort to divert the conversation. "It's the annual booze-up when the locals can get lost in a crowd and do some of the things they snigger about the other three hundred and sixty-four days. It's as well they do; it gives you something to clear up. If they all became too holy, you'd be out of a job. They ought to pay you on piece-work, so much a soul saved. Perhaps your visitor was an inspector sent over by the bishop to check up on you."

He could think of nothing to answer these bitter words and once more felt the awful silence gathering in from the rooms around them.

"Though whatever it was they paid you in this game, it would only amount to pocket money. I suppose I'd have to look around the Sales for a cheap line in sack-cloth if Daddy didn't keep up my allowance. We shouldn't even have that old rattle-trap of a car if Big-hearted Arthur hadn't taken pity on you, 'to help you make your pastoral visits'. Isn't that what he put in his letter?"

The bitterness in her voice distressed him. Then quite suddenly, exasperated by his silence, she pushed back her chair.

"I'm going away," she said, her voice rising, "I've had all I can stand."

"Away. But where?" he asked helplessly.

"Anywhere, anywhere to get away from here... from you. We're finished. There's no sense in going on like this."

"We were happy enough once. You must have cared for me then: you married me."

"Did I? I wonder! More like I married a schoolgirl dream. Girls from dormitories are terribly holy." She laughed jerkily.

"We're young yet. We could go away. We could begin again. Think how it will distress your father and mother..."

"Why should I? They're not married to you, marooned in this awful village. They should have locked me up until I came to my senses."

"I'll leave here. I know this house is terrible. Just give me the time to look around. Be patient for a little longer. A new house, new faces; perhaps if we adopted a child..."

"Leave here! Have you any option! You're finished in this parish. Row after row, ever since you came here. The holy water, the people's warden, the stewardship fiasco... You've failed; they can scarcely wait to be rid of you."

She stood up, pushed aside the pots and walked to the door.

"Georgie!"

He heard her footsteps along the stone flags. He heard them on the gravel. A few minutes later he heard the engine of the car.

"Hi!" Herbert Ruskin called from his window to one of the children returning home from school. "Hi! Wadja know?" Nick looked up and grinned.

"The world's biggest waterfall is the Victoria Falls, the world's highest building is the Empire State Building and the world's oldest man was Methuselah."

"How old was he?"

"Nine hundred and eighty-five and 'full of years'."

"I bet he was. But what about Enoch?"

"What about him?"

"He was older than Methuselah: he didn't die. It just says that 'he walked with God'. He didn't keep to the rules. Are you going to the Feast this evening?"

"Well, Dad's still pretty ill so I think I'll stay in. The aunties wouldn't let me go up to see him this morning so he must be pretty ill."

"He'll get better, but maybe you should ask them again if you can go up: he'll want to see you. And look - tell him I said, 'Give her full boost'. Tell him that; he'll understand.

And here's half-a-dollar in case you're able to go and see the Snake-Woman."

"Thanks, and I'll remember," said the boy. "'Give her full boost.' He once told me you were the best pilot on his squadron, Mr. Ruskin. He said you always knew what the form was and didn't flap around like some others he could mention."

"Jolly good; isn't there any more? I can take in any amount of that kind of line. I'm glad that someone else knew that I was a star of screen and stage. Well, I had my moments, I suppose; don't we all. To change the fascinating subject though, how was Field-Marshal Prosser this morning at the Battle of Minden? Did she get all her fire-power in the right places? Well, and here comes one of her N.C.O.s with his baton in his knapsack. My, he looks worn out. It must be all that homework he has to get through at night. Lance-Corporal Croser, mangled but still on his feet! Shock more than shrapnel though, I should say! Peplow wouldn't have unlocked the squadron safe and served him a tot of rum unless he dripped blood; he'd have had to make do with a Benzedrine pill."

Mr. Croser looked with hostility at his fellow lodger and entered the house, glowering.

"And here's Thickness. I know him. Redoubtable fellow - I can read it in his face. He's got Character. Hi Thickness!"

Thickness halted truculently.

"His name's Edwin," said Nick. "He's awfully good at Arithmetic, especially Problems."

Herbert Ruskin bent farther forward to examine him and swiftly selected a suitable key to unlock this unpromising countenance.

"Believe in treating everybody alike," he said. "Absolutely

fair treatment is my motto. Right, Nick?"

"Right, Mr. Ruskin."

"How much did I give you from the Mullett Charity?"

"Half-a-crown."

"Then Thickness gets half-a-crown too."

Edwin Thickness flushed. Ruskin caught the flash of independence in his eye.

"Well," he went on, "can I spend it on myself? A Feast is no place for a man without his legs. Anyway, it has to be this way; it's one of the strict rules of the Charity. All you have to do is to think about Mullett as you spend it. Catch."

Thickness caught. "Who was Mr. Mullett?" he asked grudgingly.

"Hiram Mullett, oh, he was a sort of Transport magnate, Big man, great patriot! He died to save the Lords and Commons in Parliament Assembled, as well as the Beer Barons and the Pools Princes. He left this money for kids to have a good time before 'ever the evil days come and the years draw nigh when thou shalt say (reluctantly), "I have no pleasure in them",' as he put it. He never used one word if he could find a dozen of someone else's. Oh, there's one thing I forgot. Are you English?"

"I suppose so," said Thickness anxiously.

"That's very important. Mullett was very keen on that, being a great patriot himself; he disliked the Scots and even the Welsh. But 'Thickness' sounds a good old, solid English name, like Mullett…"

This was how Peplow found them.

"But I've met Nicholas before," he said. "We were at Church together. I didn't realise until later that I knew your father."

"Now listen for the good old memories to roll back,"

Ruskin said drily.

"Had you seen me before, then?" asked Nick, "when I was quite small?"

"When you were a baby. I saw you once then; you were in your cot."

He avoided looking at the boy.

"Here?"

"No."

"Where?"

"In Kent... near Dover. Your father was living in - in a kind of villa. I suppose you would call it a villa. Nineteen-ten, I should say... very red brick. In fact quite an odd building on that site. It really belonged to a suburb. It had a name; Pioneer House? Something like that, an un-rural name. 'Enterprise House,' that was it. It lay back off the road. But it scarcely was a road; more of a lane, wouldn't you say, Ruskin?"

"How should I know?"

"Well you went there once, didn't you?"

"Did I?"

Peplow did not answer him; there had been an edge to his tone.

"Did you know my mother, then?" asked Nick.

"Well I scarcely knew her, except by sight. Too bad!"

"We haven't a picture of her at home."

"This boy here, Thickness, is good at Problems," said Ruskin. "Aren't you, Thickness?"

Thickness glowered.

"Perhaps he could solve yours, Peplow."

"Arithmetic problems," Nick said.

"I'll have to go for my dinner," said Thickness. He opened his hand and showed the half-crown again. "Thanks," he added.

"You too, Nick," said Ruskin. "You'd better go too. And don't forget that message to your father, remember!"

He turned to Peplow who had come upstairs and was seated again on the sofa.

"Now you can tell me all about Minden."

"Me tell you!"

"I've never left this house since the day I came here. Did you meet any of the local worthies?"

"I had coffee with the rectoress, if she's a worthy. Anyway, she's not quite the usual type that clergymen marry, those I know at any rate. Do you count her as a 'worthy'?"

"An unworthy, the Serpent in our Paradise. Even that awful fellow across the Square in the butchery is prepared to pay a couple of lamb chops to have a sniff. She's living on tick. Her father's a retired army man so she hasn't any great expectations even."

"Domestic trouble?"

"Husband can't keep her happy. Did she talk much?"

"A little. Can't say I was interested particularly. I'm out of practice with people."

"You'd soon pick it up again if you lived here. Meet anyone else?"

"A poor old thing in an advanced state of religious mania."

"Mrs. Loatley? Well, well, well, now there's a story. Her husband used to be quite the life of the local party, much younger than her. They say he had a heart attack or something nine or ten years ago. The landlady says you could sometimes see him sitting in the garden in fine weather up to two or three years ago. I think she's got him somewhere around the house still but the locals would like to believe she's twitched up his heels in the bath. You don't seem very interested?"

Peplow ate steadily, catching the irritability in the other's voice.

"It's beyond me," he said.

"Come on, Peplow, you can get off that horse. For God's sake be human for once."

He fairly snapped out the words, his face quivering, hands trembling.

"Let's stop all this 'It's beyond me, I'm not interested,' stuff. You know what the form is as well as I do. You always did. You knew: Bellenger and her, and me, didn't you? Perhaps no one else did - but you did. You knew more than any one of the three of us. You fitted the lot together in your filing cabinet of a head. You weren't the adj. for nothing. You didn't stop being one when you were off duty. People talk to you. God knows why! She did, didn't she? before she left Bellenger and the kid? What did she say? And Bellenger, did he ever know the truth? You've come to see Bellenger, haven't you? Did he send for you? Why are you here? What are you going to do?"

The words came tumbling out. His voice had risen and he slammed his knife and fork on to the half-eaten plate of food.

Peplow too had stopped eating. He had become very pale.

"No, no," he said earnestly. "Really, Ruskin, it's not like that at all. I didn't know either Bellenger or you lived here. Honestly! It's something quite different, something that only concerns myself."

He rose quickly and went to the window.

"To tell you the truth, I'd half-forgotten it all. As far as I'm concerned, it's dead and done with. What you did or didn't do then was your own business."

"Will you be coming again after today?"

"No." He turned. "Anyway, it *is* finished, isn't it? You and her?"

"I'm afraid not," Ruskin answered.

Their eyes met, searching and finding nothing.

Afternoon

FACES TURNED towards the afternoon. The face of Edward Bellenger, still as soon it would be in death, a blind drawn over a mind groping deeper and deeper into memories of a past summer. Herbert Ruskin's face, like the face on a Roman coin, lip trembling, eyelid twitching and, sometimes, passing across it like a shadow, the face of another man.

Mr. Croser: a fleck of lunch adds texture to his face, a face too indeterminate, irresolute, too ill-equipped for his accumulating problems. The Rector's stubborn, frightened; his wife's brooding, discontented. Edwin Thickness's, his sharp little brain ready to sink its teeth, his grey eyes darting like a stoat's; Nick's large-eyed, wondering...

Miss Adela Prosser's face, eyes pricking, neck flushed, Miss Lydia Prosser, exaggerated calm covering the ache to hurt and hurt again. Mrs. Loatley's, eyes dark, opaque, the eyes of a patient farm animal.

The young fair-man's humourless, laughing face, flashing his teeth as he had seen the film stars do, and Peplow's aloof, the correct, regulation bank-counter face.

Faces peering forward, beyond the afternoon and towards the night.

And Effie, blue eyes protruding ever so slightly, pouting as she slothfully pulled on her uniform, putting her palm close to her lips, breathing raspingly out three times and then smelling quickly. Sour! She always smelled like this when he had upset her the night before. She wouldn't give in to him, she wouldn't give in to him; he must marry her first.

Groping into her handbag's litter, she found an anti-bilious tablet and began to suck it. Then she flopped into a chair and studied her afternoon's engagement list.

"Mrs. Studley, Mrs. Cope, Mrs. Marwood, Miss

Kettlewell, Beryl Foulds."

"Oh, Glory!" she said aloud, thinking of the afternoon's long hours on her feet and feeling tired already. She sat stupidly gazing into the mirror, scrutinising a face which would never launch a thousand ships, seeking reassurance from the bright red mouth, pink cheeks, yellow lacquer-like hair.

Oh God! she thought, I wonder if he really loves me? What if he throws me over? Where shall I find anyone else in a hole like this? He's been ever so broody lately. I'm sure there's someone else, but, here, you can find out everything about everybody else and nothing about yourself. And he's so unreliable. He'll let me down, I know he will. Oh, Sid!

The first client slipped in.

"How hot it is, isn't it?" she said. "It's like it was at Ostend last year and I'm sorry I'm late but I couldn't park in my usual place, no, only a rinse and a set, the grey's coming through again at the roots."

"I hear that Mr. Bellenger is in a bad way," said Effie. "A person was telling me the doctor had said he won't last till tomorrow. He's expected to pass away any time."

"Doctors oughtn't to say things like that," said the Client, made over-critical by the heat.

"Well, that's what this person said, though I agree with you. I thought to myself at the time, 'Doctors oughtn't to tell personal things like that!' Mind you, he can't complain: Mr. Bellenger, that is: he's had a good innings. I heard from this person that he was seventy."

"Then he can't grumble," said the Client comfortably.

"But you couldn't call him an old man, all the same," insisted Effie. "He was in the War, they say, the last one. He was an officer. They say he flew in a bomber. And then there's that other business too."

She felt that it was time for her client to show her hand and left her surmise in the air. The other woman too knew the rules and did not shilly-shally.

"What will happen to that boy?" she asked, guessing correctly.

Effie finished her clipping. Besides being kept in the third person, this kind of gossiping had to be desultory or one might get a reputation for tittle-tattling.

"This person told me that Mr. Bellenger's grown-up daughters had said that they wouldn't keep him when their dad had passed away. They said that he would have to be put into a Council Home and that no one could make them keep him he wasn't their responsibility because his mother was still alive somewhere and it was up to her to come for him and why should they be landed with him."

"Poor little lad! But isn't there some place for ex-servicemen's children? I was reading about it in a magazine and he's quite a nice little boy, isn't he, quite good looking, isn't he?"

"My friend says he's quite bright and will pass the Eleven Plus with ease for the Gornard Grammar School. He says his compositions are very imaginative."

The Client had a girl of eleven and the mention of the Eleven Plus so depressed her that conversation ceased.

Effie's friend rubbed his second finger along the side of his nose, down the fold of his chin and rubbed his mouth. It slipped along the grease brought out by the heat. Then he smelled it, rancid, with just a trace of the beef sausage he had eaten for lunch. He rubbed harder and the smell was stronger. He cleaned the finger on his trousers.

"Only one pair between two," he cried petulantly at the girl giving out the scissors.

"Please, sir, I can't cut with this pair," called out Thickness.

"It's always you. Why do you always get the broken pencils or cracked rulers, or the blunt scissors! Always you... never anybody else! Don't you just love to make trouble!"

"Please, sir, it's the monitors," Thickness answered simply. "They put them aside for me; they do it before they start."

"Oh, we don't, sir," the two girls cried shrilly.

"Give him another pair before he starts crying," ordered Mr. Croser. "He's never satisfied, that's why we all love him. If we don't give him the best of everything I expect his Mam will come up about him. He's very important."

Thickness grinned victoriously at the girls and scrutinised the new pair.

"Now we're all ready," Mr. Croser said impressively. "We are going to make an envelope. I'm sure we all agree that's a very useful thing to know how to do."

"Can we have the one we made last week, sir, to take home with us and show people?" a girl asked.

Mr. Croser remembered with disgust the pile of pawed, Stone Age stationery he had trodden into the waste basket.

"No," he said. "That was only a practice attempt. You can all do much better than that."

"Mum says envelopes only cost 12 for 6d.," said Thickness. "She says they're not worth making. She says the only man who ever needed to *make* an envelope was Robinson Crusoe. She says it's something better left to machines."

"Your Mum!" Mr. Croser said scathingly.

"Well, that's what she said."

The lesson dragged on. The oblongs of cartridge paper were defiled into soiled and gaping wallets, smeared with paste and sweat so that Mr. Croser, tired and angry from unavailing salvage efforts, began to cuff and slap his way into righteous indignation.

"An envelope!" he jeered. "This an envelope! My godfathers! How far do you think this would carry a letter, even if any letter, even a begging letter, could be persuaded to enter it? Why it would disintegrate before it even reached Gornard."

He looked at the phlegmatic faces and his fury cascaded.

"You'll do it again. You needn't think you'll beat me. You won't. You're going to do it again. You'll make an envelope if it takes from now till Doomsday."

He ostentatiously pulled out his record-book, found "Handwork" and in the section under next week's date, wrote, "Making an Envelope (cont'd.)," and slowly read it aloud with apparent pleasure.

Thickness stared calculatingly at the top of his head. His grey eyes glistened.

"My Mum says when she went to school, they made little tea-pot stands and egg-cosies out of raffia, useful things you could take home with you," he said. "She said her teacher used to say unless you could use a thing, what was the use of spending time and the ratepayers' money making it?"

Mr. Croser rushed down the narrow gangway and slapped him very hard across the face.

"Well, there's something you can take home," he panted.

"I expect my Mum will be up," the boy managed to falter. "She says teachers aren't allowed to hit children's heads."

Mr, Croser's body contracted with hate but he was saved

from further folly by the arrival of a monitor who said that Thickness was wanted at once by the Head Mistress.

The boy stood up. A red flush already showed on one side of his face. Their eyes met for a moment. A bell jangled distantly.

"Stand," he ordered. "Turn. Forward from the back. Monitors, begin clearing up into the cupboards. You can go to Miss Prosser, Thickness."

When the last child had gone he lifted his desk lid and resting it on his head, stared unhappily into the untidy darkness.

Thickness was more relieved than surprised when Miss Prosser asked him where he lived. For two or three days he had been expecting and dreading a very different enquiry.

"Let me see, Edwin Thickness," he said. "It is in my admission register but I ought to know your address without that, oughtn't I? Yes, of course, you live near Mrs. Loatley, don't you? Do you ever run errands for Mrs, Loatley?"

"Errands, Miss?"

"Yes," she said sharply. "Errands! Do you run errands?"

"Yes, Miss," he muttered.

"What errands do you do?"

"I go grocer's, Saturdays. Sometimes I take parcels to the Post Office."

"How often?"

"Not often, Miss."

"How often? Every week, every fortnight, every month?"

"Not as much as that. Not very often."

Miss Prosser struggled to contain her irritation.

"Where do these parcels go, Thickness?"

The boy looked quickly up. Somehow he knew that they had strayed out beyond the shallows of casual talk into a deeper and more dangerous current of conversation. So he did not answer. Miss Prosser looked carefully at him. She too knew that she had overstepped the mark.

"One side of your face is red, Thickness," she said abruptly. "Has someone hit you?"

"No, Miss, no one's hit me."

"Are you quite sure?"

"Yes, Miss."

"Then why is it so red?"

"I been rubbing. It's itching."

She dismissed him and then, following him from the room, walked rapidly up and down the rows of bleak clothes-pegs, angry at her crudeness, vexed that she had let the boy guess that she was pumping him.

It's the Feast, she thought. It's what Lydia said at breakfast, bringing it all back. She does it to hurt me. It's stupid of me letting her play me up like this. It was scarcely anything while it lasted and it came to nothing. If only he'd told me, if only I could see him again, only once. If only I knew if he really cared then... Marriage, it's a prison. Some shut in, some shut out. There's something awful about it, something secret. Why did it have to happen on that night of all nights? If he'd dropped dead, that would have been the end of it. But to know that he's still there! He must think. He must remember.

Almost knee deep among the haulms, Mrs. Loatley nudged sideways along the trenches, banking the earth around the rows of potatoes. The red cotton square around her hair gave her a peculiar African look, and this was emphasised by her primitive tool, the heat and the rhythm of her jab and scrape. She did not like gardening but she did not mind it. There was plenty of land and time, vegetables were cheaper to grow than to buy and she made herself believe that, despite her age, the outdoor work was good for her even when she went on for too long so that she became pale and her hands trembled.

She was thinking about her morning visitor. There was something unusual about him. Why was he spending a day in Minden? Who had he come to see? What had he come to do? Whatever it was, it meant a great deal to him. His mind was bent completely to it, nothing else mattered to him.

And yet he was a man you could talk to. You felt he was a man who would understand.

She reached the end of the row and methodically turned into another. Jab, scrape, jab, scrape. I'd like him to know about me and Fred and all that business... I've not been myself ever since I got up... there's something queer about today... things seem crowding in on me... it's as though it's getting near the finish of something... maybe it's the weather, we'll have a storm before midnight... jab, scrape...

The mood of hopelessness engulfed her. The task suddenly seemed pointless and, letting the hoe fall and lie among the potatoes, she walked slowly down the overgrown path and went into the house.

The sun had moved across the south and no longer shone into the room of Edward Bellenger but he did not know it for he felt no desire either to see or to hear. He wanted nothing except to be left alone by the river, green under the trees, with weeds like a woman's hair under water, fallen star petals floating downstream, cool, dark, inevitable. And sounds in the trees, in the water, everywhere.

He wondered where she was. Did she ever think of him, of the boy? Surely something of that summer, some fragment, must have lodged? She *must* remember.

I was there, he thought. That was the only reason. It might have been anyone, it happened to be me. She gave herself thoughtlessly, without feeling; she used me as one uses a room on a journey. One stays briefly and forgets.

He remembered the early mornings soon after dawn when he had slipped from the bed and crept barefoot across the linoleum to a wide-open window looking across the kitchen garden, the fields and woods to the dark line of the Downs. And she had slept on like a child, one arm thrown carelessly across the faded counterpane, her long, dark lashes touching his heart more almost than he could bear.

We lived together like strangers, like travelling companions thrown together on a journey, he thought wearily.

When he had returned, dazed with weariness, from the long night-patrols over the Channel, she never asked him about how things had gone and he had never tried to tell her, for they had seemed only unimportant interludes until he could be with her again. Only once had she seemed to care. The night after he had seen an Albacore, its tailplane sheared away, dive into the sea, he had imagined he could see young Brightwell's despairing figure struggling to the surface in the darkness. Then he had cried aloud in fear, seeing again the drowning face, and had started up, and there was her hand on his wrist, steadying him; nothing more. But he had known that, for once, she knew, and the trembling passed and he had slept again.

She never gave us a chance, he thought, and after the baby was born, she must have counted the hours till she could go.

The Squadron, of course, had found out and had insisted that he bring her to parties in the Mess. She had gone, dressed as casually as at other times, a pullover only half-concealing the shape of advancing pregnancy. He remembered the bright, tight-waisted wives cluttering the bar, their voices shrill with gin, and this girl, scarcely speaking or smiling. He remembered her candid grey eyes, the long upper-lip, and, remembering, the agony of her going returned again.

"The old bastard! How does he do it?" That's what they must have asked. And that, doubtless, was the least coarse of their questions.

In any other circumstances, the younger men would have been sniffing around but now, when they were losing a couple of crew almost every week, they were engrossed with mortality and passed the time moaning about lack of leave, hanging around the office or bar, dozing in the ante-room, dissipating the long interludes between action. Young Ruskin, fair-haired, gay, bright-faced; she had sat talking to him for more than an hour once: they had laughed together, two of an age. He had watched them and had been afraid. Was this the boy who would take her away from him? But only a few weeks later, low over Knocke, Ruskin had gone too. He had seen the tracer stream out at him from the airfield defence posts and his aircraft slowly twisting through the air until it hit the ground and exploded in a cloud of fire and smoke.

And she had never asked what had happened to Ruskin.

I'll never know, he thought, I'll never know. Where did

she come from? Where did she go?

Everything had seemed the same when he had returned to the cottage one morning; a spade blade deep in the border, the green door ajar, sunlight on the threshold, the table laid, even soup rumbling in the pot. But she had gone: he knew at once that she had gone. Even so, he had rushed up into the bedroom. The bed and the cot were made up, fresh flowers were in a vase but the expensive watch that he had given her was ticking away on the dressing table; the baby's clothes were there, but her own had been taken away. He remembered turning away from the desolation towards the window, staring unseeing at the sun-drenched garden. He had been there still when a neighbour from down the lane brought a letter and the child.

The word had spread round the Squadron but no one, not even the adjutant, spoke to him about it. Yet it was always there; the curiosity, the pity?

How often since then he would have liked to talk about it to Ruskin in Minden and how often he had meant to do so. He had half expected Ruskin's version of the affair to go round the town and he wondered when and how it would reach him. But this had never happened; no one except Nick even knew that they had met before.

We are always alone, he thought, no one really knows us and yet, when we are gone, some part of many others goes with us.

Once more his thoughts and memories submerged in the greenness and sound and the room darkened around him.

Peplow stood motionless at the foot of the bed.

Another world, he thought. Bedrooms in the daytime are another world. And the bedroom of a dying man! They should make us go into a dying-house like the Chinese.

The Old Man of the Sea lay very still, his square and stubborn head pushed into the pillow.

"He's gone off again," whispered the daughter. "He's been like this three days now. Sometimes he's asleep, sometimes he's awake. Why don't you wait here for a while and see if he comes round?

"Dad," she said, "it's a Mr. Peplow come to see you. He says you know him."

The dying man did not stir.

"He's gone again," she repeated. "He's been like it for three days; he's in a bad way. You can stay with him for a few minutes."

The door closed softly behind her.

"Hello, Peplow!"

The eyes had not opened. Until the lips moved again, he thought it was imagination.

"Peplow!"

"Hello, old man... Ruskin told me. How are you?"

"Finished, thank God!"

The long mouth twitched. It was no more than a breath, shaping words.

"Peplow..."

"Yes."

"Do you remember?"

The time for discretion had passed. He knew at once what Bellenger meant.

"Yes, I remember her."

He waited for more questions, knowing that, this time, he

would answer truthfully.

But the eyes still did not open. For a long time there was no sound but the faint breathing, growing more shallow, its intervals imperceptibly increasing. He stayed there for a long time but Bellenger did not speak again, and after a time, he quietly let himself on to the landing again.

"It was in his wallet," said the elder daughter. "It's her all right. Look, he's got his arm round her. How old was he then? Fifty-two... fifty-three? And just look at her – twenty-four, she couldn't be more than that. Fancy! Younger than his own daughters! Isn't it revolting? And see how he's looking at her, as soppy as you like, a real wipe-your-feet-on-me look!"

She turned the picture over.

"Well, would you believe it!" she exclaimed. "Listen to this, 'Taken by Ruskin, Sunday, May 22.' So that horrible Ruskin knew her. Would you believe it! I expect he's told everybody: it's probably all over the place now."

They stared again at the picture, the immense curiosity and interest in their faces cancelling everything that they said.

"Well, you've got to admit it but the old boy looked smart in his rig-out. And you've got to admit it, he wasn't a shirker like some. Flying at his age!"

[She stood by his side among the tangled boughs and shadows of an orchard which they would never know and in a time that was gone. Dark and cool and lovely in a white cotton dress, and gloves.]

"Look, she's wearing gloves," they cried. "Little puss! Keeping herself clean for the bedroom! Gloves!"

[She was smiling at the camera, eagerly, impulsively. It was a moment caught among a million, of which they would know only this.]

"What do you suppose she's smiling at? Thoughts? That Ruskin man? Her clever little self?"

[The ruffled grass hid her feet; in a patch of sky a cuckoo would be calling as it flew; there would be foxgloves in the hedges and, beyond them, farther still, valley after valley and folds of orchard-covered hills, rolling into the blue distances that they would never see.]

"It's been in his wallet all the time," the elder daughter said again, "all these years!"

Once again they stared at the picture, as though by staring they could wring out the answer to many questions that had puzzled them for so long.

"We felt we had to call you," Bellenger heard his younger daughter saying. "The doctor says he's going fast and though he's past understanding, we felt we had to have you for our own satisfaction. Maybe you could say a prayer or something for him? Don't take any notice if he doesn't seem to hear. It's this door here. Don't feel you have to stay long; after all you have your own business to go about, haven't you? The world can't stop."

A moment later the Rector entered and Bellenger knew at once that he was being looked at. Effortlessly, he disengaged his mind and listened again at the clock and was quite startled and annoyed to hear the Prayer for the Dying being spoken above him.

"*'Give him unfeigned repentance for all the errors of his life past... that his sins may be done away by Thy mercy and his pardon scaled in heaven before he go home and be no more seen...'*"

He found that he was listening with very close attention to the words. It surprised him.

"'*Yea, forasmuch as in all appearance, the time of his dissolution draweth near so fit him and prepare him, we beseech Thee, against the hour of death...*'"

The voice stopped and was followed by a stealthy movement towards the door.

Edward Bellenger roused himself to a supreme effort. "The boy!" he whispered.

The movement ceased.

"The boy!" he repeated.

But once more, his mind disengaged. Had she ever loved the child? Had parting from him been hard? The woman down the lane had told him that she wept as she left the baby behind. Did she ever think of him even if, now, she had another family? Was his loss a secret scar marking her life for ever? Did she ever long to see Nick again?

"All I have done, I would do again," he whispered.

The door closed quietly.

"I would do it again," he murmured into the gathering silence.

Now I wonder, thought Herbert Ruskin, as he had wondered for ten years. He's not like me to look at. But he's not like the Old Man either. He could be anybody's. I ought to feel proud that I could have sired him. Once I might have been, but not now. Why did I get myself involved with her of all people? Women were plentiful enough, God knows. The station was thick with Waafs; there was Margate, Ramsgate, Broadstairs. Why her? Bellenger's woman!

Remember Pollard and Whiteparish, the day they bought

it. Only an hour after the news went round, less than an hour, other bods calmly cleared out their lockers of everything eatable, tins, bottles, fags, the lot. "Well, what of it?" they said. "Can they use it now? If we cop it, you can have ours and good luck to you."

And that's what I did when we wrote the Old Man off; I took his woman and said, "Tomorrow it'll be my turn." How was I to know he'd turn up again? God knows. I felt a mean enough bastard when he did.

He lit another cigarette and stared moodily across the Square to the hillside and the church, remembering the hot bicycle ride to the red house isolated at the end of the lane.

And it was Peplow who told me to go, he thought. Damn it all, he made me go. 'I'm absolutely bogged down with all this bumph,' he had said; 'I simply haven't time to go see her. It isn't as if they were married; she's not his legal dependant; she's not Official. He didn't draw an allowance for her. (He didn't even try to, like Musgrave did.) It's bad enough having to churn out the same old sob story to his daughters. I've taken it up with the Wingco and he says someone *must* tell her. You're not flying tonight; you've got the job. Look, I tell you what - you can borrow my bike, but don't lose it.'

Cold devil!

Riding through sunshine and lanes dappled with the shadow of leaves to the house lost in the heat and silence! The gate had whined as it turned and she had looked round as she sat, almost hidden, in the overgrown grass which once had been a lawn. Unhurriedly she had pulled the cotton dressing gown across her breasts and thighs. So this was how she welcomed him home from the night-shift, he had thought admiringly. Excellent. No wonder we scarcely saw him in the Mess! Then, when he had recited his unconvincing piece about the search going on and the chance of his rubber dinghy being seen by coastal shipping, she had invited him in for a drink. Was it then that it began - as they crossed the threshold? Didn't their arms brush and hadn't she looked suddenly up, letting her wrap open? The next moment his back was against the coats on the wall - he remembered Bellenger's cap, falling from a peg above him, slithering ridiculously from his shoulder on to hers and then to the floor - and she was pressed against him, neither speaking, passion stirring in their warm and eager limbs until, still silent, there seemed nothing else to do but to climb to the cool back room looking over towards the orchard covered hills.

When he had returned to camp in the morning he had told Peplow he had passed on the message and had then cycled on to spend the night in Folkestone. "Bad show!" Peplow had said. "But we can't do anything for her. Now, if they'd been married, she'd have had a pension. Well let's hope he hasn't put her in the family way. She can always go back to her people; no one need ever know unless she tells them. It was an interlude, part of her education you might say. Thanks Ruskin!"

Next day he had returned in the afternoon to the utter stillness of the lonely house, to the half-dream of utter abandon, exhaustion and sleep. Four days and four nights; a huggermugger of memories. Breakfast in the stone paved kitchen, the first cigarette of the day (passed from one to the other) on the bench beneath a chestnut tree, warm still nights, passionate greetings and farewells, the explosive violence of their lovemaking. Neither spoke again of Bellenger.

And so it was, returning after dawn from a patrol of the Cherbourg Approaches, hurrying to the mess tent to bolt some breakfast and get away to her, the news splashed over him so that he stood shocked: "Amazing! Wonderful! The Old Man's back! They took him home an hour ago."

An M.T.B. returning from a night sweep had picked him up - alive.

Ruskin squashed the cigarette on the sill and flicked the butt into the Square.

"Alive!" he whispered.

He had seen her only once again after that, months later in the dusk, one rainy evening when she already was grown big with the child and moved slowly, carefully, the water dripping from her mac. She had told him that she was sure it was his child.

"It is, it is," she had repeated. "When can I come to you?"

"I'm almost through my tour of ops; then they'll post me to a training station as an instructor, to Devon or Scotland I should think. You can come then."

"What about your leave? Why not then?"

"There isn't going to be any leave for anybody. As Monty moves north, Jerry's pushing his merchant shipping up the coast each night - to Ostend and the Dutch ports. Group's ordered us to take up the old rag-bags even on moonlit nights; we've become expendable. But Mullett and I have only three more trips to do and that will be it; they're bound to give me fourteen days' leave before a posting."

Had he really meant to take her away from Bellenger or was it only an interlude? Really, for him hadn't it all suddenly ended when someone shouted, "Heard? Bellenger's back. Amazing isn't it?"

It was impossible to see it now as it was then. Each week

one crew, often two, was lost. And there were no replacements. Hadn't his taking her been a gesture? At what? Death? Affecting to despise those who had gone down into it? They were theatrical times: the young were dying faster than the old. And Bellenger was back.

She must have read his thoughts as she had stood submissively under the dripping boughs in the lane through the orchards, her face pale, a wisp of damp hair across her forehead. Her long fingers had gripped the turned-up collar of his greatcoat (the child she said was his in the womb between them), eyes large and feverishly searching his face. There had been the heavy feeling of an unfriendly fate around them.

Then it was all over, and he stayed watching helplessly as she sloshed away in her wellingtons through the rain-filled ruts and the gathering night.

[A pandemonium of cries across the Square; it was afternoon playtime. The children crowded to the rails to talk to the postman on his round.]

Herbert Ruskin swung his chair and stared with sombre eyes at the face before him in the mirror, fleshy, loose, repulsive.

I am another man, he thought. The other went up in the flames on the perimeter track at Knocke, and this lived on.

After that, there had been one or two almost incoherent letters forwarded to him during his long illness and convalescence in German hospitals and several since his return but he had only replied once or twice, repeating firmly that he did not wish to see her or hear from her again. She belonged to the other life when he was a whole man. She belonged to his last summer.

The letter addressed in the frighteningly familiar hand

still lay where he had pushed it across the table. He took it hesitantly; then, suddenly, tore it open.

"...I still feel the same. I always shall. You can't go on refusing to see me. I won't let you hide yourself away any more. I think of you all the time, I need you: I shall never be happy unless we are together. If we could only talk it over, things would straighten themselves out. You must give both of us another chance. I am coming tomorrow (Saturday), and I shall arrive on the earliest train. We'll make it work; we must. We'll find a cottage like that other one - at the end of a lane..."

When the dread note went round saying that only the boys and men teachers were to assemble before the Head Mistress, everyone knew that the parochial guilt of the lavatory scratches had been established and that the universal sin of maleness was about to be punished. The lines gathered in utter silence before the dais.

"Cross-legged, sit," ordered the Chief Assistant. The lines sank like Bantus before the baas. The wall clock ticked on across the stillness.

Miss Prosser rose from her chair and motioned to him and he opened the Punishment Book and began nervously to unscrew the cap of his fountain pen.

"I have told you all before yet it stems that you have to be told again and again that I know Everything which goes on in my school. Everything, yes absolutely Everything! There is nothing happens that I don't hear about. I can see into all the hidden places."

This Hebraic pronouncement plunged round and round the room. It was as if the air refused to absorb it.

Once more the clock punctuated the frightened stillness.

"I can see into all your minds; and I can read what is written there..."

This too began to clatter round the walls.

"I know the identity of the person who wrote that Dirty, Filthy Word on the Toilet Walls. I know him. He can't hide from me."

Mr. Croser stared anxiously along the lines and tried mindreading too. To him, everyone looked equally suspect and, outstanding in his guilt, the Chief Assistant who was unscrewing and screwing the cap of his pen. All at once, he pictured his own face as he must appear to Miss Prosser - alert, wide-eyed, guilty.

Heavens, it couldn't have been me! he thought fearfully. I couldn't have done it in one of those traumas we had in Psychology.

There was another awful pause.

"I know the Name of the person who did it. Oh yes, I know *his* Name. But I am going to give him one small last chance to redeem himself. I am going to let him stand up and confess before I call out his Name. That Boy, stand!"

Mr. Croser saw two small boys, heads hung, bodies sick with fear, climb unsteadily to their feet. Two, he thought. She only said One. Why did the other fool stand up? And then a third, half up, to the side, at first not noticing the others who had preceded him. Thickness!

Thickness, half up, in a haze of panic, counting silently, "One, Two, One, Two!" trying to make his limbs bend back to the ground again, trying to change his expression from fear and mortification into amiable curiosity! But he could not move. There he stuck, half up, half down, the horror at his own stupidity written large over his face.

Mr. Croser tried to whisper, "Sit down, sit down, you

fool," but he was dumb, listening to the Head Mistress cry triumphantly.

"Oh, so there were three of you! Three of you!"

The pause.

"Come out here."

Miss Prosser drew the cane from its hiding place behind her bookcase. It was very long; one split end had been bound with Elastoplast.

"Put the date and write down their names," she said to the Chief Assistant, "and then enter up the number of strokes which I shall give to each. I will sign it when I have done."

The lobster flush had re-appeared on her neck and now enveloped her left ear and temple, her eyes were bright and brimming.

She pushed back the cuff of her blouse, raised the cane and brought it down again and again, at first deliberately, then with breathless speed.

The shock of each outrageous slash fell on an Assembly already unnerved by the second boy, who had begun calling out for mercy and collapsing into an animal-like blubber before he was even hit. As for Thickness, his red and warty hands shoved deep into his armpits, sick with pain and stumbling back to his place, he looked full at Mr. Croser, a core of defiance peering from the mask of pain, but found on his adversary's face instead of exultation, horror.

Dropping her cane on the desk, Miss Prosser took the pen and tried to dip into the pot. The nib's point struck like a beak on a stone. She prodded again; once more it struck the edge of the pot.

"It's a fountain pen, Miss Prosser," the Chief Assistant stammered, pushing the book towards her. "The ink's in it already. You don't have to dip."

Her hand was trembling even more violently now and her "E" was a cryptic wavering line. At "P" the nib stuck like a dart in the paper and a blot gathered around it. She could not make an "r". She, too, stared fascinated with horror at her own hand and the almost unrecognisable "E. Pr…" Then, signature unfinished, she shut the book with a slam and, in the utter silence, they heard her sharp footfalls grow fainter along the stone floor of the cloakrooms.

"Stand!" ordered the Chief Assistant in a low, apologetic voice. "Turn! To your classrooms, file!"

When the trembling and nausea had passed, her little office suddenly seemed as unbearable as the thought of the enormity of what she had just performed and, putting on her flowered hat and locking her door, Miss Prosser hurried out of the playground. Despite a call at the greengrocer's to buy some early roses, she was back at the tall stone villa six or seven minutes later.

She went straight up the gloomy staircase, took off her tweed costume and dust coloured blouse, washed and then changed into the dusky-red tea gown she had bought at Easter. After a moment's hesitation, she rubbed a tinge of rouge into the slack of her cheeks, pinned on a handmade Celtic brooch bought on a holiday at Oban, and went downstairs.

Her sister immediately turned her novel spine-upwards.

"You're early, Adela," she said. "Have you had a difficult afternoon. An inspector or some funny soul like that?"

"I felt a migraine coming on and there was nothing needed my attention at school."

"Well, you're not growing any younger. You can't expect

to pitch in like a thirty-year-old any more. Those funny people at County Hall know how old you are - they can't expect what they once did of you. We have to watch the blood pressure at our age."

"It was only the heat. Actually I had a quite pleasant afternoon. Just as I was leaving a child gave me these roses. Funny little creature! I felt just a little guilty taking them but one can't refuse a child." A look of grim amusement passed over the face of her sister.

"But all the same, I suppose you often do," she said. "And what about your teachers, do you ever have to refuse them?"

"We are a happy little staff," replied Miss Prosser. "We work together and there is no question of refusing any privileges the regulations allow me to grant."

"It always amazes me how men can work under a woman. To me it seems odd. Men like to be Big Master."

"My men aren't like that. On my staff we all are Teachers. Some are male, some female, that's all."

"It's the Managers' Meeting tomorrow, isn't it. How will you report on that Croser man? Is he going to be sacked?"

"Mr. Croser? There's nothing to report that time won't cure. He is very young and will improve. He is responding to training. On the whole, we get on very well."

"Well, that isn't what you let slip last autumn. You said then you'd have to get rid of him. I distinctly remember you saying he had a disturbing influence. You said then that he had a wrong attitude to his work. I remember you saying it. Really, how undependable you are getting!"

"Well, if I did say that, then he's made some improvement,"

"There's a lot of talk about him in the village. From what I hear from the daily they say he's got a little harem in the district. It's going the rounds that he's running around with the rectoress as well as that fat girl. I'm surprised he's any strength left for teaching sums."

"I never enquire into the private lives of my staff. What they do after school hours is their own affair. A teacher has a private life like anyone else."

"Do you bully him all the time for it, Dear, or only when you're not feeling too well?" said her sister in an overly sympathetic tone and ignoring Miss Prosser's protestations. "It must be rather nice to do it. I read all about it in a book by a German. It's an outlet for sexual repression, he said. I always laugh about it afterwards - when I've been sharp with the daily. Poor old us!"

Miss Prosser bit her lip and did not answer, but her silence brought no respite.

"Are you going to the Feast tonight, Adela?"

"You know that I never go, so why do you ask?"

"Oh, hoity-toity! You *are* upset this afternoon about something or other. Never mind, I'll find out about what you've been up to at school: I can always pump one of the children. You were fond enough of the Feast once upon a time so don't sound as though you've never heard of it before. Now I wonder what *did* happen on that Feast Night ten years ago? That *would* be interesting to know, very interesting. Or let's say what might have happened if Father hadn't stopped you. It's as well I found your melodramatic little note before you slipped out through the front door and 'out of our lives' …as you poetically put it. You wouldn't be so high and mighty now if you'd half a dozen of your own kids in a back street and getting up at six to get your husband off for the factory hooter, that is if he hadn't already run off with your savings and a pretty little typist."

Miss Prosser had become very pale.

"Dad was a fine man," she cried. "I loved him and I respected him but listening to him that night was the silliest thing I ever did. It was more than that - it was the wickedest. If I'd have gone as I meant to do and done what I meant to do, I'd have been a happier woman and a more useful one: I might have been a mother. I knew what a fool I'd been when I sat in my room and heard the night train leave. I knew it then, and I've known it every night since. Every night! 1 think something died in me when I heard it. Now are you satisfied?"

"Who was he?"

"No. I shall never tell you that. It's the one little morsel you haven't managed to worm out nor ever will, thank God. He told me that I'd never go through with it when it came to the point. And he was right. I gave up happiness for respectability. And now I'm like you."

Miss Prosser began to laugh hysterically.

"And now I'm like you," she cried again.

The Rector's Warden, a farmer, was just scrambling into his Jaguar when the Rector cycled up the drive.

"Blast!" he muttered, crawled reluctantly out again and said with a fair semblance of affability, "Only just caught me, Rector: I was just going to have a look at my beasts; I expect you're on a similar job."

Like most self-effacing men, the Rector was incapable of the preliminary circumlocutions which disarm; he only turned red and looked away.

"Look here," he said abruptly, "the P.C.C. must do something about the state of the churchyard. The graves are in a shocking condition, even some of the box-tombs are completely overgrown. It's a reproach to The Church. There must be no more of this shilly-shallying. I'm looking to you to influence tonight's meeting into allocating money for the work."

"Well, you know what was said at the last meeting, Rector."

"Yes, and I know that it just was not good enough. I refuse to accept the decision. The necessary money must be found."

"Well, I'm only one, you know, and I'm an incomer here like yourself. When longstanding folk are against anything, fellows like Lamb the butcher, it's a dickens of a job to move them. They just say 'In our dad's time, etc., etc.,' and once they've said that it's domino: you can't change them. Village folks are like that. I know. If it had been a meadow I'd have cleared it myself with a mower before tea-time. It's all those danged heaps that's the trouble. It's all got to be done by hand. You couldn't even do it with a scythe: you can't get a swing at it. And the heaps'd take off your point. It's a job for a sickle and that's a slow job. It'd cost fifteen quid even if a pensioner did it, and still look rough."

"Well, then the P.C.C. must find the fifteen pounds. There's scarcely a family in the town which doesn't have some relative lying there. Do they like their own people lying in a wilderness?"

"It's the money!" the Warden said, contriving in farmer fashion to give this pronouncement an awful solemnity. In fact he liked the sound so well that he repeated it, adding, "It's tight."

"Why, the cost of wreaths at a single funeral would pay for it," the Rector exclaimed indignantly. "The people can find money enough for their Pleasure, their Pools and their Television; is it too much to expect them to pay for the care of the hallowed ground where their forefathers lie?"

"What about that twenty quid Sarah Lessing left you to use as you thought fit. Wasn't that for Church purposes?"

"You know very well that I intend to use the bequest as an offering to the Society for the Propagation of the Gospel, stipulating that it should be used in Sierra Leone. I feel quite sure that Miss Lessing did not mean her legacy to do the work of... of the pinch-penny people of this parish."

"Well, you must admit she'd get something out of it, my way," the Warden replied. "After all, she's there and not in Africa."

"That money shall never be used for that purpose. It was meant for Our Lord's Work, not to save work for the people of Great Minden. And that is as far as I intend to discuss it."

"Well, Rector, I can see we're getting nowhere, and I have my beasts to attend to. But look here, I tell you what I'll do, I'll pop round to sound one or two others on the P.C.C. I'll do that. I'll find out what they think about it."

"They'll think whatever you tell them to think - you and Lamb," the Rector said bitterly, but the loudening roar of the car engine drowned his words. The Warden raised a hand, smiled encouragingly and was gone in a flurry of gravel.

"The Rector's on again about t'Yard," he told the butcher. "He's going to raise it again at tonight's meeting, I can see that. He seems to have got it on the brain. He's just been on to me about it, called the parish 'pinch-penny', 'stingy', and I don't know what else. You should have heard him carry on about it."

"Well, he can carry on until he's under it before I'll vote a brass farthing to it. The old rector paid for it hisself, and the one before him too, it's the way it's always been done in Minden and this chap can do t'same - definitely."

"Well, you've got to admit he's not so well fixed as the last one," the other said dubiously. "In all fairness, you've got to admit that. The poor devil must be pushed for money, especially with that wife of his."

"He can afford that car, can't he? Love-nest on four wheels, is my name for it. I saw her and that clanged schoolteacher in it close on midnight yesterday. No, he can cut it himself; he's got all day and every day except Sunday to do it in. Hasn't he? Definitely he has. He doesn't need six days to make up a sermon; it's a prince's life. He wants to try a bit of work like the rest of us; that way he'd learn where the Money comes from. The sooner he pushes off the better. They never should have sent him here. Town chaps definitely don't understand us country folks. They're not used to real people."

"Well, I said I'd see you," the farmer said cheerfully, "and I've seen you."

"Look at his wife, look at the way he lets her run loose. It drags us all down. The danged Baptists are laughing up their sleeves you can bet. Let him bring her to heel before he gets on his high horse and tells us what to do and what not to do. They're in debt all over the shop. They owe me more'n five quid and do you think I'll ever see it? Some blasted hope! I'd have her in County Court if it wasn't for the pleasure them Baptists'd get. I'll never see it again. Five quid! My missus let 'em run it up last time I was in bed with lumbago, and I don't let her forget it. Don't talk to me about cutting graveyards."

"Then you're against voting money for it?"

"Definitely! I'm definitely against it. You can say I'm definitely against it. Not one brass farthing!"

"Then we can tell him we can't do anything about it just

now. He won't like it, but there it is. He'll just have to lump it."

"I'll say nothing to you nor no one, I wouldn't say to his face," cried the butcher. "What I'll say behind a man's back I'll say to his face. It's my way. But he'll not look me in the face since I asked him when he was going to pay that five quid. I've talked it over with the wife. Mind you there was a bit of humming and hawing but she sees it my way now neither of us sets foot in that church again till he goes. We shall go over to Gornard if we go anywhere. A man that can't rule his own wife, I've no respect for him. And I'll tell him to his own face. Definitely!"

"Just my own feelings," said the farmer. "You've summed it up perfectly. Well I'm glad that's settled. Here, remember you mentioned a bit of beef? Well I could let you have a young bullock on the Q.T. next week. You can look 'em over in the pasture down by the station. Pick your own. I don't see why the cities should get all the home-grown and us local folk have to take Argentine. It'd have to be cash, mind you; no cheques."

"How much?" asked the butcher, his tone suddenly flatter.

"Have a look at 'em first, then we'll talk about it."

"I can't go above market price. There's the risk while it's rationed. There was a Lincolnshire chap fined two hundred quid only last month."

"You have a look at 'em, then we'll think about it; they're real good, solid stuff," said the Rector's Warden. "And I'll work in with you tonight about the graveyard: we won't play."

His wife looked up when he returned to the farm.

"You didn't mention the car to the Rector," she said anxiously. "You promised that you wouldn't. I mean about his wife using it."

"No," he replied and grinned. "Anyway it isn't a car anymore; it's a mobile love-nest. Butcher says so."

"Oh, you didn't mention the car to him, did you; he's such a big ignorant lump. I mean you didn't say that it was you who'd lent the Rector the car?"

He laughed and shook his head.

"Why ever did you call it a love-nest?" she asked, examining her knitting with a sudden interest.

The Rector's Warden laughed more loudly still. "For pastoral visits! Pastural visits more like! Well, at any rate it's the right colour."

"The P.C.C. can't pay you a great deal, Thickness," the Rector said, "but with your large family every little helps until you obtain regular employment again. And it's a healthy job up here in the fresh air."

Mr. Thickness looked dubiously at the burial pasture.

"It's got a bit thick, ain't it? I mean, look at it. Up and down an' all. I mean, how'd I get a scythe in among it? I'd never get t'blade in, would I, and if I did, these stones'd knock me point off."

He looked depressingly around him.

"The railings too. Look at them railings round them stone boxes. They'd knock me point off an' all. It's not a straightforward job, is it, I mean just look at it."

"Well, you can't expect the grass to drop off just by looking at it, man," the Rector said testily. "We've all to do something for our money. We mustn't for ever be counting the cost."

"There was a time I'd have run through it," said Mr.

Thickness with a spurt of unconvincing confidence. "Yes, I'd have just run through it. I'd have done it in a morning, I would. Now, it's me blamed back. If it wasn't for me back, blame it, I'd have run through it in a morning, aye, less'n morning, I would. I've done it afore. Folk'll tell you."

"There's no need to rush through it," said the Rector impatiently. "If you get through it in a week, it would be quite satisfactory."

"I got something just here. They couldn't get it out. It's cruel when you bend. It stabs into me back. Doctors seen nothing like it. They say it's six inches if it's an inch. Cruel! Shouldn't ha' got it but for that Sergeant. 'Get out there you English bastard, get out,' he shouted. Kicked me. Next minute he'd had it in the head and I got this. They took me pension an' all. They'd never get me to go again. He was always kicking me. And look what it got him."

He stood in gloomy silence, brooding on the ruthless generals and fierce Scots sergeants who had flung him, Mr. Thickness, into the heat and forefront of the battle and then left him naked and defenceless, something six-inch long in his blamed back, before the Public Assistance Board.

"What was you thinking of payin' for the job?"

"I think five pounds is all we can afford. But I'll add another five from my own pocket."

"Ten quid! I mean, look at it. All ups and downs and them stones. It's a sickle job. It'll be all bendin'. Them iron railins. And I haven't a sickle anyhow."

"Look, Thickness, I agree with you, ten pounds isn't much but it's something and the work would occupy you until you found regular work. You must think of your wife and family and the little extras the money would buy them."

"Think of the wife! Let her think about me! Think of me

wife! What if I was to tell you she's gonna sling her hook and go off wi' a feller from t'Feast? What about that? It's what she said. Leave me wi t'kids and slope off."

"Oh, surely. We all say hasty things in a tiff."

"She's gonna sling her hook. I know. Don't ask me: I know. I can tell she means it. She's been working up to it. Who's gonna look after t'kids? I mean, I can't afford to have a housekeeper in like you could if your missus went off. Here you go on botherin' me about cuttin' this blamed grass and I've got all this on me plate. Me wife goin' off, and me wi' a handful of kids!"

"You must try and dissuade her. The Marriage vow is sacred; it must not be broken. Ask your wife to make a new beginning. It may be that you both will have to make concessions. Have a frank discussion of your difficulties. Find employment. Pay her a fair proportion of your wages." Like many well-meaning people, he became very bold when advising others.

"Are your difficulties physical or psychological?" he demanded.

"We got no difficulties," replied Thickness sullenly. "She suits me all right most times. I got no complaints. A lot of fellows got worse women."

"But you have just told me that she says that she is going to break up the home."

"Maybe I did, but we got no difficulties. We was all right till he came sniffing around last year. She's my woman: what's he want to come sniffing around for? I knew how it would be as soon as she seen him again. He's younger than me. I bet he didn't do his bit. Aye, such as him was cock o' the walk when they sent us lads overseas. And when they got us there, they put dope in us tea to keep even us minds off women."

"You must think of your children," said the Rector sternly, "and of your Marriage vows. My advice is..."

Thickness burst into tears.

"What's he want to come swaggering around for?" he blubbered. "He's got a woman of his own; I seen her. What's he want my woman for? It ain't right. I'm going to see the British Legion about it."

He shambled off.

"The grass, Thickness, the grass?" the Rector cried.

"Cut the danged stuff yourself: I got too much on me blamed plate without it. She's my woman an' I'm gonna have her. I'll have clothes off her back an' lock her in the house afore he'll have her. I'll learn her what she can do and what she can't do. She'll find out who's boss. You can keep your danged grass."

He set off at an absurd trot down the hill.

Mrs. Thickness stood, back to the chair, black hair rolled tightly in curlers, eyes bitter.

"Aye, if he'll have me."

"And what about t'kids?" he muttered.

"They're thine as much as mine. Tha canst do as tha sees fit, poor kids!"

"I can't look after 'em," he said helplessly. "The Council'll have to have 'em. I'll have to go into lodgins."

"If anybody'll have thee. Who dost t'think'll want thee layin' round t'kitchen all day long and all week long, under other folks' feet."

"It's me back."

"Thy back! It didn't stop thee saddling me wi' more kids,

did it? Tha doesn't notice thy back when tha's in bed. That's thee all right. That's thee. Tha makes me sick to vomit."

He jumped up and stumbled towards her. Immediately she snatched an empty milk bottle. "Don't! Just don't! It might make me sorry."

He halted, a small grubby man, his finger nails bitten to the quick.

She said fiercely. "Them days are ower, Tom Thumb, an' tha knows it. Tha'll knock me about no more, by God. I don't know why ever I let thee start. I was a great soft lass. My dad beat me and I let thee beat me. But he was a big man, not a banty-cock like thee. Thee - and thy back!"

She suddenly lunged forward and before he could raise his arms, she had crushed him to the stone flagged floor, rammed down his shoulders with her knees, clutching his thin hair. His fists beat ineffectually at her heavy sides, his short legs kicked at the air.

"Now, mi Little Man," she laughed, punctuating her words by banging his head on the stone slabs. "Now who's maister here? Who?"

He did not answer, only stared furiously past her breasts to her passionate face.

"Who?"

She tilted her body forward, grinding his shoulders until he screamed.

"Who?"

"You! You!" he gasped.

Placing her hand across his nose, she pushed herself from him, allowing him to shamble off and flop on to the sofa. She scornfully turned her back and propping the mirror behind the tap, began to take out her curlers.

"That settles it then," she said carelessly. "Now that tha

can't manage me any more, that takes away thy last attraction."

Mr. Thickness made as if to rise to this challenge but thought better of it.

"He'll knock thee around. Tha won't be the only woman there. He's got a lass half thy age in his caravan already…, aye at this very minute."

"Maybe he has, but she won't stay there," she replied confidently. "Any road, tha'll ha' t'bed all to thisself tonight. If tha gets lonely, tha can think on where I'll be. Tha knows what I'll be doin', doesn't tha! I'll ha' another maister."

She turned and grinned victoriously at him.

Fascinated, he watched her draw her hands slowly along her thighs and up to her breasts.

"Aye, I'll ha' another maister," she said complacently.

The young showman and his elder brother, Artie, sat on the steps of the former's caravan dragging at fags, basking in warmth and idleness.

"I seen thee with same woman as last time we was here. They can smell thee out. Is she wed?"

"Aye."

"Old hands suit thee best?"

"Less t'teach 'em."

"Smashin' figure," said the elder brother. "Tha can pick 'em. What about husband?"

"He's nowt. On Assistance. She can't get him to work. He won't get out o' bed."

"Don't blame him if she's there. What about her kids?"

"What about 'em. Nay, that's his problem. There's places they can put 'em into. She's leavin' him an' comin' wi' me, permanent."

"Is she, by gom! Tha can pick 'em all right." He lowered his voice.

"What about t'other wench. Goin' t'keep 'em both? Two hens i' t'nest? Is tha?"

"Gi' me a coupla quid an' she's thine. I'll make her come to thee. If I say so, she'll come. She knows me: she'll come. But it's going to cost thee a couple quid."

"Coupla quid?"

"What's couple quid. Eighteen, that's all she is. She'll see thee all right; she's a bit o' hot stuff."

"An' tha thinks she'll come?"

"Aye - if I say she'll come, she'll come. Gi' her a touch o' thi belt if she acts soft."

"Happen tha'll want her back?"

"Happen I will, but not for a week or two. I like a change."

"Happen I can take on t'other then?"

"Happen tha talks too much. Coupla quid - that's what I said."

The elder brother half grudgingly fumbled in his pocket. "Tha'll see she comes. If she's not there I'll have mi brass back?" he kept muttering anxiously.

"It's no use carrying on," the young fairman told the big girl sagging on the caravan's bunk. "It's no use at all. Tha's gotta get outa here. I shan't keep on telling thee an' blubberin' won't help thee; it only spoils thy chances of ever getting back. Tha come of thy own accord. An' now I'm gettin' shot o' thee."

She whimpered.

"An' where'll I go?" she sniffled. "I can't go home now any more.

"I tol' you. Artie'll have thee. Tha can move in wi' him tonight an' if tha plays thi cards right, happen he'll let thee stay. But he don' wanna bag o' blubber roun' his neck. Tha gotta do what he says. If tha does what he says he'll treat thee fair. But tha's gotta gi' him what he wants and no hanky--panky. An' tha's gotta stay off other chaps."

"I don't want to leave here."

"Well I'm not goin' off to t'North Pole. I'll be seein' thee. But not here. Understan' that? Not here. I din' have other women here when you was here an' it's gotta be same now. But I'll see thee. Tha needn't tell Artie that. I wanna change and I'm gonna have a change. To listen to thee it sounds like End of World if a chap wants a change... I'm not married to thee an' I din' ask thee here. I've kept thee here more'n six months an' I've given thee spendin' money. Now I want shot o' thee. Another woman's movin' in wi' me."

The big girl moaned.

"Well I've told thee. If tha's here a minute after dark, tha'll know about it. Tha'll get what tha got i' Doncaster. Things'll get smashed an' it won't be tea cups. I tell thee Artie nor nobody else'll want thee after I've finished."

The girl lumbered to her feet, her heavy breasts pushing against the cheap soiled blouse.

"Fred, don't send me off," she cried. "I can't bear it. Not now. I feel queer. I want you, Fred. I don't want anybody else. You needn't marry me - not if you let me stay till I feel better."

She stared wide-eyed at him.

"I love you, Fred."

The young man took one swift pace forward and hit her with his open hand across the side of the face. A trickle of blood oozed from her mouth and all at once her face collapsed in an agony of weeping.

Mr. Thickness stood nervously at the foot of the caravan steps and looked at the Proprietor's knees.

"It's the kids," he mumbled. "If it wasn't for the kids, I wouldn't have come botherin' you. But how'm I going to see to 'em if she goes? I've always played fair wi' her; except for mi fags, she's allus had t'Assistance money."

"Maybe she's only talking," said the Proprietor.

"Nay, maister, she's means it all right. She's mad on him. I know her and I know she's mad on him. She's going off to him all right."

He paused.

"Unless you can do something, maister," he added miserably.

"How old are your children?"

"Edwin's eleven, Joe's eight, Gloria's seven, Cary's five an' Marilyn's three."

"Why did you keep bringing these poor children into the world if you can't support them?"

"They just kept coming, Maister. We didn't want 'em."

"Why is it you don't keep a job?"

"It's this back of mine, Maister. It's the War. They gave me a pension for it and then They took it away. I got to have a sitting-down job. It's me blamed back."

The Proprietor looked down at the spiritless face.

Poor woman, he thought, tied to *that*. Always hanging about the house under her feet, wanting to lech around with her at all hours of the day, too gutless to grow a few vegetables in his garden or even wash himself. Poor children!

"I wouldn't have come," Mr. Thickness went on, "but I

knew you were a religious man and you wouldn't want..."

"I'll see to it," the Proprietor said shortly.

"Thanks, Maister, I knew that you'd see to it. Folks said I ought t'see you."

He turned away.

"Here," said the Proprietor. "Here, and look me in the face for once."

The pale eyes in the wrinkled old face were hard.

"What you want is some backbone, man. You want to get off your idle backside and get yourself a job - and keep it."

"It's me back..."

"There's only one thing your back needs and that's a bone up its middle. A woman wants something else from her man as well as another baby every couple of years. Bone lazy fellows like you ought to be operated on."

The Proprietor stood up, pulling down his broadcloth jacket, and pushing the ends of his green silk scarf deeper into his armpits.

"But I've said that I'll see to it," he said, "and I'll see to it for the children's sake."

The letter lay among the circulars and the bills. Georgie read it in the postmark "Stratford-on-Avon". There really was no need to open it; the page inside merely elaborated what she already knew.

"...there it is. I can't turn it down and you wouldn't want me to, I know. You know what it's like in this kill-your-own-grandma job - turn down an Offer and you don't get another. So I'll be here all next Spring and Summer and well into Autumn. Julian and Fenella musn't change schools just now so Pam will stay in Town for their

sakes... as well as for Tiddler's. So, darling, even though we can't make the Clean Break you wanted, we can still see Lots of each other. I've my eye on a Splendid little cottage no more than five miles from here but Wonderfully Lost - and you can come whenever you can get away. Haven't you a Sick Sister you can nurse for a month at a time?!! Believe me, I'm Desolate at the way things have gone..."

And so on and so on, wrapping lies and excuses round the unspoken core - that he would not leave his wife and his children and his little world. And yet, he must have the cake and eat it, a town wife and a rural mistress tucked away in some godforsaken rutted lane, waiting with supper and bed and a balm bath for the frayed ego of a small-part actor who licked the collar chafing his neck.

So that was over.

Very well! Then Croser must be made to toe the line. She crumpled the letter into a ball and threw it decisively into the basket. That was the end of that.

She found her husband sitting on an old kitchen chair under the apple tree. The book he had been reading had dropped down and was half hidden in the overgrown grass. When she spoke to him he started and then smiled nervously.

"It's very pleasant out here. I came out because it seemed so close in the house. Are there many people in the streets yet? If you care to sit here a while, I'll make a pot of tea and bring it out to you."

"Look," she said, "it's no use beating about the bush. I'm going away tonight."

"Away?" he faltered.

"Away, and I shan't be coming back. I'm leaving you. I can't stand living in this ghastly backwater any longer. I just refuse to go on being punished for the mistake I made when

I married you. I'm going while I've still enough sap in me to enjoy myself."

"Where are you going?"

"London."

"Alone?"

"No."

"But Georgie, does he love you, does he really love you?"

"Love! What's love to do with it. He's young and he's willing. He can give me what I want - he can give me what you never could."

The Rector had become very pale. He rose from the chair like an old man.

"Georgie," he muttered.

She took a step forward.

"In fields, by the hedges, under haystacks! The whole town knows it."

He turned blindly as though trying to escape into the tangled boughs of the tree. She could see his shoulders shaking and the sight goaded her on.

"You should never have taken me. You cheated me. You don't need a woman. One of your own hassocks would do." She turned to go.

"And don't look for me. When I'm tired of him there'll be another man and another. But I'd rather sink to a brothel than come back to you."

Shuddering and pressed against the tree, he heard her walk leisurely away and, after a time, a door slammed. Somewhere near, a wood pigeon resumed its calling across the warm summer afternoon.

The Canon debated the lesser evil, a walk up the Rectory drive or scratches from the protruding bushes on the paintwork of his new car. The debate was brief; lunch at the Palace had been very, very good.

"Ah," he said, "ah, His Lordship asked me to look in on you."

He usually called the younger clergy by their Christian names but he had been unsure of this man right from their first meeting and now he felt pleased at his perspicacity. For a moment the Rector almost answered "The Bishop may have done; I did not" but he restrained himself, feeling some compensatory pleasure in watching the other's discomfort wedged in the narrow utility armchair.

"Ah, coldish in here, even on a day like this," the Canon said, even now not noticing how pale and ill his host looked.

"You should visit us in December."

"Ah yes, these immense rectories and vicarages..."

"You are Chairman of the Diocesan Committee which refused my application to have something more suitable built in the village."

"Money, my dear man! Or lack of it. You can't imagine how worrying it is."

"Yet you agreed to a similar scheme for Gornard. And the incumbent there was a younger man."

"I am only one of a Committee, my dear man. You can depend upon it that the two cases were most thoroughly gone into. You do not know the whole story."

"No, that is true, but I should very much like to hear it."

"Come, come, this really is not what I came to see you about, and I have to make another call this afternoon."

And the better to accomplish his mission, and aware of

the rising pitch of his voice, he paused, breathed deeply (as his wife had suggested) and injected what he believed to be an avuncular benevolence into it.

"His Lordship wished me to sound…" (now is that the word I wanted? he worried) "to sound you about the living at Nettleton. Would you be interested in it. No, no, wait, I haven't finished; it is worth forty pounds a year more than your present living and…"

"And since poor Egger's death, hastened on by the disgraceful living conditions of his rectory, it has been combined with vacant parishes at Arley-in-the-Hedges and Arley Stoke; and the new incumbent will be expected to scurry round and round (at his own expense) to administer artificial respiration…"

The Rector's voice, aggravated by his harrowing day, was shrill with indignation.

"Really! You read things into what I say which simply are not there. His Lordship, knowing how things stand with you, merely wished to help…"

"Knowing what things?"

"That is not for me to say," the Canon replied prudently.

"You mean that the Bishop thinks it would benefit my parish if I left it?"

"I did not say so."

"I wish the Bishop would speak as forthrightly to the laity as he does to the less exalted clergy. But since laymen appointed him, no doubt he knows on which side his bread is buttered. It is monstrous that one who never ministered as a parish priest should presume to censure one."

"He is not censuring you," the Canon interposed impatiently.

"What does he know of my difficulties? Indeed, how can

he?"

"He only wished to help you, man."

"Then let him speak plainly to the laity about their Christian duty as stewards of Our Lord. Let him tell them of a diminishing priesthood, the poverty-stricken families of clergy scratching for a living in barns like this. Let him tell them of the souls lost overseas because of their miserliness towards our sacred mission..."

"Oh, come, come..."

"Fifteen pounds - that is the cost of tidying my own churchyard and the churchwardens will not authorise it. Fifteen pounds! The burial place of their own people!"

"Perhaps you did not approach them tactfully. As my good wife tells me, 'Kid them into doing it.' Sometimes these good people need a little prodding, a little admonishing perhaps, but I have noticed that a joke at the right time usually does the trick. One mustn't make an issue out of things."

"But it is an issue - the Duty of the People to God."

The Canon knew that he was being drawn on to uncertain and perhaps holy ground. He stepped back swiftly.

"Ah," he mourned, "if only you had been as fortunate in your wardens as your predecessors was and Tallboy before him - a wonderful man, a great diplomat, Prosser the father of your present Head Mistress. A man of God, if ever one lived. Well, there it is; he has gone before and we must do the best we can with what is left.

"Well now, would you like me to tell His Lordship that you would like a little more time to think about Nettleton?"

"I would not."

The Canon's patience suddenly collapsed. His face reddened, his wife's warnings were forgotten.

"Now," he said in a cold, controlled voice, "I am going to speak plainly to you, my dear man. I am going to speak very plainly. No one in our diocese likes what he sees in the parish of Great Minden. Please *do not* interrupt me. We see an empty Church, a stubborn priest, a recalcitrant Parochial Council, a diocesan quota unfulfilled, the domestic life of its rectory a by-word in the County. *And this has to change.* We have tried our utmost to avoid a break. We have offered you a new living in which to make a new beginning. And you have refused. Very well!"

He wriggled out of the chair and stood up.

"His Lordship has desired me to say this to you and I shall say it - 'The incumbent of Great Minden parish is advised to put his house in the order that befits a priest.'"

"You insult my wife," cried the Rector, white with anger. "Please leave my house and... and tell the Bishop that listening to gossip ill becomes his high office!"

These last words were uttered to the sound of his guest's footfalls in the echoing corridor and to the vigorous closing of a door. Only then did he realise how his legs shook and his voice trembled and, leaning his head upon the mantelpiece, he wept again.

The last half hour of the day dragged on its way.

The class slumped in their trap-like desks and looked impassively towards, but not really at, Mr. Croser who stood leaning heavily on the tall desk.

"At last," he said dully, "there were only nine lean horses left. How many, Bellenger?"

"Nine, sir."

"What is a lean horse?"

"A thin one, sir."

"There were only nine lean horses left. What had happened to the rest, Thickness?"

"Died, sir."

"Wrong."

Thickness, his duty done, lay back against the desk bar.

"Don't look so pleased with yourself, Thickness. Everybody sit up."

The class made a stir of shoulders.

"You, Bellenger!"

"The garrison had eaten them, sir."

"Correct. The Blue team can have a point." He pushed a blue button one space up a string.

"Things were bad. Nine lean horses as I've said, and a pint of meal each day. They ate dogs, cats, rats, mice and dried hides… Look here, Elsie Perrin, doesn't this interest you?"

"Yes, sir."

"Well, then, look intelligent - and sit up and stop chewing your handkerchief, you're not besieged in Londonderry…"

No one tittered; no one even smiled. The room was hot as an oven. All round him he could hear the treadmill clicking - a distant class drearily straining at "It was a lover and his lass," one nearer chanting "Thirty pence are two and sixpence, thirty-six pence three shillings, forty pence are three and four pence, forty-eight pence, four shillings, fifty pence…"

In the hall a sweating student-teacher was harassedly cajoling an exhausted group to "Heels raise; knees full bend, backs straight; head - rest. Ready! Press! Press! Press! Press!"

Mr. Croser passed his handkerchief daintily across his nose and licked the concealed acid-drop lodged between his lower gum and his cheek.

"Famine - starvation," he said impressively. Looking swiftly at the half-concealed text book, "One man remained so fat, while the rest were almost skeletons, that he believed he was in great danger. So he hid himself in a cellar for the rest of the siege. Why did he think he was in danger, Thickness?"

"From the enemy's cannon balls, sir, because of his size, they were more likely to hit him than thin people."

"Oh, you fool. Anyone answer!"

He rushed down the first gangway, struck the boy across the back and began shaking him.

"Now will you wake up. Why did he think he was in danger?"

"He was a Roman Catholic, sir."

Mr. Croser clutched his forehead and rushed to the desk. "My God," he hissed. "My God! Teaching!"

The bell rang.

Instantly from all parts of the building, hinged seats happily banged back and children shuffled and clattered to their feet. An assortment of evening prayers were briskly sung and then each room poured out a column of children. Only the singing class remained; the bell had caught them in the middle of a verse,

> *"Between the acres of the rye*
> *These pretty country folk would lie."*

They sang into the guilty silence.

Croser imagined Miss Prosser walking menacingly towards the classroom.

"Poor Everett's for it if she heard that," muttered the Chief Assistant, "and he probably thinks the verse has something to do with telling fibs."

"Well, hasn't it?" said Mr. Croser with a leer.

"You ought to know. There's been your girl friend's car parked outside my window since ten to four. Whose rye field are you going to tumble about in?"

Mr. Croser pushed his way through the jostling children and emerged with the vanguard into the street. He was hot, harassed and very irritable. He had half believed the Chief Assistant was codding, but there it was against the opposite verge, the familiar dark red coupé. He angrily crossed the road and pushed his head awkwardly into the open window.

"I thought we agreed you weren't to come here," he said furiously. "Everybody'll be talking now. Maybe you don't care, but I do. All the kids'll be running home now, spread it around. Of all the damned stupidest things to go and do…"

Georgie pressed down the handle and pushed the door against him.

"Get in," she said. "We can't talk here. For goodness sake keep calm and get in. Here, have a cigarette: you need one."

"I can't stay more than a minute," he muttered. "I've my tea to get and then I have to go out. I've an engagement."

She ignored this and drove off.

"Prosser's been helling you again," she murmured. "Never mind, I'll make it up to you."

He felt her gloved fingers run lightly along his thigh, shivered and then lay back, blowing clouds of smoke through the open window, gradually forgetting the humiliations and anxieties of the day.

"Forget it," she went on. "You'll see - just give it ten minutes. What's it matter anyway? *We* know what we want, that's the important thing. Why let that desiccated spinster get you down? You know what her trouble is, don't you?

Didn't you have to study all about it at training college or whatever they call the institutions for churning out teachers? Watch out…"

The track to the mill was rutted and overgrown and the car bumped and slid along between trees and brambles. Getting out, they mounted past three rickety landings to the topmost floor, bending low to pass beneath the rusting machinery. For a moment Croser paused, looking down to the reed-choked pool.

Summer… summer…

I never have any time, he thought. They're always on at me. If it isn't one it's another - the landlady, Prosser, Effie, this one. It's nice here: it's like that picture I was looking at, those flowers in the water, the white ones with the yellow middles, that shadow, the heat. Maybe I should buy a box of paints. It would be good for me, calm my nerves. I could go off on Saturdays and Sundays with a vacuum flask. I could buy a bicycle and Effie could come on hers and then sit and knit.

I could get a headship in a little village school, Group Nought or One. We could live in a converted mill with a thatch. We could have a seat on my carrier to bring the baby out on. We could… The heat and the heavy silence of the afternoon gathered comfortably around him. Summer… summer…

"I'm here, darling. I'm ready."

She had spread out her silk dust coat on a bed of sacks and was lying with one hand behind her head, relaxed and expectant. He sat clumsily down beside her and fumbled for his packet of cigarettes but she turned towards him, reaching up and pulling him down towards her.

"I can't wait," she muttered, "I can't wait."

Edwin Thickness, too, had not stood upon the order of his departure from school. Eschewing the delights of horsing around, he raced hot-foot home to the Row and only slowed to a casual walk when he approached the backyard. But his dissimulation was wasted. One pace through the open door was enough to tell him that what he had feared was true; the house was empty. Dinner pots, greasy and unkempt, littered the table, the beds were unmade, scent which his mother splashed over herself before going out cloyed the air. Two of his brothers followed him in.

"Get us sommat to eat, Edwin," one said. "Mum'll be gone a long time."

Oh, so he can tell too, thought Thickness, rather surprised at the sapience of one so young, as he flicked the switch of the electric kettle.

"Man came and turned it off, Edwin - after you'd gone to school: the same as turned it off last time. He knew just where to look for it."

"Mam started crying," said the other.

"Water's just as good," said Thickness, rinsing out three breakfast mugs and filling them at the bucket. "Where's He gone?"

"He was in the snug at t'Fusilier. I saw him through the frosted glass."

"Aye," said Thickness bitterly, "he has money for t'booze but when I wanted a couple o' bob to go on t'school trip he hadn't any then. No fear! Booze, that's different. Booze and fags!"

"Will tha booze when tha grows up, Edwin?" asked the youngest brother anxiously.

"Nay, that I san't. I'll have holidays and I'll buy a fishin' rig-out an' I'll not get married an' have any kids. I'll see as

I'm not poor like us. Tha bet I will. I'm goin' to be like Mr. Croser an' not have a wife. I'll live in lodgins an' be independent."

Thickness sat down at the table and thought how Mr. Croser brushed back his hair and smoked and didn't say prayers. He just mutters, he thought, and in hymns he moves his mouth but he doesn't make any noise. He knows plenty too about battles and the Bible. I'll be real sorry when I have to go up into the next class in September. I wish he liked me more. I don't think he likes being a school-teacher.

"I wish Mam would come home," said one of the brothers. "Dost t'think she's run off, Edwin?"

Thickness turned savagely and struck him across the cheek.

"Well, Fred Jarvis's mam ran off," the child sobbed. "An' when she'd gone, his dad put Fred an' his sisters in a Home. I know a lad who saw them there. It's at Seaside. He said he liked it there better'n here."

Thickness weighed the portents of the day, considered a Children's Home, and his proud soul quailed.

"Heavens, how long a day lasts when one isn't working for someone else!" thought Peplow. "It just goes on and on; there seems no end to it. Or maybe it's these country towns. Time doesn't seem to have the same dimensions. There should be a new reckoning. Nine hours equals one city day; forty hours equals one country day. I should have come to live in a spot like this when I was demobbed instead of beating my brains out in the city. Think of all the hours I've sat in parks, trying to escape from the other ten thousand milling around behind the laurel bushes. And I could have been here, at this pool and not another soul around - only Tom. He would have liked it. We could have come here to fish - and to have one of our little talks.

["Who was the world's greatest batsman, Dad?"

"The world's greatest batsman undoubtedly was the famous Doctor Grace. He had the biggest average, the biggest aggregate, the biggest beard and the biggest feet. Bowlers were afraid to bowl within his reach."

"Did you see him play, Dad?"

"No, but maybe your great-grandfather did, Tom."

"Dad, are we well off?"

"No, not very. Comfortably off, I think you could say. We have enough. We're just about all right. Not too little, not too much."

"Is that why we don't have a car?"

"Yes, I suppose so. But I expect we'll get around to it some day."

"Would you like to be rich, Dad?"

"Who wouldn't? But it's not Everything. Don't forget that. I'd rather have Mummy and you than a Million. There's other things beside money you know. There's Honour and Courage and a Good Name."

"I'll write them in my book. But I'd like plenty of money too."]

He started. Had Tom ever asked him those questions? These conversations continually talking themselves out in his head - had they really had them? The eager voice - why couldn't it be still like the eager body. Why couldn't it draw back into the dark? Why couldn't it die too?

In the dark rides between plantations of water-lilies, fish moved lazily around. Dragonflies cruised close to the surface, rested on green islands of leaf, explored the air-currents among the rushy borders. He sat down on the crumbling prow of the mill, his legs dangling, all at once drowsy in the heat and stillness.

I seem to know this place already. Ruskin, Bellenger, that poor old hot-gospeller, the boy Nick. Half-a-day ago Minden was only a name on a railway timetable, a place where a train stopped, a place to get off at and to do what I came to do.

A moorhen, bowlegged, walked away down the track, snipping here and there in the verges, turning off at last into the ditch's green jungle. A cuckoo was calling, insistently, monotonously. He scanned the trees, but the sound still mocked him.

When it was over and the thing done, what would people here say? "I think I remember him but I'm not sure - yes, there was a stranger here - I think he was tall - yes, I remember speaking to him. No, not at all the kind of person you would imagine. No, quite definitely not the type I'd have said would do that sort of thing."

And what would Ruskin say? And Bellenger? But Bellenger wouldn't know. Once again his thoughts darkened. I used to be afraid when I was as close as this before. That night in 1944, for instance, with Dexter dying in my arms, and flak everywhere, like an orchard in blossom...

A herd of black cattle moved, Indian-like, across the gap, swallows dashed across the borders, spread their wings suddenly, stalled and flashed back. A bee buzzed at his hair and instinctively, he struck it. It was dead before it reached the surface of the pool, one wing broken and bent awkwardly, dipping into the water, floating like a strange flower, an idle current drifting it to the fringe of lilies. A dragonfly hovered, flittering momentarily above it, then spurted away. Immediately he was sorry at what he had done - senseless, unnecessary.

Behind him, axle deep in nettles and grass, was a farm wagon rotting in retirement, wearing away in the weather. What had saved it from the axe, the saw, the wood-pile? Its gently curving lines, its memories, indolence? For a moment he was abashed by the permanence of the place and the transitoriness of those who had made a mark and were gone - the mason, the tree-planter, the wheelwright, the wagoner. Death and partings hung in the heavy cloying smell of the may and the kelkin; it fitted the heaviness of his mood.

The sound of a car's engine roused him. He recognised them at once - the woman bold and uncaring, the younger man, his demeanour half reluctant, half eager, sidling behind her into the twilight of the derelict building.

The Morris stopped long enough for Croser to wriggle out and then was driven discreetly off across the lower end of the Square.

Hell! he thought, crossing the road before going in the same direction. She'll kill me if we go on at this rate. I can't take it - not on my landlady's feeding. I'd need a diet of caviar and stout to keep it up. It's all right for her: she can loll around in bed all day, she doesn't have to slog her guts out wearing out blackboards like me. She's never satisfied, she's never had enough, that's her trouble; she ought to see a doctor about it.

He turned in to the Square, was checked in his usual path across it by the paraphernalia of the fairground and was forced to pass along the shop fronts.

What I need is a good lie-down. In fact, I'll have a good lie-down. Then I'll pick Effie up and we'll go to the Pictures at Gornard; it'll be cheaper than being robbed here, and I'll be resting.

He explored his pockets. Beside the four pound notes he had saved for his holidays there was nothing but a shilling and a half-crown. I'm not breaking into them, he thought bitterly, not even for the Empress of China, so it's no Pictures. Just a walk in the blasted country! And it's going to stay a walk and no other kind of nonsense. I've blunted my manhood for Friday the 23rd. I couldn't even oblige the Queen of Sheba if she dropped in.

It occurred to him that he would have to pass the hairdressing shop and that it might be as well not to be seen so far off-course. If he walked back, he could go round by the other way; or could he push through the stalls and things. He decided on this latter diversion and, taking a fix on the Fusilier, stepped off the pavement. But he had hesitated too long. Even before she spoke, he heard the door slam and sensed her shape alongside.

"Good gracious, Sid, what are you doing here at this time? It's a quarter past five. Have you had your tea already?"

It's a prison, thought Mr. Croser. All day long - "You're late, Mr. Croser." "Why didn't you do this, Mr. Croser?" "Get up, Mr. Croser." "Get down, Mr. Croser." "Love me, Mr. Croser." "What are you doing here, Mr. Croser?" "Why aren't you somewhere else, Mr. Croser?"

"Got a prescription for my landlady," he said. "You're knocking off early, aren't you?"

"Well, it's the Feast, isn't it?" she replied. "I'll get in real early tomorrow and clear up."

"I bet you will," Mr. Croser said. "You're terrific at getting up early."

"There's no need to be sarky."

He already had noted her drooping mouth and resentful eyes.

They stood facing one another.

"I've got a bad head too," she added, and when he didn't answer, burst into tears.

Mr. Croser was dumbfounded.

"Here," he muttered, looking round, "come off it, Eff, what have I said?"

"It's that Mrs. Morgan and what she let slip," she sobbed. "She hinted you were carrying on with a married woman."

Mr. Croser went cold.

"She said what?" he cried indignantly. "Me! A married woman! Well!"

Effie continued to sob.

"I'll go straight round and see her about it. I shall. I'll go now. It's a Slander."

Effie stopped crying.

"Well, she didn't exactly say that," she snuffled.

"Oh, she didn't," said Mr. Croser. "Then I'd like to know what she did say, the old stinker!"

"Well, I don't really know but she left it lying on my mind. All afternoon. Oh, Sid, it isn't true, is it?"

"Haven't I just said so? Of course it isn't true. Me! A married woman!"

He knew that the danger was past and pressed to the attack. "I'm just surprised at a refined person like you listening to village gossip," he said.

Effie began to sob again.

"Oh, Sid, I do love you," she choked. "You know I do, don't you?"

Mr. Croser glanced guiltily over his shoulder again; the butcher, from his doorway, was sardonically watching them.

"Oh, all right, all right," he muttered angrily, "only don't go on about it; you've got that damned meat-merchant laughing at us."

"He's always peeping," Effie said vindictively but suddenly calm. "Especially at us girls. I've heard things about him, things I can't repeat."

"He hasn't bothered you, dear?" asked Mr. Croser with a sudden access of righteousness.

"He once asked me to sit by him in the pictures at Gornard."

"He did!"

"And he once told me he liked girls with big busts."

Mr. Croser looked furiously over his shoulder again.

"Why he's old enough to be your grandfather," he growled. "For two pins I could bust his big fat nose for him. And I will if you like. Just say the word, that's all."

"You don't look very well," murmured Effie maternally. "You look real pale. Have you been studying too much? I think you've been overdoing it."

Overdoing it! thought Mr. Croser, that's a laugh!

"It's the heat," he said. "I say, I'd better go."

"I want you to come round about six-thirty. I want you to meet my Uncle. He's going back at eight. You know, the one in Business I was telling you about. You said you'd like to meet him. He might do something for us."

Mr. Croser was considering what excuse would sound most convincing when she began to brush his trousers.

"You're all dirty," she exclaimed. "Anybody would think you'd been lying down on a meal-bag…"

"It's the chalk-dust," Mr. Croser said swiftly. "I'll be around about twenty-five past since you really want me to." Effie's big blue eyes moistened again.

"Oh, Sid," she sobbed, "I can't help it. It's only because I love you so much."

"Not here," said Mr. Croser hastily, giving her a firm push. "There's people about. Twenty-five past, at your place. Wait till then."

He walked jauntily off; the various transactions of the last hour had repaired his self-esteem. I'll be damned if I'll go off with her, he though, jettisoning the promise he had given Georgie at the mill. Damn it, she's pushing forty. She's *passée*. She's had it. Now Eff, she's got years and years of it left. She's got nubility. And I bet she'll wear well.

Evening

Mr. Croser's landlady was maintaining the perverse mood of the morning and, instead of showing the Rector into the sitting-room, she sent him unheralded upstairs so that when his discreet tapping was unanswered and he gently opened the door, his wife's lover was discovered, legs lasciviously apart and collar undone, sleeping off his exertions.

"Mr. Croser," he said, and repeated it several times with loudening tones until the sleeper stirred and at last, sat up very suddenly.

"Mr. Croser, I've come to see you about my wife."

"Your wife!"

"Yes, she says that she is going away with you."

"Me! Going away with me!"

Mr. Croser struggled reluctantly into wakefulness.

"Yes. I am told that there is a liaison between you."

"A liaison!"

"And I've come to beg you not to do it."

"Not to do what?" asked Mr. Croser stupidly.

"Not to take advantage of her. She is so easily swayed by a stronger personality. Perhaps I've not given her all the attention she needs. Perhaps I've not given her all the love she needs. Perhaps I should not have asked her to share the life of a country priest when I could not give her the things to which she was accustomed. But I made a sacred vow to care for her. And that is why I am here."

"Well it's very nice of you to call. But I think you've not got the right story. I don't know who's been telling you things. I think you've made a mistake. Well, you see, I do know your wife. I'm not denying I know her. Because there's nothing to be ashamed of" (Mr. Croser's brain was struggling into wakefulness again). "We're just good friends, you see. We met at, at, well we met on a Ramble and got into conversation and we found that we had similar interests, as it were. It's not so easy as you must know, a man in your position, to get intellectual conversation in these backwaters, is it? My home's in the North you know, in Castleford. It's different up there."

"Are you telling me that you do not intend to go away with my wife?"

"Certainly I'm not going away - with anyone's wife. How can I go away with your wife when I'm engaged to be married? In fact I was just setting off to see my young lady when you called."

"Oh!"

"Yes, my young lady and me have made certain Plans for the autumn. I hope nothing you've been saying has got to her ears because, if it has, then I'm going to see someone about it. Why, it's scandalous. My young lady wouldn't like it at all. It's a bit thick I must say."

"And you are not leaving Minden tonight?"

"Of course I'm not leaving Minden tonight. How can I? I have a job to go to in the morning. How can I leave my job; it's not the holidays. What would Miss Prosser say?"

"Perhaps I've made a mistake," said the Rector in confusion. "If I've annoyed you, I do apologise. Only, you see, I feel a deep responsibility for my wife. She is restless and unsettled and highly strung. She isn't at all well, in fact. Things have been very difficult for us."

"I'm sorry," said Mr. Croser, "but I don't see how I can help. We were just good friends, if you follow me."

"In a way, she's like a child. I can't explain it, but she is. She's so impulsive. Sometimes it's quite difficult. Please try not to see her for a while, will you?"

Mr. Crosser suddenly made up his mind.

Why not? he thought. She doesn't give a damn for me. She's too forward. She'd throw me over as soon as look at me if someone she fancies more turned up. Anyway, she just uses me like a vacuum cleaner.

"Anything you like," he said. "It's all one to me. If you think our little friendship upsets her, very well! But you've got to tell her not to bother me. I'm quite annoyed about the fuss. There's my young lady to consider. You've got to remember that. It's not me alone. Well, you'll have to excuse me, I'm just on my way to see my fiancée" (he emphasised the last word).

He got up from the bed, feeling like a film star going off into the sunset at the end of a feature; very noble but very broken-hearted.

"Well, Uncle, I know it's only a council house but it's a corner one and only one side's on the Estate. The other side is next to a privately owned house and he's a bank clerk and his girl goes to Miss Kettlewell's private school. We don't have anything to do with the people on the Estate and Dad pays the rent by post so the man doesn't call."

"What's wrong with living in a council house?" asked the Uncle. "The rent's low, too blamed low with the rest of us slaving to subsidise you all. I wish I could get a council house and have the ratepayers pay my decorating and plumbing bills. You're lucky."

"Oh, Uncle, you know you wouldn't live in a council house, not in your position."

"My position! Good God, girl, who do you think I am - Lord Nuffield?"

"Well, you have an Office and you have men working for

you. You don't have to go out at seven in the morning like Dad does and come home dirty at night. And you have a car, not a bicycle like him."

"If your old dad's not got all the money he ought to have, it's because he's had to dress you and your mum like a pair of peacocks for twenty years."

"Oh, Dad's all right, but he's a bit dull. He never says anything. Work, and Saturday afternoon watching the football and reading the paper, that's all he lives for. I'm dying for you to meet Sidney."

The uncle grunted.

"Sidney's a certificated teacher. He went to the grammar school and to a college. He's ever so clever; he can talk French."

"Fat lot of good that will do him. I know his sort; never have any money, always whining that the world owes them a living because they can talk French and have a certificate. Lazy devils usually. I had one work for me in his holidays. Sat on his bottom smoking and sneering and when he left we missed two quid from the cash box. And I couldn't pin it on him neither," he added savagely.

"Oh, Uncle, you'll not find Sidney's like that; he's a gentleman. Mummy says he's a gentleman."

The Uncle looked with distaste around the over-stuffed room and wondered when his brother would be coming so that they could go down the street for a pint.

"Uncle!"

Uncle grunted.

"Uncle, when Sidney comes I wish you'd tell him about your Business. You know, all the men you have working for you and your big house, and about the gardener and the garden-fête you have there - you know."

"Why should I?"

"Well, because it would be sort of nice."

"Oh, so you're ashamed of living in a council house and having your dad come home dirty, are you? I suppose your smarmy threadbare school-teacher thinks he's a cut above you, does he? I suppose you wouldn't like me to talk lah-de-dah, would you, and tell him I go out chasing foxes six times a week?"

It was a pity that the front door bell interrupted him because he was just warming up.

Mr. Croser, standing on the doorstep, quoted silently a context about Samson he had been made to learn by an unusually zealous master in his school-certificate year,

> *"His servants he with new aquist*
> *Of true experience from this great event*
> *With peace and consolation hath dismiss'd -*
> *And calm of mind, all passion spent."*

Just my views, she just about sucks you dry, he thought. Chews you up. I feel as limp as him. Another year of this would have killed me. It's all right at the time, but afterwards! I just hope that Effie isn't expecting me to perform tonight, too.

The Uncle regarded him balefully; it was evident that he had been tried and sentenced in place of the man who had decamped with yesteryear's two quid and all other men who could talk in French.

"Evening!" said he briefly.

"Uncle was just telling me about his cruise," Effie said. "He and Auntie visited seven countries in a fortnight... Italy, France, Venice, Africa, Spain... and what were the others, Uncle?"

"Aston Villa," said the Uncle un-accommodatingly. Mr. Croser laughed brilliantly.

"Did you put in at Marseilles, sir?" he asked incuriously.

"Where? Never heard of it."

"Southern France."

"Oh, you mean Marsails."

"I expect the French say it your way, dear," said Effie, "and the English say it Uncle's way."

"Did you enjoy your cruise, sir?" Mr. Croser asked.

"No"

"Oh."

"I loathe all foreigners and their food and their filth and I loathe the sort of folks who go on cruises. They're too damned lah-de-dah, except for the bumsucking stewards, who're a damned sight worse. God help me never to go farther than Skegness again."

Having made this pronouncement, he sat comfortably back and stared steadily at Croser, who, feeling himself not quite up to arguing with the unconvincible, put on an outrageously false smile and kept nodding his head. Effie, still battling desperately, however, plumped down beside her uncle and asked to be permitted to fill his pipe.

Mr. Croser had had a harrowing day. He had tasted wormwood and gall and the world seemed full of tyrants bent on his humiliation so that this picture of uncle and his pink, purring niece suddenly revolted him.

"I say," he said unconvincingly, "I've just remembered an education meeting I should be at; I must run, I'll see you later on, Effie - ten o'clock at the usual place. I must rush. Goodnight, sir. It was very nice to hear about Marsails."

All this time he was moving to the door but when he had opened it his self-control basely deserted him and he hissed

"And I hope you didn't catch anything there."

Effie caught him at the front-door.

"Oh, Sid, you spoiled everything. He'll never give you a job now if you need one. I don't suppose he'll give us a wedding present even," she wailed. "You're so temperamental."

But the day's events had been too much for Mr. Croser and speech normally would have been beyond him, had he not tripped and skinned his knuckle against the wall. When he had finished cursing, Effie took away a hand from her out-raged mouth and exclaimed, "Oh, Sidney! You with a college education!"

The uncle listened appreciatively.

"Ah well," he muttered, "I reckon there's more to him than I thought. 'Caught something,' eh?"

Until someone hurried nervously forward and brought him a chair, Peplow stood irresolutely on the threshold, at the bar between the sun's glare and the dimness of the house.

"Mrs. Loatley said there might be a newcomer," she whispered. "Here's a hymn-sheet - numbers three and twelve."

When his eyes had become used to the change of light, the wail and wheeze of a harmonium drew them towards its player. It was Mrs. Loatley, grey, stiff-faced, respectable, blackbloused and brooched, pressing down on the yellowing keys, squeezing out the plaintive songs of Zion.

> *"In the Sweet By and By,*
> *In the Sweet By and By,*
> *We shall meet, we shall meet*
> *In the Sweet By and By..."*

Apart from it being written for illiterates, it's not a bad hymn, he thought. Sounds quite attractive - a kind of celestial Costa Brava; we all ought to be hurrying there, like poor old Bellenger. Like me.

The eight or nine women sank happily on to kitchen chairs. Another, dowdy and furtive, sidled to the front.

"'When the Trumpet shall sound' is my Text," she said boldly.

Peplow looked at the picture of a cat in a gilt frame on the wall, fierce eyes staring from its furry head. Then he thought about his feet for he had been on them a long time and he crumpled and straightened his toes. Delicious! Everyone should wear too large shoes. The various topographical features of the room ebbed and flowed in his consciousness like hills disappearing and appearing from the mist - the hats of the disciples, a bacon hook in the beam (wonderful hanging place for throats), the cat, prehistoric and savage, crunching birds' bones. The fierce and glittering cat. And Bellenger blind-flying now, coming in on the beam... He placed a hand over the twitch that had begun again under his left eye and tried to control it. The day, the day, the oncoming night!

Far too soon they were singing again.

> *"Ah Beulah Land! Sweet Beulah Land!*
> *As on thy shining shores I stand,*
> *I look across the crystal sea*
> *Where mansions are prepared for me..."*

Then it was all over. Dim curious faces were turned towards him. He thought, They will tell people, "Yes, he sat close to me... as near as you are. No, he didn't look that kind at all." Or maybe they will say, "Yes, it was written all over him."

He rose to go. Mrs. Loatley leaned forward from the harmonium and touched his arm. He saw another woman glance quickly at them. Was there something queer about her? Was she that kind of woman? When the reluctant company had left, Mrs. Loatley closed the outside door and came back. He waited in an agony of embarrassment for her to speak.

"What are you going to do? I've been watching you. You're not here ordinary are you? There's something queer about today; I just seem to sense things. Sit here for just a minute."

The heavy scent of the elderberry flowers drifted into the house. He turned irresolutely towards the door. Mrs. Loatley looked down at the keys of the harmonium; she was pale.

"Let me help you. Won't you tell me what it is that's oppressing you? What is it that you came here to do?"

Peplow shook his head; he felt very tired. "I enjoyed the meeting," he said.

"Shall you visit Minden again?"

"No"

"Never?"

"Never."

He turned once more and went out into the sunshine.

Edward Bellenger's fingers no longer played with the coverlet. His breath, in increasing intervals, came and went in shallow gasps and when silence came, it came unnoticed.

Petals like stars falling from the darkening boughs floated away on the water, turning gently and swinging with the current and, below, in the green depths, weeds streamed out like a woman's hair, rising and submerging again. Petals like stars and leaves falling, the sound of water… until darkening sky and the low confusion of sounds merged into the night and silence.

A breeze from the garden soundlessly closed the door.

The boy stood in the hall and listened to the voices.

"What did Minchin say?"

"Just what I said all along."

"We needn't keep him here?"

"Well, he did go on about trying to trace her but when I pinned him down to it, he said that we had no legal responsibility to look after him and that it was really up to the mother."

"Did you remember to mention it?"

"Mention what?"

"Well, who's going to look after him…?"

"No, I didn't. Hang it all, he's only ten. We can't just pitch him out like that. I mean it's his home as well as ours. He didn't ask to come here. I mean you can't blame him, can you? It's *his* father that's gone, as well as ours."

"That's all very well, but what about her? Why does she have to get away with it? He's more hers than ours; you've got to admit that. I mean you have to admit he isn't really our responsibility, now is he? Don't tell me there aren't ways of finding out where she is. How do we know that that Ruskin doesn't know where she lives? We might find something among Dad's papers about it."

"Well, that's different. As a matter of fact I had a feeling when I was talking to Minchin that he knew more than he was letting on. I suppose he's got Dad's papers, the Will and all that. For all we know perhaps Dad appointed a guardian for him and…"

The sitting-room door was pushed to and, after a few moments, Nick tip-toed past it and up the staircase. The door of his father's room was shut and, on the landing, the silence seemed to gather round and overwhelm him so that he began to cry softly. For several weeks it had been quiet here but now there was a cold stillness, a hush. Half reluctantly, he turned the knob and went in.

In his office at the city station the young police inspector wondered angrily why these things happened to him. It was like anonymous phone calls about bombs on planes; one knew that there wouldn't be one but there had to be a time-consuming search because no one would take the responsibility of not searching.

"So what it boils down to is that you're asking me to look for your husband because of a feeling you say you have and because a weapon is not in the place where you last saw it," he said wearily. "And where is this place, Madam?"

"At the bottom of his handkerchief and sock drawer, upstairs."

"He shouldn't be in possession of a revolver; you realise that?" The woman simulated a massive sigh of exasperation. "We shall have to take action. It is an offence to own a firearm without a licence and I suppose he hasn't a licence. It's a very serious offence. Why did he keep it?"

"What has that to do with it? I've told you that the Bank says he hasn't been there today. I've told you what I'm quite sure he's gone to do, and you still sit there asking me stupid questions."

The young inspector flushed.

"I'd advise you not to adopt that tone with the police, Madam."

"And why not, if the police are just going to sit and draw pictures on their blotters?"

He looked down at the flower-embowered cottage.

"You must answer my questions," he said doggedly.

"Well, keep them to the point then. I don't think you mean to do anything. I think you're trying to put me off. I'd like to see the Superintendent."

"I shall make a report to him."

"When? Tomorrow? Next day? Next week? When you've built that house and grown the roses? I'm going to ring the Superintendent in half-an-hours' time. And if you haven't done something, I shall go on to the Chief Constable, even if he's half way round the golf course."

The policeman felt a spasm of cold fury and his legs began to tremble.

"That is all, Madam. When we hear anything we shall let you know immediately."

She laughed ironically.

When the door had slammed behind her, he rang the sergeant.

"Look, I want a summary of a case - a boy called Peplow, run down by a lorry, about a year ago. Oh, you remember it? What? He was playing on the footpath outside his own house. The driver was a fairground operator. Yes? Defence was loose steering gear. Why didn't he stop? Oh, the usual one, didn't know he'd hit anybody... Witness? No, no, I said 'Witnesses?' Only the father. Well what did he see? He claimed they both looked back and laughed - yes? Said that the man we put in the dock was not the driver - look, are you sure about this? Then I suppose he was acquitted because of lack of evidence? How old was the lad? Ten... poor little devil."

"So that business isn't finished yet," the Superintendent said, leaning back. "Well, I thought we'd hear about it again - just one of those feelings one sometimes has. No one in Court was very happy about it, except the defendant and his brother."

"Then you didn't really believe that it was faulty steering gear that caused it?"

"No one in Court did. They had twenty-four hours to fix that before we found them - as well as to sober up. No, the whole damn business was unsatisfactory from beginning to end. Now don't quote me here - I'm not convinced that the chap we prosecuted was the driver. This chap, Peplow, swore it was the brother who did it, but we had to assume his evidence was prejudiced."

"But why should the wrong man let himself be put in the dock?"

"His brother was a stronger personality - it was made worth his while. He was just plain stupid. Take your choice. Why his brother didn't want to carry the can, that's another matter. It makes sense; his record was dead against him - two successful prosecutions for drunken driving, another for wounding his own wife, another for assault on the police. He's a real Masterpiece. Britain at her best!"

"I don't think I'd like him," said the young inspector.

"I was told that his legal wife was in here only a couple of weeks ago; she's not had maintenance from him for a threemonth. I tell you what, ask them down below; they may have found out where he is. You'll have to follow it up."

The inspector grunted.

"What a business! Blast! Do you seriously think this man Peplow has really gone after him?"

"Could have. Sounds in character; he's that quiet sort. Why else would a bank clerk take a day off? They're a class on their own. And the gun; that needs some explaining. Might be off his rocker; you never know. Did you get a description from her?"

"Dark grey suit, striped tie she thinks, no overcoat, neat."

"Neat - that's very enlightening. Look for a neat man!"

"Well, that's what she kept saying, 'He's such a neat man.' Damn it, sir, people don't take off like that and work off a grievance a year later. At the time - O.K.; we know they do. But not wait a year…"

The telephone rang.

"Sorry," the Superintendent said, "I'm afraid that they've found him for you. Place called Great Minden, out in the wilds. You'll have to go."

"Great Minden! Found Peplow?"

"No, the driver in the manslaughter case. Unless he's left his father's business, they say he'll be there. It's the annual fair there. Good hunting! Lovely pair, these brothers - you'll enjoy meeting them. Of course, you could always get there too late, and let Peplow get at him, couldn't you?"

"Well, there's a fat lot to go on, sir," the young man said. "Just because he's gone and the gun's gone! Apart from that, we only have his wife's second sight. That's not much to send me haring off to a place at the backside of nowhere to look for someone I've never seen in the middle of a fun-fair. And I wish you'd seen the wife; she's unbalanced. Looked neurotic to me. There's probably another women in it and she won't say so. She'll wait till he gets back and then pretend she thought he'd gone to this place just to annoy him!"

The Superintendent pursed his lips. It would be very awkward if anything serious happened and the woman complained or, worse still, went to the newspapers with the story. It sounded a bit far-fetched but then, one never could tell.

"Look," he said firmly, "you'll have to follow it up. I'll fix it with the County. As soon as you reach Minden, contact the local sergeant - They'll have told him what it's all about. And keep me in the picture. You have my private number. Give me a ring no matter what time it is. Part of the job, my boy. Anyway I'd like to know. Come to think of it now, I remember that chap Peplow's face when they brought in the acquittal."

He reached for his In-Tray.

The open suitcase lay on the unmade bed. With all The Paraphernalia of Flight in it, thought Georgie: dressing gown, underwear, soap and toothbrush, aspirins and a half-eaten box of chocolates. She closed it and snapped the lock.

And that's all, she thought. I've lived in this house for months like a lodger and the only things I want to take away fit into this case. She looked at the Van Gogh print of scorching fields, the half-empty bottles on the dressing table, the dead flowers on the window sill. Somebody else's room, she thought - it's To Let. I don't think there'll ever be another room I want to own. Or a home. I hope Croser won't want me to follow him to a new usher's post to live in a council house? How long is it going to last?

It's like an infection; when will I be free of it? One minute we're well and then we're ill. It's like someone creeping up behind us and knocking us down. When will Croseritis pass off? There's only one thing certain - I shall be able to leave him without a second thought. No more harrowing exits! I'll just go out to the shop at the corner and that will be It. Then, I suppose, he'll slink back to his fat Clarice or whatever she's called.

There was a timid knock on the door.

"I don't want to see you," she said very distinctly. "Go away."

"Georgie..."

Croser doesn't want to go away really, she thought. He wants to stay on here and bully and be bullied.

Hesitant footsteps drifted away down the corridor.

He doesn't even care too much for me as a bed-mate. He wants someone shaped like an overstuffed pillow that he can roll on and off and start snoring again. Ye Gods what would they say at Hassocks if they ever saw him! Daddy or Pete Jagger! "This is Mr. Croser. We live together in sin. Isn't he a devil? Sorry, he doesn't have another suit. Yes, he always wears a pullover under this waistcoat: his auntie knitted it for his birthday."

She began to laugh softly.

The room had darkened. Outside the garden was still but, beyond, she could hear the crazy song of the steam-organ.

Boob-a-doo
You and you
Wadja goin' to do?

That's my music, she thought. Tonight here, tomorrow in another place and then another after that, until one is sick of the tune. Then one changes and begins all over again.

She pulled the suitcase towards her.

"Now, Room," she said softly, "The lodger's going. You're vacant again, Fully Furnished."

His two sleeping brothers beside him in the bed, Thickness lay awake under the back bedroom window.

Somat's up, he thought. There's somat up between Mam and Him and it's worse'n usual. Mam's been queer all week. It's somat to do wi' t'Feast? Why did old Croser gi' me that bob at home-time? Does he know somat? I'm going to stop playin' him up. He stammers when Mr Prosser comes into t'room. Happen he's scared of losing his job and goin' on t'club like Him. There's somat wrong wi' Dad. Mam says He doesn't want a job. She says He just doesn't like work. She says He could get a job tomorrow if He wanted to. He oughta get a job like other kids' dads. He oughta take me and Mam and t'nippers to t'seaside like other folks do. I'm sick of hearing what other kids have. I hope he gets a job at Christmas so that man from Uncle Frank's Christmas Appeal doesn't come round wi' presents. My kids'll never have presents brought round by people they don't know, at Christmas. Mam's goin' off. She's had enough. She's going to leave us. Then He'll have us put away.

A single note was punctuating the shrill noises of the Feast.

Somebody's dead, he thought. Happen it's Nick Bellenger's Dad. Why's his Dad so old? Mebbe it's his grandad and he just calls him Dad.

I wonder where Mam is. Happen she's gone out to t'boozer and'll be back soon...

But he knew that she wouldn't.

Then, all at once, he sat up and slipping from the bed, went down the stairs to burrow under them until he found the only book in the house. It was Fox's *Book of Martyrs* and his father had given it to him when he had found it among the unsold litter after an auction sale. "Full of history and religion," he had said. "My old Dad in Yorkshire gave it to me when I left home. I carried it all through the War. I read it from beginning to end."

Mr. Croser liked history and no doubt read it with the facility and pleasure that he, Thickness, read the comics. Tomorrow he would give this book to him. It would be a sign of a new era of peace between them. He propped it against the bed as harbinger of better days and climbed in again.

NIGHT

In the darkening bedroom the Rector sat among its disorder of unmade bedding and scattered clothes, it was still heavy with her presence - an over-sweet smell of powder from the pillows and the dressing table, the dressing gown still trailed across the carpet where she had carelessly tossed it the night before, jumbled heaps of film magazines, a dying geranium clamped in its bone-dry pot, the memory of her heavy limbs turning sleepily and the dark warmth of her body.

His work here was over and he had accomplished nothing. What would the parish remember in a dozen years time, what would it remember in five years, or even two? "It was in That One's time," they would say, "the one whose wife left him."

That is what they would remember, nothing else: the one whose wife left him. And yet it was for her sake that he had left his industrial parish and put aside a hope of some years in Africa. He had supposed that here she would find activities similar to those she had been brought up among. He had foreseen a growing family of exuberant children, even the shared pleasure of skimping and saving for ponies and prep. school and, for themselves, the occasional hoarded supper out and a show. Instead, childless, ignored by her social equals, covertly watched by the townspeople, infatuated with a lecherous nobody?

I can lose myself in the Work again, he thought. I can start again. Perhaps I can forget. There's the Mission Field, India, West Africa; I have no ties now. There is still time to do something worthwhile. It's not too late.

"It's not too late."

He jumped to his feet and shouted through the open door, his voice echoing wildly along the empty corridors of the darkened house, "It's not too late, it's not too late."

What would she do when Croser tired of her? She had no money, no profession and she was lazy. She was too proud to return to her parents. Either she would be driven to return to him or to be passed from man to man. He twisted around and buried his head in her pillow.

He lay there for a long time.

It was dark when hammering at the outside door roused him but he did not go to it or answer. After a time he heard the visitor moving away, his feet scuffling in the gravel, the rattle of a bicycle. Then the sound of movement stopped and someone shouted, "Is anybody there?"

The voice from the darkness and the succeeding silence seemed strange, supernatural. Words like stones thrown into a pond and instantly lost!

"They sent to say that Mr. Bellenger has passed on."

He moved to the window and saw a red rearlight wavering and dwindling; the messenger had gone. Groping his way to the kitchen, he freshened himself under a tap, then slipped out of the house into the churchyard where the great medieval building, rearing above him in the darkness, had an unfamiliar, hostile look; not a church now but only a very old place, outlasting generation after generation, garnering for itself a kind of renewal from the decay of humanity.

He remembered his pride in the days when he had walked around it like a captain seeing his first command. My church! The buttresses, the carved tympanum, the great curves of the nave arcade, the chancel arch, the altar! My church!

He pushed through the heavy door and on through the curtain screening the tower chamber, ropes brushing his face, and then swung the big tenor bell until he heard its muffled voice in the tower above him.

One for each year!

At the edge of blare and brilliance of the Feast below, older people would be counting now. In cottages in the hills too. Was it a stranger or some old friend unexpectedly gone? Someone old, someone young? Keep counting.

Twenty-three... twenty-four... The end of an old man's life and of his own love. Thirty-one... thirty-two... He had been that age and she eighteen when they married. Forty... forty-one... Time passing but no end to bitterness. How imperfect we are! How can we comprehend the meaning of things? Keep counting... fifty-five... fifty-six... This man, Bellenger, how would his God judge him? As a libertine in his old age, as a man who loved a small son, as one who had not laboured for the Kingdom? Sixty... sixty-one. The bell rolled, the rope spasmodically rose and fell. He let it slip through his hands and gradually the confusion of noise inside the walls sank and the church once more was still.

Peplow leaned heavily on the bar and watched Artie's reflection in among the wine bottles and tumblers standing on the shelf before the grandiose gilt mirror. A violent face, he thought. The face of a bully. Plenty of wind, some steam. The face of a man who could beat a woman. The face of a man who could kill a child, and laugh.

He turned quickly away, realising that the other had become aware of his scrutiny, but it was too late. Artie already was swaying sideways towards him, thrusting his red face at his own, over-aweing him with his immense body.

"Tha'll know me agen, mate? Got thi eyes full or dost want a closer look? Has anybody told thee thy nose is a blasted sight overlong?"

And with a quick movement for so big a man, he gripped Peplow's nose between his great flat thumb and forefinger and squeezed. It was agony. Ineffectually, he tried to tear away the other's wrists but it only made the big man increase pressure. His eyes began to water so that the room and everything in it became indistinct except the overwhelming pain at his nose.

He heard another voice, the barman's.

"Here, let him go, chum; let him go. Let him go or I'll fetch a copper."

"All right, all right, but he was staring at me," the other grumbled. "He wants to remember me; happen he will now."

Peplow fumbled for his handkerchief and rubbed his eyes.

"Look at him, blubbing!" the showman laughed. "Shouldn't let fellers like him into pubs. Give him an orange squash in t' kids' room."

The Law told them that they were free from guilt and they've cleaned it from their memory, like a slate, thought Peplow. He can't even remember me. He can't remember me in the witness box or even that it was me who stood up in the middle of his lying testimony and shouted "Liar!"

"Now go off home like a good chap and come back tomorrow," the barman was persuading Artie.

"All right, all right, but no one stares at me."

He turned suddenly towards Peplow, making him involuntarily step backwards.

"And I've seen thee before," he shouted, clumsily arranging his features into a menacing glare. "Where have I seen thee before?"

There was a silence, each man facing the other.

"Well, wherever it was, don't thee let me set eyes on thee

again."

He lurched for the door, purposely crashing into Peplow to tread heavily over his feet, before disappearing into the darkness.

"Never mind him, sir," the barman said. "It gets a bit rough most Feast times. Us fellows can't really do much about drunks like him… except try to get rid of 'em somewhere else before they get too rough."

He stopped speaking and looked up, he was alone in the bar.

Outside, Peplow leaned against the wall. For a moment it seemed that Artie had disappeared. There was no sign of him in either direction and yet it was impossible that he could have reached the first group of people in so brief a time. It was then that he heard the blundering noises in the backyard of the inn, and the splash of urine against corrugated iron. He slipped swiftly from the footpath and into the darkness, moving certainly towards the shuffling. Almost before he knew it he was close behind the big man.

"Hey," he called roughly and, feeling the other turn, struck with all his strength at the middle of the shape, and then again and again as it tumbled forward, clawing at him. Large hands fastened around his neck dragging him down. Immediately he jerked up his knees in successive piston blows. There were two sharp cries of agony and the grip loosened, allowing him room to strike savagely out and up again. The brief struggle ended as swiftly as it had begun; he felt the body slip down his own until the face came beneath his knees. Then he bent, gripped both sides of the head and struck it against the flint cobbles.

Now what? His overmastering wish had been to hurt the man. Well, he had hurt him; now what? He must wring the truth from him, wring it, squeeze it, batter it out.

A few steps confirmed his guess; a stream flowed across the foot of the pub yard. He dug his fingers into the shoulders of the unconscious man's jacket, dragged him like a sack to the water's edge, arranged the head and then pushed it below the surface. The reaction was immediate; Artie began to flap his hands, jerk his head and make incoherent noises.

Peplow pushed the head under water again and the revival accelerated.

"Let me get up. Let go of me." He began to struggle violently so that Peplow's anger blazed up again and, using a fist as a hammer, he struck him repeatedly in the face until he lay still.

"Listen very carefully and don't move or I swear I'll hold you under till you drown," Peplow said softly. "I am the father of the boy you ran down a year ago."

"Never did."

"Listen, I know you did. Who was driving? You or your brother?"

"Don't know what tha's talking about."

Peplow placed one hand over the man's forehead, forced it under the water and counted to twenty.

"Now will you tell me?"

The only answer was a renewed struggle to rise. Peplow forced the head under again.

"Now."

"It was him - he always drives."

"Tell me the rest."

"That's all."

Once again Peplow pushed down and this time counted to twenty-five, terrified arms threshing in his face. "He was boozed up."

"Go on. Was my boy on the road? You said he was on the road."

"No, he was on the footpath."

"Well on it? Near the gate?"

"Yes "

"The lorry ran on to the footpath?"

"Yes, he was boozed up. He was driving all over the place. He'd been up twice before. He gave me hundred quid to say it was me. Here, let me go, mister. I told you it wasn't me who was drivin'. What are you going to do?"

His voice was hoarse with panic.

"I'm going to kill him."

"You've nothing against me, Mister. I couldn't help what he did. I won't tell him you're here."

"I've half a mind to finish you off too, you drunken, lying swine." (His pressure on Artie's face increased again and the impotent struggle to rise began again.) "But I won't."

He rose quickly to his feet and, stepping back, straightened his tie, and after a minute the other scrambled up uncertainly too, wiping the water from his face and began to move forward furtively.

Then it seemed as though all the agony and hate of the past months surged into Peplow's arms and he struck time and time again into the collapsing and groaning body until it sagged to the ground and was still. Then he dragged it by the legs to an outhouse, stuffing it away with his feet before bolting the door and leaving.

From the hill, the bell's last sound beat like a pulse, a ground bass to the reeling music in the Square. They heard it standing at the gates of isolated cottages between dark woods or lost in fields, at the open-windowed parlour of pubs, faintly across water holding the last of the light by the ruined mill.

By its own steady rhythm it broke the rhythm of restless living, and people paused for a moment, suddenly out of time, and purposeless. It did not occur to Mrs. Loatley, in the quiet bedroom, that one of The Millions had slipped off before the Day.

Who is it - who is it? wondered the elder Miss Prosser. Is it old Bellenger? Has he gone then? Dragged down at last, brought to his knees like an old goat, his horn broken, the taste of dust in his mouth? And where's Adela gone? Did I go too far? If she goes before me, how will I manage alone?

And Mr. Croser: They oughtn't to let it be rung. It's depressing. Anybody would think we were still in the Middle Ages. It's only these futile prehistoric places like Minden where they keep it up. Round Castleford they don't. Somebody's dead. So what! It's just irritating.

Still trembling from his exertions in the yard, Peplow leaned against the high wall in the darkness. So the Old Man's gone and I didn't tell him I knew, he thought. What will that funny little kid be thinking? Crying his eyes out on the pillows? Asleep? If only there was some way of hunting her up and letting her know about the boy.

Funny, two from the same outfit coming to a full-stop on the same day in this one-horse spot! Not over the sea or on the runway or plunging into a convoy's firework display, but here. And he remembered his own place, the house by a great tree, back from the railway, candlelight flickering in an upstairs window.

Without Bellenger, even a Bellenger lying helpless and bedbound, Great Minden suddenly seemed emptier to Herbert Ruskin.

"Part of my life's gone with him," he muttered. "Except for him and Peplow, I'm only as old as the time I've lived in this room. Only he in all Minden knew Swingstead, the grass runway between the woods, the tents in the pasture, the ops room in the decaying farm, the intolerable beauty of that last summer, the frightening moon in the shelterless night sky. Only he knew the narrowing road through the orchards. Only he knew her and that faint warming smell of her body, the touch of her cool hands."

The bell's last stroke and the sound died away, blotted up by the dizzy uproar of the Square, lost among the tree-hung hills, a thousand fields, and the sky.

The two policemen found the young showman making an adjustment to one of the generators. The young inspector looked distastefully at him.

"Are you Frederick Dolan?" he asked.

"Why?"

"Never mind why. Are you Frederick Dolan?"

He did not answer.

The sergeant nodded.

"I have to warn you that the father of the boy who was killed by a lorry in which you were said to be a passenger is believed to be in this village. We believe that it is his intention to do you an injury. He is believed to be wearing a dark grey lounge suit and…"

The young man laughed.

"Are you kiddin'? He's got nothin' on me. M' brother was acquitted. And we can take care of oursen. Thanks for nothing."

He turned away.

The young inspector controlled his rising anger.

"It is my duty to warn you that he is armed," he said coldly. The showman laughed again.

"Sounds like t'pictures," he said.

"We shall do our best to protect you but you will have to give us your co-operation. You will appreciate our difficulties in this crowd and confusion. I advise you to remain in the company of others until you hear to the contrary from me. Right?"

There was no reply.

"Do you understand?" the inspector repeated sharply.

The young showman straightened his back, grinning insolently and placing his tongue between his lips, made an emphatic razz.

"Where is your brother?"

"Look for him. Me an' Artie can look after oursen," he said. "We don' like coppers breathin' down us backs."

"It's peculiar," said the Minden police sergeant, "but it's possible. And I *did* see a fellow like the one you describe in the street this morning; he was dressed a bit smarter than most of the folks round here or I wouldn't have noticed him. If it's the same one, I saw him going into old Ma Loatley's earlier this evening."

The phone rang.

"You were right, sir," he said admiringly, "the landlord of The Fusilier has found one of the Feast fellows in an outhouse and says he's in a bad way. I'll take you round there."

They found Artie lying on a horsehair couch in the back parlour, pale and bruised but conscious.

"How did it happen?" the young inspector asked briskly.

"Chap went for me in the dark."

"Know him? Can you give us a description?"

Artie shook his head.

"Oh, come along, man. Strangers don't attack men your size."

"I've told you. Didn't know him. Couldn't see him if I had."

He paused and added, "He hit me from the back anyhow."

"How did your hair get wet?"

Artie shrugged his heavy shoulders.

"Search me!"

"Can you think of anyone who would want to attack you?"

"Me! No! I never done nobody no harm."

"Was it a man called Peplow?"

"Told you, didn't know him in the dark."

"You were acquitted in a hit-and-run case less than a year ago, weren't you? You and your brother."

Artie did not answer.

"Peplow was the name of the child you ran over. Was it his father?"

"I told you once; I don' know who done it, Fellow jumped on me back. I gotta go now."

He scrambled up and walked shakily off. Outside in the street he met the big slovenly girl.

"Fred said you wanted me, Art," she said uncertainly. "He said I could stay with you. He says he don't want me back."

"Where is he?"

"He's having somebody else."

"I said 'Where is he?' you stupid bitch."

"Don't know."

She began to cry.

"Then go and fin' him quick. An' tell him that the kid's dad is looking for him."

"Which kid?"

"He knows which kid. Thee fin' him or don' bother comin' roun' to my caravan tonight. Clear off."

When she was gone, Artie leaned across the wall and vomited into a garden.

"Gotta fin' him," he muttered. But his head sagged lower until he cradled it on the bricks. Then he was sick again.

"A man called Thickness has been to see me," said the old Proprietor. "He says you are carrying on with his wife and she is going to leave him. He says he has four children, all under twelve."

His son did not answer.

"Is this true?"

"He's crazy. What should I do with his wife? When I get hitched up again it will be with a woman a lot younger'n her. Think I'd saddle myself with four kids?"

"Nevertheless, that's what he told me. Do you know his wife?"

"Sure I know her. Everybody knows her. There's one in all t'villages. Ask Willie, ask Artie, ask all t'lads. Everybody knows her."

"Why don't you leave her alone?"

"She chases after me. I can't dodge her, that's why."

He grinned.

"Women go that way about me," he added.

"I got two sons," the Proprietor said bitterly, "I brought them up as well as I knew, gave them schooling I never had. And they both turn out to be liars and lechers. Thank God your mother never knew it."

"Now, Dad, there's no need to…"

"I haven't forgotten," he almost shouted. "Liars - lechers and drunkards. You killed that child a year ago when you were drunk. You struck him down on the threshold of life, and you felt no remorse nor pity…"

"The Court said we was clear."

"The Court! The Court didn't know you were liars like your father did. You killed him and you left him lying there. You left him like most men wouldn't leave a dog. Then you lied and perjured, you and my other son. Sons! You killed him and you drove away your wife. You broke her heart with your ways. What are you, men or beasts?"

The young man's face darkened.

"Hey, steady on. I can only take so much, y'know."

"*You* can only take so much!"

The Proprietor rose with startling suddenness and grabbed his son's throat, squeezing it with his square-ended thumbs.

"You can only take so much!" he cried again, his voice thick with disgust. "You leave those children's mother alone. Leave her alone. You swine wallowing in your own muck! Get out."

He flung his son heavily against the door.

"The Court!" he shouted again. "Aye, maybe you deceived that Court, but God is not mocked!"

When Lydia Prosser was in her most overbearing mood she blew her nose like a trumpet almost continuously and explored its most obscure cavities for remnants of mucus, rooting them from their hiding places, blowing them to the entrances of her nostrils, corkscrewing them out with her handkerchief. She did this sitting square before the fire or the TV according to her humour, screening them from her sister, the bottom button of her dress undone, its hem pulled up above her fat knees. And she chewed liquorice-toffee sweets, prising them from her teeth, enjoyably sucking them to another part of her mouth. She would do this for an hour at a time, and if she could have found a little girl to fan her, the picture of oriental self-indulgence would have been complete. Its ultimate pleasure was the almost unbearable annoyance it gave to her sister.

"There's one of your letters I forgot to give you," she said, "It's from that W.E.A. man."

"You shouldn't have opened it."

"It was addressed to Miss Prosser, that's my name."

"But you knew from the envelope. Look, it says 'Extra-Mural-Board'. You knew it was for me."

"It says 'Miss Prosser' too, and I'm Miss Prosser."

She leaned back to enjoy the quarrel, ready to take down and open the packages of wounding jibes she had stored up all day.

Vexatious tears pricked the schoolmistress's eyeballs and she felt the tell-tale flush inflame her neck, fearing to be drawn into another exhausting defeat. But she could not trust her voice and, taking the opened letter, she ran upstairs. It had many encouraging things to say about her little Memoir "carefully written... the right style... grasp of the significant events..." He would certainly advise her to have it printed especially if it could be amplified in any way.

Miss Prosser became very attentive. She really was in no hurry to finish her work. For about three years it had given her an excuse to withdraw from the domestic battlefield and had provided a topic for talk on holidays or with the few villagers she still knew.

["How is your little biography progressing, Miss Prosser?"

"I do hope you won't forget to mention your father's stand on the Old Workhouse, Miss Prosser."]

She folded the tutor's letter of opinion.

Yes, that's very true, she thought, it does need a few more human touches in it - ["What was he like at the seaside?... remember him when you were a child... try to put in a few ordinary details; they would contrast and thus emphasise the more public side of your father."]

There was the old railway trunk in the attic; they'd emptied all the odds and ends from his bureau into it after his sudden death, meaning to go through them some day. She would look there. It would take her mind off the day, off her sister, off the Feast.

A single dormer window lit the attic, a large arched room which lay up the final staircase, itself shut off by a wall-papered door from the lower house. It was one of those remote rooms so still that the air seemed dead, and Miss Prosser found herself listening to her own footsteps, the pushing around of boxes, rustling of old newspaper cuttings, even her own disturbed breathing. She nudged out the domed black trunk, tugged it below the window and opened it. By its side she dragged an empty packing case into which to empty what did not interest her.

A fat layer of newspapers to begin with, marked in red pencil, her father's letters to the press, reports of Council meetings, the menu of a presentation dinner in his honour, an account of his unsuccessful parliamentary campaign. She put them aside.

A thick envelope, Adela's School Reports. She smiled

with pleasure, remembering his pride in her successes, and began to read them. The marks were high, her form position always in the first three. Teachers' comments were "Thorough in all she does" and, "a joy to teach", "hardworking and conscientious", "one of our best girls", "should have a successful career"...

"Should have a successful career"... Well, she'd done all she'd been told to do. "Work hard": she'd worked hard. "Aim high": in those days to be a Head Mistress herself had seemed the very pinnacle of glory. She'd passed exam after exam, harvesting at twenty-one a sheaf of certificates and diplomas.

Her old form photograph was there. Out of the thirty only three had gone into the sixth; the rest had fallen by the wayside, become hairdressers, clerks, telephonists, most of them marrying young to bear the children she would teach.

"Should have a successful career"...

She squashed the tokens of success back into their envelope.

Then a layer of Diaries - terse entries "Council Meeting 7", "Meet deputation 8.30", "X", "Men's Group 7.30", "X.X", "X"...

She flicked through them, still depressed by her thoughts, wondering what the crosses meant, year after year, some even on blank pages, sometimes five times a week, sometimes seven, never less than four. And at regular intervals no crosses for six or seven days. Crosses - what for? And why this regular gap? Couldn't be meetings? There wasn't a monthly holiday from meetings. The word "monthly" struck her like a blow in the face. "No," she thought wildly "Not that! He couldn't mark them with crosses!"

She rifled the pile. Nineteen-thirty, the year her mother died.

April 27th. No crosses after that, no crosses for a month before it! But before that they stabbed monotonously backwards, five one week, four, six, five, five...

Miss Prosser's eyes widened with horror. "And marked each time with a cross!"

The diaries thudded into the packing case.

And now books, books in brown paper covers, books without names... She opened one and read, her eyes dilated. It slid from her hand and lay opened at a revolting drawing. "No," she moaned, "No!" Another book; Great God, were they all like this! Another - another - and now packets of postcards, clippings of pictures...

Nausea enveloped her... she felt faint and sick and found that tears were coursing down her face, blinding tears of utter misery. Whimpering in an agony of wretchedness she flung herself on the bare boards, her head cradled in her thin arms. She lay there for a long time. After the first anguished minutes, the horror of her discovery was lost in the sudden knowledge that she was completely alone and had been alone for many years. And after that, there was the bitterness of remembering all she had lost because of it, so that she moaned like an animal wounded and waiting in a thicket of fear. The cosy comfortableness of life had been snatched away and a vision of waste land and wind, a naked prospect stretched before and all around her. And she, herself, utterly alone.

As the light faded, a feeling of intolerable restlessness drove her downstairs to snatch a coat from the rack and rush into the streets and the organ's wilderness of sound.

"No, it isn't exactly that," Effie said, moving restlessly on the settee as her mother probed at her love-life. "I just feel sometimes that he doesn't know his mind. Sometimes he seems frightened at the idea of settling down. And you can't talk to him about it; he gets mad so easily nowadays and takes offence."

"Well, he's in love with you in his heart of hearts," her mother said soothingly. "You can tell he is by the way he looks you up and down. Sometimes he looks as if he could eat you. Your Dad never looked at me like that. All he did was to plump himself down in a chair and talk at your grandad about football. Then when it got to be ten he'd get up and say, 'Well, I got to go now,' and look at me out of his eye-corners. Romantic! But your Sidney adores you. It's ever so plain. I don't see what you're worrying about. Perhaps it's the weather. It upsets some men. Maybe his landlady isn't feeding him too well. He needs plenty of eggs to stimulate him; I read it in an American magazine."

"Do you think…"

Effie suddenly stopped.

"Yes, dear?"

"Well, I mean, do you think he expects more of me?"

Her mother, who was a sensible woman, instantly gave her mind to the problem and did not pretend that she could not follow the new drift. She groped in the boxroom of her memory and came back with the phrase which her husband used to justify his weekly half-a-crown on the pools.

"You have to speculate in order to accumulate," she answered sagely.

"Sometimes he goes on as though he's not content with just kissing, and once he began to swear and wouldn't say why…"

"Men are queer," her mother said enigmatically.

"Queer?"

"They don't see things as we see them and besides…"

This, she decided, was as far as she could safely go. If ill came of her words, they were vague enough to be squared in her conscience. If propitious, then her daughter would forget them. No more was spoken. Indeed the comprehending silence and a slight heightening of Effie's colour were more eloquent than words. The inconclusive "and besides…" flowed imaginatively on, gathering tributaries of concealed meanings, eddies of nuance, to become a deep channel of certainty in both their minds.

At last Effie stood up, pushing out her breasts, a Boadicea girding for victory in defeat.

"I'll be late in," she said simply. "Tell Dad not to wait up for me." She went upstairs to prepare herself for the glorious sacrifice.

There she turned sensuously before the long mirror and turned again before going so close that her nose touched the glass before beginning to pencil in her eyebrows. Her mother watched her admiringly.

"I love you in that red coat," she said. "It flatters you. Gives you something, if you know what I mean. Nothing cheap about it. You can always tell quality when you see it. Those lovely buttons! You can always tell a garment by its buttons."

Effie stepped back a couple of paces and turned quickly so that the coat swirled and hissed around her.

"It's the silk," she replied. "It just has that something. Sid likes me to wear it; he says it does something to him. He likes the sound of it. He says it puts the East in his mind."

"Isn't it wonderful what an interest he takes in the way

you dress yourself! Now your dad, he never took no interest in my things. It's never been no pleasure dressing for him. He never notices."

"Do you think he likes Sid, Mum? Dad, I mean. Sometimes I don't think he does. They don't have much to say to each other when Sid comes round."

"Well, what do you expect? Whatever can your Dad find to talk about to anybody except Football and the Club. He won't even talk about his job and they say he's ever so clever at it. He just hasn't any ambition. He's not like Sidney, a pusher. My! I envy you. If only I had my time again! When they make him a head-teacher, they'll ask you out to all the big do's, opening bazaars and chairwoman of this and that. And you can carry it off too, with your figure."

"Oh, Mum, don't go on; we're not married yet."
"Sometimes, he looks as if he could eat you," she repeated.

Effie could believe that. Sometimes she had thought that he was trying to.

There was a painful silence as Effie reluctantly began to prise her feet into stiletto-heeled shoes.

"You haven't given in to him have you, dear? Not yet I mean?" her mother said, looking at the ceiling.

Effie did not reply.

"Look Eff, why don't you make him toe the line tonight? Make him fix a date, make him want you and want you till he can't wait any longer."

The hobbling skirt, a sheath imprisoning her legs, the confining bra, the crippling agony of her shoes! He makes me tie myself up like a damned parcel, Effie thought rebelliously.

"You funny old Mum," she said, "Don't worry, I'll see to His Lordship; he's had his fling for long enough."

Mr. Croser threw his sports jacket over a chair and loosening the zip of his worsteds, sprawled on his bed. When he had arranged an empty tin of throat-pastilles on his stomach, he lit a Woodbine. Everything was moving too swiftly for him.

Another day like this and they'll be sending the van for me, he thought.

He lay, looking desperately at the ceiling and knew that it was the hour of decision. The tune of the organ surged and ebbed in and out of consciousness.

You and you
Boob-a-do
Wadja wanna do...

He blew a cloud of smoke and suddenly knew what *he* was going to do. She's no good for me, he thought. She's right out of my league and it's no use kidding myself. A couple of months and she'd look at me as though she's never seen me before, that's what she'd do. Then she'd be away with one of her own lah-di-dah sort and cheerio Sid and thank you for Nothing.

Eff's my sort. Young and plump and not too smart... a bit countryfied, but mouldable. There isn't any need for her to grow fat like her mother if she's taken in hand young enough. Some of these new towns are letting council-houses-without-waiting to anybody who'll teach their horrible kids not to break open the gas meters, and you can furnish on the Never Never and Eff can go out hairdressing and help pay for it all. Wrapped in a pillar of smoke his mind raced prophetically forward, a long vista of carefree pleasures stretching invitingly ahead of him.

Well, that's a weight off my mind. Effie!

Now that new assistant at the Co-op. Now, she's an

interesting piece. They say that she'd left her husband even before he went to gaol. She'll be about thirty, the intense kind...

He lit another cigarette and that was when Georgie slipped in. She was wearing her red leather coat, unbuttoned, and a silk scarf round her hair.

"Lazy bones," she said, "not packed yet?"

"For Pete's sake! Don't forget the landlady. She doesn't allow girls - women visitors - in the rooms. She's dead strict about it. If she comes in now, I'll be out on my ear. Look, wait in the street, I'll come down in a couple of minutes."

She sat down quickly beside him and when he tried to rise, pushed him back and leaned over him, so that he could not straighten his arms to push her off.

"The landlady!" she mimicked. "Here's a fine thing when a man cares more for his landlady than he does for his mistress! Where's the young hearty that tumbled me only two or three hours ago? You didn't push me away then. What's your precious landlady to do with it, anyway? You won't need her bedroom any more. You won't have to worry about a landlady tonight; I'll be your landlady."

"I'm not going, Georgie," he muttered. "I've thought it all out and I've decided that it would be better for both of us to call it a day. Better for you - definitely."

To his dismay she took this without surprise. "You're joking."

"I'm not. I've thought it all out. Really. It wouldn't work."

"It seemed to be working down at the Mill this afternoon, whatever 'It' is."

She ran her long fingers along his leg.

"Don't fight it: everything's going to be all right," she said with just a trace of irritation in her tone. "You can't keep on living in a hole like this, being roughed up by Prosser whenever her complexes feel raw. This isn't Life. Look at it - linoleum and a pocket of red pencils!"

"You're not really in love with me," he said sulkily.

"Love, love, love!" she cried angrily. "I've heard enough about Love for one day. You know what you want and you know that I can give it you. What else do you want me to do? Make bells chime in your head whenever you see me? Grow up. You're not sixteen any more."

The rhythm of her fingers became more insistent. He felt the cool, smooth leather, its dry smell mixing with her perfume. She bent more heavily upon him and engulfed his person in a sudden access of passion until he responded. Then she drew away and would not let him draw her down again.

"Tonight - wait till then. And tomorrow too. And all the other nights after that..."

Mr. Croser looked hungrily up at her.

"What about your people, what will they say?"

She straightened her skirt and did not reply.

"I don't know anything about you really," he complained. "You've never told me much about yourself, about Roedean and hunting and your brothers in the Army."

"That's behind me," she said, "thank God!"

"Don't you miss it all? Living in a big house, servants, stables, posh house-parties and all that?"

"No, why should I?"

"Well, it's a bit of a come-down, isn't it? I mean, look at it sensibly. Married to a parson, running off with a school-teacher."

"You don't know how dull it was."

"You're damned right I don't, but I'd like to. It all sounds

O.K. to me. I'd rather ride to hounds than be ridden by Prosser. And Roedean! You should have seen the awful council school I went to and the kids that went along with it."

"Only people matter."

He drew her down again and for a moment she submitted, relaxed and compliant, covering his body, sinking again into a wild darkness. Then she stirred and twisted away.

"We've got plenty of time. Wait till tonight. Just wait - we can lie in and talk tomorrow, after the maid's brought us a cup of tea. There isn't time now. We'll be together all night."

She stood up and looked down at her dishevelled and defeated lover. She felt quite sure of him now. "I'll pick you up in half an hour. Here, by the door. You have to pack now."

A moment later she was gone and Mr. Croser was left not with his last sight of her at the door but of her lying luxuriously by his side after early morning tea... talking about Roedean.

"Do you think it was him, sir?" the sergeant asked.

"Certain of it. Wouldn't have put him in the shed otherwise. He means business. It's serious. Look, we must find him. What's your nearest station?"

"Gornard."

"Well, ring them, put them in the picture and ask them if they can spare a couple of men. I'll be trying that Loatley woman to see if she knows anything about him. And look, when you've rung Gornard, go to the middle of the fair near that statue would be a good place - and we'll just have to hope that he'll be washed up to your front door. There's no other way of getting hold of him in this mob."

He turned back to the landlord. "Tell me what you can."

"Well, medium height, on the short side, striped tie, neat looking chap. Kind of chap they get behind the counter in city shops; wouldn't have thought myself he could have tackled that big bloke. Quiet, inoffensive chap he looked to me.

"Ever seen a picture of Crippen?" the inspector said irritably. "You can't tell 'em by their staring eyes, you know. If he happens to come back here, try to get someone to go for the sergeant; he'll be close to that statue you have."

He hurried out.

"Bag o' nerves!" the landlord muttered. "Crippen!"

Later, when the Inspector told his wife about this particular evening, he said, "And one of the most peculiar things about it was an interview with a Mrs. Loatley. Queer old stick. Grey, sixty-odd I should think. That's the word, grey. Fits her appearance, personality, home, the lot. Seemed oblivious of the fair raging over the garden wall. In a world all of her own.

"Oh yes, she'd seen Peplow but didn't know that was his name; she hadn't enquired it. Well, was it right that they'd met and talked at least twice during the day? Yes, it was. Had he told her what he was doing in Minden? No; she'd supposed he'd come for the Feast. Or he could have been a solicitor, perhaps come on that particular day to see about a will or something.

"Then why had he been at her particular house? Because he was interested in Religion. (She pointed at a bill hanging on the gate.) So all you talked about was Religion? Well, he wasn't a man who talked much; but whatever he was wanted for, he was a good man at heart, a very good man. She was sure of that.

"Could she tell me where he was now, where he could be found? No, she couldn't... oh, yes, she'd just remembered. He said he was going to Gornard. (It was so obvious a lie, I didn't bother to say so.)

"And then she looked at me, her eyes wide open, with a please-believe-me-even-if-I-don't-believe-myself expression on her face. I could have laughed. Quite frankly I sympathised with her. I didn't really care whether he pulled it off or not. But, at the same time, I kept thinking 'If he does and I don't arrest him, it's going to pull me down a lot of pegs on the promotion roster...'"

From Peplow's seat on the churchyard wall, Great Minden lay spread-eagled below: the four writhing arms of roads, its heart the Square, pinned to the plain by a confusion of light and sound. The truth choked from the second brother had locked his determination and, once again, he was waiting. For the first time that day he wondered what his wife was doing. Within a few days of the accident she had had a nervous breakdown and when she had returned after living with relatives, they had become strangers, neither able to bridge this gulf.

She had not even asked where everything had gone, the toys, the clothes, the little bed. A party of scouts haphazardly collecting for a jumble sale had called one Saturday afternoon during her illness. He recalled their confusion as he had taken them into Tom's room and told them to take everything.

"There's such a lot. Can we come back tomorrow?" they had asked, but he had insisted that everything must go now, that day. And after that, they had worked in silence, their leader directing the removal in a subdued voice, hurrying them on so they could escape from something he did not understand.

[The little pile of picture books from Tom's earliest years - that had been the hardest link to snap, memories of his own joy in buying them as he came home from work, the plate pushed back, the scramble to his knee - "And see this man, he's a sailorman and he's going to..."

"What does he say, Daddy?"

"He says, 'I'm a sailorman and I'm going for a shipload of oranges for Tom.'"

The bright books, cheap and thin, the holy word of God!]

And she had never asked... the tiny clothes which tore at his heart as they lay without a living child inside them, the mittens, bibs, squares, the coat with the velvet collar, the brief history of a life. His fingers closed and unclasped over his palm and his heart tightened. He began to tremble violently.

It's true, he thought. I'm round the bend. They knew it at the office; no wonder they began to look away whenever I came in. I suppose they told their wives about me. "He's cracking up, he can't go on much longer... the Bank has offered him a month off, they say, but he won't take it. You can see he's getting worse every day. Poor devil!"

Tomorrow, they'd know and understand.

Would they?

He glanced at his watch; it was time to go down now. He shrugged, slid from the wall and set off downhill along the lane leading to the Square. As he approached the darkened terrace where he had seen Mrs. Thickness at her window he encountered parents with tired children returning to outlying farms and villages, and then drunks and lovers spilling over into the fringe of night from the noise and glare hedged in by sides of shops and houses.

He pushed along the edge of the Square, past the school, the Post Office, from whose window he had watched the Wreathing, the fat girl's saloon, the butcher's shop, all like discarded stage props shoved back now from the action of the day, until he stood briefly below Herbert Ruskin's window.

Here! This was the place.

He stepped off the pavement and allowed himself to be carried along by the crowd into one of the four avenues leading towards the steam-organ and the statue.

"Just a moment, sir."

A hand gripped his arm and he was pulled firmly against the pedestal. It was a police sergeant. "May I have your name, sir?" the man shouted.

"My name? Why?"

The crowds pressed all around them, their two faces were scarcely six inches apart.

"A man was assaulted in the town this evening earlier on. I think you may be able to help with our enquiries. Can I have your name, please?"

Peplow gave the first name that came into his head. The sergeant looked closely and disbelievingly at him.

"Have you any proof of identity, sir? Letters, documents?"

A sudden movement of the crowd forced their bodies half sideways so that they wedged together and Peplow felt the revolver pressed painfully between. He forced back his head and immediately saw that the policeman had guessed.

"I must ask you to accompany me to the police-station, sir." As the grip on his arm tightened, a sudden eddy of movement pushed them apart and Peplow, turning swiftly, drove down the edge of his right hand at the sergeant's wrist and, released, twisted away and plunged down an alleyway behind a row of stalls, making blindly for the edge of the Square.

"Here - come in here."

He obeyed instantly, almost collapsing into the garden's dimness.

"It's the police, isn't it?" Mrs. Loatley said. "They've been here asking about you - a young man, an inspector."

Peplow leaned against the wall, struggling to regain composure and breath, more dismayed at the indignity of flight than by the narrowness of his escape.

"Sorry," he said, "I hope that they didn't upset you."

"I told him that you'd gone to Gornard."

"Thanks, but I don't think they believed you."

The high wall of the garden hid the Feast but its glare lit up the higher branches of the bushes and trees, throwing intensely black shadows below and behind them, reflecting the whiteness of the elderberry flowers so that they glowed theatrically.

"You didn't...?"

Peplow shook his head.

"Leave it then; it won't do any good."

"Just let me stay here a minute or two."

"They might come back. Come into the house. I know how you feel but it doesn't do any good. It doesn't pay to go against the Law."

"The Law! The Law that hangs you if *you* kill with a gun and lets you off if you kill with a car?"

"I mean God's Law," she said. "The Great Judgement Day when the nations shall stand before him in their thousands and ten thousands..."

They spoke in low voices in the dim passage, curiously intimate like old friends, like accomplices.

"It is not for us to judge," she went on. "Mr. Loatley - I didn't judge *him*."

The name startled Peplow. Mr. Loatley... he had not considered that there must be or have been a Mr. Loatley. "Mr. Loatley?" he repeated stupidly.

"It's not for us to judge," she repeated, "I didn't judge him even though I knew what was going on. He couldn't hide things. When he came in late. One, Two, sometimes Three in the morning. I got used to that. I knew there was another woman and I could bear it. I was older than him and I expected it. That sort of thing doesn't hurt so much when one's past fifty. But leaving me, that was a different matter. The house was in his name, the savings were in his name, and the furniture - he'd have sold it over my head in a fortnight and left me in the lurch to pick up a living as best I could. If he'd only been straightforward about it instead of planning to march off and sell me up through a solicitor. Do you know what he did? It was the last straw. I found that he had taken my ring, my engagement ring, the ring he had given me before we were married. I couldn't forgive him that. That was the bitterest moment. And, of course, as I said, I knew all about it, even the time of the train they were going to leave on. I found his case all packed. I knew he'd have to collect that and I waited for him up there on the landing."

She pointed up behind her and he glimpsed the white painted banister.

"I heard him coming quietly up the path and into the passage. It was terrible. Then there was an awful silence. All at once he fell. I could hear him struggle to his feet. And fall again. I could scarcely bear it but I waited. He crawled up the stairs. Can you imagine it - crawled on all fours. At the top he pulled himself up by the post. Sweat was pouring off his forehead, his face was flushed and his tongue seemed caught in his teeth.

"'Emily, I've...' That was the last thing he said."

"A stroke?"

She nodded, "It was God's judgement."

He followed her up the staircase and to the white door at the end of the landing.

"My husband!" she said bleakly, and entered the room.

Reluctantly he crossed to the bedside. At first, in the gloom, he could only see a dark head, featureless on the pillows. Then when a candle had been lighted, he saw the man's pale eyes and, below the single sheet, the feeble stir of hands.

"My husband!" she said again. "For seven or eight years after it happened he could get about a bit... sitting around the house or the garden. I had to dress him - even feed him. But that's finished now. I can't bear other people to see him now. Her, for one! I couldn't bear for her to see him. Not like he is now. And he wouldn't want people to come and stare at him and go away and talk. I've never been able to bring myself to let anybody see him like this except the doctor."

The swirling lights of the Feast sent shadows spinning crazily around the walls. Her husband still looked steadily at the ceiling.

"He doesn't understand anything. He's like a baby. I have

to feed him with a spoon. And what will happen to him if anything happens to me?"

She pushed back the sheet and took the thin hand in her own. "But I didn't judge him," she said once more. "Not like you. 'Judgement is mine, saith the Lord.' Leave things as they are; it's not for us to judge, or punish."

"You are a good sort," Peplow said. "I shan't forget you. You'll manage somehow."

She didn't reply, and he turned quietly and hurried out of the house and across the garden. The elderberry flowers still glowed in the half-light. There is something primeval about them, he thought. Something possessive as though only they belonged here, flowering on and on, May after May, outlasting the houses and the town and all those who have or will live here.

In the bedroom, the steady, rough breathing never altered; the long pale fingers never ceased to twiddle with the edge of the sheet, the pale blue eyes never moved away from the dark ceiling directly above them. His wife looked indulgently down at him. It was almost time for the other woman to pass and she moved to the window but not so near that her shadow might be seen through the net.

"If you were well again, Alfred, well enough to walk again and carry that suitcase - it's still there as you left it - would you go to her? She's ten years older now and she looks it. Mind you she's not forgotten you. Don't think that. She never speaks to me but I can see it in her look: 'Where is he?' She just has to carry it around with her like a cancer eating into her life. She never can be sure why you didn't come to meet her on the night train."

Bending her body slightly forward but approaching no nearer to the window, she watched Miss Prosser hurrying past on the opposite pavement.

"Now - look," she murmured indignantly, "Go on, look."

And there it was, the swift, furtive glance upward at the window and then the hurrying on once more.

"They laugh at Hell, Alfred, the unbelievers," said Mrs. Loatley, "but it's here, it's all around us. Adela Prosser, you know don't you - you've spent ten years there? And you can *never* have him now."

She suddenly pulled back the thick net curtains and stared down.

She stared down as though turned to stone: Miss Prosser had turned suddenly and, as though caught by a hook, their eyes met.

Peplow stood quietly in the shadow. Now that the time had come, he felt quite impersonal. Revenge seemed to have no part in the business; he wanted to be finished with the job, to be quick and clean and then to go. This time he avoided the avenues and moved gingerly through the alleyways behind the sacking of the stalls until he was only a pace or two away from where he had last seen the young showman. He was still there, checking the evening's takings at his dart stall.

"When's Artie comin' back?" he asked irritably. "He's been gone more n'hour."

"Found hisself a local wench. Some o' these country bits are on t'slow side," his assistant sniggered. "Here, look at that copper. What's he hanging about for?"

"Search me! Pity he's got nowt else to do. Well, I'm off. Got to see a man about a dog. Bring t'brass round in t'morning - not too early. I shan't be back tonight."

"Mind her husband don' catch thee."

"If she don' mind, I don'. He's only a little runt; we can fettle him up in t'kennel."

The sergeant, tangled up in a sudden surge of the crowd, missed him by only a few seconds, turned to the dart stall and appeared to be asking questions before pushing hurriedly away in the opposite direction.

Peplow moved out into the stall's light.

The assistant spat.

"Coppers!" he said. "Nosey bastards! It's a pleasure to send 'em chasing their own tails... Here mate, have a bob's worth o' darts. How steady's your arm?"

Peplow took the six proffered darts.

Eight, he thought, I'll put all six in Eight.

"Eight," he said.

Dart after dart thudded home. Scarcely an inch separated them.

"Here," called the man as he turned away. "You get a coupla prizes for that or one big 'un if you like. What about this pig?"

He thrust a china pig at Peplow who mechanically stuffed it into his pocket.

"You got a steady hand, mate," the man said.

The Feast reeled noisily on, a clearing of glare and confusion in the darkness and stillness spreading out from the surrounding streets to the hills of dark fields and the plain, and he knew that it was time and moved two or three paces from the street of stalls and sideshows into the shadows of a rope tangled alley and there unwrapped his service revolver from a handkerchief. The brass and copper-ringed cartridges bedded snugly in their chamber; half-fascinated, half-repelled, he stared at them.

Suddenly he knew that he was not alone and, turning sharply, he found Nick, his eyes wide and startled, looking up at him. He snapped shut the weapon and slid it back into the inside pocket of his jacket.

The boy spoke first.

"I saw you come in here," he said. "I wanted to tell you that my father is dead."

"What are you doing out here alone?"

"I slipped out. The house was so still. I was frightened."

"Where are your step-sisters?"

"In the front room. They sent me to bed."

"You shouldn't be here."

Even as he said it, Peplow recognized its stupidity. What was the boy to do? Stay cowering and grief-stricken in a friendless house?

"Go to Mr. Ruskin. He'll look after you."

"What are you going to do?" the boy asked. He did not answer. "You don't look like you did this morning. You look different." Once again the crazy song of the steam-organ flowed across their consciousness and between them. They stared at each other's face, neither moving, the boy's eyes dark and large.

"Is it to do with the boy you told me about, the boy who was run over?"

Peplow nodded.

"Shall I see you again?" the boy asked.

Peplow shook his head.

"Go to Mr. Ruskin," he said. "You can tell him you've seen me. If you want to tell him what you saw, you can; he'll understand then. You're a good boy. I'm sorry about your father: I liked him very much once. And your Mother too, but Mr. Ruskin knew her best. He'll tell you about her. I know you want to hear."

Nick turned away, his head hanging.

Peplow stretched forward, took the narrow shoulders and turned him round. The boy's eyes were bright with tears.

"You're a good lad," he repeated and, bending, kissed his forehead, at the same time blindly thrusting the china pig into his hands.

A moment later he was alone, and turning, he walked swiftly to the caravan and pushed open its door.

"What the hell!"

The showman, one leg in a pair of trousers, one out, swung round as he entered.

Peplow shut the door.

"Listen," he said. "This has got to be quick so I'm not going to talk much. There are six rounds in this revolver and if you come any closer you'll get at least two."

The young man shrank back, face pale, hands ineffectually pulling at a single trousers leg.

"You remember me?"

The man nodded.

"I've come to kill you for it."

"They'll get you. The coppers are in Minden looking for you. They know."

"He was ten when you mowed him down. He was dying when I picked him up."

"The jury said…"

"This is the jury."

Peplow raised the heavy revolver and levelled it between the shocked eyes.

"No… please! No! No, don't!"

All at once he collapsed - so suddenly that Peplow's shot tore above him through the wall. His hands clawed Peplow's ankles.

"No!" he sobbed. "No!"

Peplow kicked into his face, but he clung tighter, grovelling and whimpering with terror, as he felt the revolver's muzzle pressed against his scalp.

Then just as suddenly, revulsion swept over Peplow, the horror of a small boy on a wall watching a shrieking pig struck by its slaughterer.

"You bastard!" he hissed. "You're right. I can't do it, even to you. You're too horrible."

He paused, gasping, and turned away. Then he turned. The snuffling had stopped, a black crafty eye was watching him.

"This is all I can do, by God!" he groaned. He dragged the showman to his feet and hit with full force at his face so that he toppled over like a doll and sprawled head downwards among the empty bottles and a chamber-pot.

And then, cursing again and again, and waving his hands in helpless rage, Peplow rushed madly into the darkness.

"This has been an unusual day," said Mrs. Loatley. "Not so much what has happened but what might have happened, or may happen. There is something queer about today. I felt it when I got up. I've felt strange all day. To begin with, I thought it was the elderberries, the heavy smell; but it wasn't. It's something all around me. Maybe it's the heat; but it's not the first hot day I've seen. No, it's something else, not that."

The room had become quite dim. The bowl of white roses, the green tablecloth, the bookcase, drew away, shedding shape and colour.

"I think I'll make myself a cup of tea before I go up to Alfred again."

She left the front room and was in the passage close to the umbrella stand when the terrible pain struck like a knife in her side. Her legs crumpled and gasping for breath, she sank, her head grotesquely tilted, her tongue protruded beyond her lips.

For a moment she gave way to intense terror. I can't speak, she thought. It's a stroke. I'm lying here like an old coat fallen from its peg.

And so she was, a dark bundle of clothes scarcely distinguishable from the floor in the gathering darkness.

Who'll care for him now, she thought fearfully, who'll care for him? The knowledge of her helplessness flooded over her and she began to whimper.

Far away, or so it seemed, she heard the hurdy-gurdy's sound and, nearer, someone knocking again and again. Is it her? she wondered. Is it her?

In the main avenue of the Feast, the crowds surging round him, Peplow was shouldered and nudged aimlessly along like a log in a torrent, dazed, purposeless, the long barren dream over. Sometimes, he felt an agony of dismay at what he had drawn back from doing, sometimes a marvellous relaxation and lightness of spirit. Sometimes he asked himself if it had been meant to end like this or if this day, Bellenger, Ruskin, all he had seen and heard, had blunted his resolution and changed his purpose.

Then, after a time the faces and sounds around became coherent again and he pushed his way outward towards the edge of the Square and up to Herbert Ruskin's room. It was unlit, and, though for a moment he did not see the young boy standing there, he sensed that the day's tide had carried others far out with it beside himself.

Ruskin's bloated torso seemed more froglike among the shadows.

The boy looked up at him. "Hello, Mr. Peplow," he said. His startled eyes searched the man's face.

Peplow shook his head. "No," he said harshly.

"Nick says he doesn't want to go back to the house," said Ruskin.

There was a long silence.

"Oh, God!" Ruskin suddenly cried out, "and I'm his guardian."

"What!"

"The Old Man got me to agree to it three or four years ago. He didn't want him to stay with his step-sisters. Everything's settled, drawn up, money for his education, the lot! Me! Me of all people! How can I look after him?"

The hysteria in his voice was unmistakable.

"I couldn't refuse. There was more to it than that. More than even he knew." His eyes flicked across Peplow's face. Even now, he couldn't bring himself to say her name. "You know."

Peplow was trembling. The reaction, he thought. It's caught up with me. The day, the heat, that blasted organ! God, I can't take much more of this. They've got to let me alone.

He stepped back and leaned against the chest of drawers struggling to control himself.

"You know, damn you. Say so. Can't you see I'm in Hell," Ruskin shouted.

White faced, each stared at the other.

At last Peplow nodded. "I guessed," he said. "She came to see me a week or so after you were missing."

"Do you think he knew when he asked me to take on this job?"

"No."

"No?"

Peplow shook his head. "You're taking it all too seriously," he said.

"I couldn't refuse him. But now it's here, what can I do? It's impossible, Nick. You can see how it is, can't you? It's quite impossible."

The boy hung his head.

Light splashed spasmodically into the room, the faces appearing momentarily from the darkness and submerging again. No one spoke. Then Ruskin raised his voice above the outside roar. "Look at this," he cried despairingly. "Read this."

He pushed the letter at Peplow.

"Now do you see how it is? I can't cope with things. It's too late now. No, please don't switch on the light."

"She's coming here?"

"Yes."

"When?"

"Tomorrow."

Was this the focus of this extraordinary day? Not the brilliance and blare in the Square below them, nor the insane encounter under the harsh light of the caravan, but here in this room caught between alternating darkness and flashes, between long silences and bursts of feverish talk?

Tomorrow - a senseless echo. Tomorrow will be different, he thought. I'll be myself, as I used to be, the perpetual bank clerk, absolutely reliable, unquestionably trustworthy - tomorrow. Well, tomorrow's not here yet. Without turning, he pushed the unread letter on top of the chest and, concealing it behind his hand and lower arm, the revolver too.

"I'd like to take Nick home to live with us - now, tonight," he said. Nick looked swiftly at him, his eyes widening.

"Will you come, Nick? I think you're a grand little lad. My wife and I need you very much; I think you know why. You could give it a try. I think your Dad would have liked it. Will you come? There'd be a sort of bond, wouldn't there? I mean both of us remembering your father."

His eyes met Ruskin's. The boy came closer to him.

"Are you sure about it?" he asked. "Would it be all right?"

"All right! More than all right! It would be marvellous for us; we need each other."

"I'd like to come then... away from here."

"It's the right thing to do, Nick," Ruskin said in a low voice. "I'd like you; you know that. But it would be better Peplow's way. You oughtn't to stay here. Look, I know. I *know*. Switch the light on."

He groped in the drawer and opened a long envelope.

"Here's the thing your dad had drawn up. Minchin the solicitor did it for him so he can change it just as easily."

He dialled and began to speak into the telephone.

"No, it won't do tomorrow. Look, it's urgent. Yes, very! You can write it in. Yes, I know it'll have to be drawn up all over again but I want a cover note, the things they have for insurance... *A Cover Note*... to show what my intentions are."

He put down the receiver.

"He's coming round to fix it," he said. "So that's that."

Peplow and the boy looked confidently at each other and smiled.

The Rector sat on a carved box-tomb, his feet on the low wall and looked over the village. The Square was a splash of light in the dark huddle of houses and the darker, vaster darkness of the encircling plain. When he had first come to Minden this had been his favourite place. "I am watching over my parish," he used to say half-proudly, half-jokingly to guests. "Keeping in touch with both the dead and the quick." But that was in the early days when he believed that there was a place for him here, when he had seen himself as one of the people, yet keeper of the Holy Mystery.

All had changed. This hill was now a refuge, emphasising his isolation from the heart of an indifferent parish that waited to be rid of him. He peered out over the darkness's immense landscape. Familiarity filled it with the shapes of woods, doll-like farms in tiny fields, lines of willows marking the courses of streams, spires and towers punctuating the distance. The land of lost content!

He felt quite sure that, this time, Georgie had gone for ever and that, almost certainly, he would never see her again. Far towards the south he saw the long lights of the night train coming away from Gornard, probing into the dark miles of fields and woods towards the glint of green and red lamps of Minden Station, and he slowly rose and turned back into the wilderness of graves, skirting an impenetrable thicket of brambles which had obliterated a score of stones, pushing past an elderberry splitting a box-tomb, knee deep in the rank faded grass, his shoes sinking into the mat of last year's unmown crop and that of the year before. A stone blocked his way, and he shone his torch at it.

HENRY LAMB
BORN 1871.
DEPARTED THIS LIFE 1941.
'Lord Thou Knowest'

"Knowest what?" he muttered. By its side sagged another stone,

MABEL LAMB
FAITHFUL WIFE OF HENRY LAMB
BORN 1880. DIED 1930.
'Remembered'

And another and another; Lambs everywhere underfoot. Probably these modest Stuart stones, names rubbed out by three hundred years of Minden weather, marked Lambs too. And below them, unmarked except by God, medieval Lambs and Saxon Lambs.

He recalled the butcher, his stupid stubborn face, his great red slaughterer's hands thrust finger-tip down into his waistcoat pockets... "The rector allus paid for it in the years gone past. In Reverend Panter's time, folks came miles to see it. An' I've heard my old dad say it was same in Reverend Tallboy's time too. I'll not lift a finger to vote the money for it, let others do as they want..."

He felt a pulse in his temple twitching at the memory. Not a single man or woman on the Parochial Council would second his motion that the money should be allocated for the work. Some had looked at the floor, some through the windows, some stared cunningly at him. No one had spoken so that in the silence, the butcher's words seemed to echo round the room and, when they had gone, he had heard someone passing the open window, say, "Well, the gloves are off proper now - Old Lamb didn't mince his words."

Standing there in the midst of the Lambs, he felt a sudden tightening of his heart. This time they should not win. As he looked wildly about him, the lights below began to rise into the air, cascading and falling and spinning and the music of the steam-organ spiralled beside them,

Boob-a-do
You and you
Wadja gain' to do...

For a moment he thought that he was about to faint and threshed backwards into the darkness, reeling from stone to stone, crawling, running, the black shapes of yews towering above him, menacing, imprisoning.

The night was full of sounds and lights but at last, seeking refuge against the great wall of the tower, he pressed his face to the rough texture of limestone and closed his eyes. And after a time, the trembling ceased.

For a few minutes he stood there. Then, quite deliberately, sensing the flow of the night breeze, he struck a match and cupping the flame in his palm, bent down and carefully lit the tinder-dry grass.

"Why don't we just drive there in the Morris," Mr. Croser asked irritably. "After all, a car's always useful, even in the city. And anyway, how do you know we're going to stay there. We might want to move on - to Bournemouth or Brighton," he added vaguely.

"Because it isn't mine," Georgie answered. "It doesn't even belong to my husband."

"But it would be useful. You've got to admit. Why don't we just take it; anyway, who does it belong to then?"

Georgie didn't reply but opened the door and got out.

"Is that all you're taking?" she asked when Mr. Croser pulled out his fibre-card suitcase, "You don't have a very large wardrobe, do you?"

She bundled her fur coat under one arm and, picking up her own luggage, made for the station entrance and waited for him by the ticket window.

"Are you buying them or am I?" she asked.

Mr. Croser unfolded two of his four pound notes and asked for singles. The booking clerk, who knew him slightly, winked.

"Singles, ah!" he said, and looking past him at Georgie, "First or Second?"

Mr. Croser leered uncertainly. "Second," he mumbled. Out on the platform they felt the first chill of the night and Georgie buttoned her leather coat.

"You'd better put yours on too," she said.

Mr. Croser saw himself in the curious eyes of the travellers, taxi-drivers, hotel-receptionists, they would encounter and chose to leave his thin, cheap raincoat rammed in the suitcase.

"I'm warm enough," he muttered.

"We'll have to buy you an overcoat. You can't wear that macintosh you're hiding, all year round. It's past its best anyway."

It's not too late, thought Mr Croser. I'm not good enough, neither me nor my macintosh already, and we've not left Minden even. Eff wouldn't have said a thing like that; I was Somebody to her. Why am I doing this?

She'll be waiting for me now. I had my feet well under the table there. This one, she's just using me because it happens to suit her. She'll leave me just as soon as look at me when one of her own set takes her fancy, someone with enough dough to buy her things and fix her up in a posh flat. I don't know why I got myself mixed up with her. She just isn't my sort. I could never take her home like I could have taken Eff. She'd laugh at Mam and Dad. She's ashamed of me already. I don't think she really cares a ha'porth for me except for what she has to have and I don't think she cares who gives her that. I might as well be a black man.

He bitterly mulled over his fascinating captivity.

"You're quiet all of a sudden," Georgie said. "Isn't it marvellous getting away for ever from this ghastly place!"

Mr. Croser tried to feel the marvel but felt only regrets at memories of egg-and-chip suppers at Effie's, with hot encounters on the sitting-room sofa as dessert, regret for the safety of the well-charted shallows he was so crazily abandoning for the hazards of the deep. The realisation of his miserable plight utterly depressed him.

"Isn't it?" she insisted. "Isn't it terrific?"

"Yes," he muttered. "It's terrific."

Peplow looked ostentatiously at his watch.

"I'm afraid we ought to be going, Rusky," he said.

Ruskin nodded.

"But I'll be back to see you in a couple of weeks to clear up everything. That solicitor will want to see me again, I suppose."

There was an uneasy pause.

"Did you get all the things Nick wanted? Sisters say anything much?"

"They were quite helpful, considering everything," Peplow answered. "They said that they'd miss him. Who wouldn't?" He looked across at Nick and grinned. "But they felt that it was a jolly good idea bearing in mind his father's wishes and considering your own feelings about it. I told them that my wife will keep in touch with them and let them know how things go. Still like the idea, Nick?"

The boy smiled and nodded.

"Well, I suppose we really ought to leave if we're going to catch that train. Will you wait for me downstairs, Nick; I want a private word…"

When the boy had gone, he tapped the revolver with his forefinger. "I see you've found it. It is yours. I hung on to it when I checked in your gear. Pray have it back with the compliments of the Air Ministry; if you don't like it around, you can always hand it in at the local police-station, or give it to the next White Elephanters who call. But mind you unload it first."

"You're a queer devil, Peplow."

"Am I? Well at this minute I'm a very happy devil too."

"Nick told me about you, meeting you among the stalls I mean. He said that you told him he could. The police had been here already, anyway. I didn't tell them a thing, but I guessed which chap you were after."

"My wife must have guessed too: I had a feeling that she knew about this."

He tapped the revolver. "Anyway, he wasn't worth it. I must have been completely off my rocker to have ever reached this stage."

He laughed.

"You knew about me and Bellenger - and her, didn't you? What happened?"

Peplow nodded.

"You wouldn't like to talk about it, would you?"

"Not particularly. Not now. I've had about enough for one day."

"I suppose you have," Ruskin said heavily. "Sometimes I think there's a pattern to things and sometimes I think that there isn't - just a crazy mess. If only we could have our time again."

He turned his unhappy eyes away, swinging his chair towards the open window once more.

"In about a fortnight then?"

"Peplow - don't go for a minute!"

"Yes?"

[He saw her again, the dark wisp of hair, heard the rain rattling in the trees, felt her heavy body straining against him, remembered the ominous feeling of finality.]

"Never mind..."

"Things'll sort themselves out," Peplow said. "They always do. Just hang on. You'll see."

A moment later Ruskin heard the street door close behind them.

The darkness in the lane was heavy with the smell of elderberry flowers overhanging Mrs. Loatley's crumbling wall and, for Effie waiting beneath it in the shadows, it was the smell of Passion.

"Like magnolias," she thought, hearing the heavy waves... ("the heavy scented waves," she substituted) beating on a tropic shore and her, a single blossom in her hair (black not blonde) being carried victoriously towards his hut of reeds by an incredibly bronzed Mr. Croser, naked to the waist and garlanded.

Her shoes nipped.

Why does he go on at me if I wear strollers, she thought, prising one bruised foot from the stiletto-heeled traps and pleasurably rubbing its toes on the back of the other ankle, but she vaguely knew that it was something to do with Mr. Croser's conception of Passion.

"Like this awful skirt," she thought rebelliously, trying to ease her stomach in its barathea sheath.

When they were married there were going to be one or two changes. She would indulge him by wearing a housecoat and pyjamas for breakfast but, after that, she would dress to suit herself... No more high heels and skin-tight dresses.

And he was late. Later than his usual ten minutes. She lifted her wrist but it was too dark to see the watch's dial. The scent of elderberry stirred in the flurry of breeze which flapped her silk coat against her thighs and the minutes passed.

He's not coming, she thought and, all at once, she knew that it was true this time. He was not coming.

Boob-a-do
You and You
Wadja gain' to do...

The tipsy song rose to a final blare, and stopped. In the following unnatural silence, she heard, far away, the night train theatrically straining along the line from Gornard.

It's going to rain tomorrow, she thought, and a pair of fat tears welled and rolled down her cheeks.

He's finished with me, she thought. I'm not good enough for him. He's thrown me over. What will they say at home?

Somehow she had to find him and get him back.

Moaning and whimpering like a lost child she pulled the coat across against her breasts and began to hobble through the Square.

Winter should be the sad season, thought Herbert Ruskin pushing aside the book of verse. Winter, bare trees, dark woods, streets under snow, an iron sky; not summer, not a night like this when the lanes are choked with growth and life. Not a night like this, screaming like a cat in the dark...

He twisted the letter in his pocket.

"I still feel the same..."

Bitterness suffused his mutilated body and he swayed uncontrollably from side to side.

"I won't let you hide away any longer. I need you. I shall never be happy without you..."

Oh God, he thought. Why did it have to happen? Why did only Mullett have to burn? Why did the clever devils have to salvage me?

"I shall come on the earliest train..."

He imagined her emerging hesitantly into the Square almost before the early morning mist had cleared, as Peplow had done. The stone horseman - and her!

I can't face it, he thought, I can't bear it.

[She was tall and cool in a print dress and they stood in the orchard of the house at the end of the lane, laughing as Bellenger fiddled with the box camera. That was the day when he knew that he really wanted her.]

He wheeled himself to the wardrobe and opened it. Above him, the slate-blue tunic, the faded mauve and silver ribbon, the two rings at the sleeves, the stain across the chest and one sleeve... his own blood or Mullett's?

"There's so much I want to see and hear about - all the people you have written about. I feel that I know them all. If only you knew how I have longed for this day to come..."

Ruskin looked back across to where the lights reeled above the raucous confusion... *"the people you have written about"*! They were all going their several ways, not gay as he had made them seem but secret and dark, confused, groping, despairing... He glanced again at the verse he had been reading

> *For the world which seems*
> *To lie before us like a land of dreams…*
> *…Hath really neither joy nor love, nor light,*
> *Nor certitude, nor peace, nor help for pain…*

He felt the words writhing on the page and his eyes darkened, his big hands clenching on the chair's arms. Above him, on the hill, something had caught fire, the flames lighting the black bulk of stone.

> "*…nor peace, nor help for pain.*
> *And we are here as on a darkling plain,*
> *Swept with confused alarms of struggle and flight…*"

he muttered, his agonised face sinking to his chest, scarcely noticing the din trail into silence and the lights on the stalls and sideshows going out or that, after a time, the Square was dark and empty and the Feast over. But his day was not finished yet.

The young showman and Mrs. Thickness came out of The Fusilier, dawdled down the footpath and stopped beneath the open window.

"I'll just slip away for a few things an' then I'll be back. Wait for me in the caravan," she said.

But the man placed his hand hard against the wall and pressed her back. Then he pushed his body against hers and began to kiss her.

"Wait till we get back," she gasped. "Wait till then. There's people here know me; we're making an exhibition of ourselves. There's all night for it."

But he only tittered and pressed her more fiercely between the wall and his own body, forcing her into the crook of his elbow so that he could hold her with his right arm and fumble with his left hand.

"You funny chap," she said softly. "Why can't you wait? Oh well..." and she too began to stir and respond fiercely, their bodies twisting and bending in the darkness.

From above their heads, Herbert Ruskin peered downwards, trying to follow their movements, trembling as wave after wave of disgust, desire and blind, angry self-pity flooded over him. At last he could stand it no longer and bending farther out over the sill, he turned a powerful flash-lamp on them.

"For God's sake, clear off into your own private pit, the pair of you," he shouted thickly.

Violently startled, they sprang apart and for a moment there was no sound. Then, shielding his face from the torch beam, the young showman drawled. "I've heard tell o' thee. Thu's t'chap that watches. We could find a job for thee wi' t'Feast '*The Legless Wonder*.' Just because thu can't get it or women won't gi' it thee, it don't stop rest of us lads having it. Well then now - watch this."

He grasped the woman and forced her head back so that her startled face was transfixed in the lamp's glare.

"Now watch to thy heart's content, Midget!" he cried viciously, at the same time thrusting his own face upwards into the light.

"Good God! You!" shouted Ruskin.

Without turning from them, he fumbled along the chest of drawers and took up the revolver. Very carefully he thumbed back the safety-catch and extended his arm.

Suddenly the lamp slipped and, falling, momentarily illuminated the weapon.

Mrs. Thickness shrieked and pushed the man away and he, recovering his wits, began to run uncertainly along the lane between the deserted stalls.

Herbert Ruskin fired.

All around the Square doors were flung open and curtains thrown back.

The revolver banged a second time and the runner staggered, threw up his arms, stumbled on a pace or two towards the statue and collapsed. Still no one moved and he lay alone, trying to call for help, staring in terror at the darkening lights before him.

A third bullet struck sparks from the statue's stone pedestal but the fourth thudded into him, so that he gave a long shudder and then was still. Ruskin drew back his arm. The bitter smell of gunpowder had filled his room. Someone was hammering at the door and shouting his name.

It was all happening so swiftly now. Far off he heard the hiss of steam. For him it had an elemental sound, the long withdrawing whine of fate's backwash.

"That's the night train drawing in," he muttered. "Peplow and the boy will be waiting there - my boy. It's been a long day."

He thought of all his long days stretching from the first train until the last. In a few hours a train would begin another day and carry another intruder into his little world. But it would be a day which he could not face.

The banging on the locked door continued. His name was called again and again. The fire on the hillside had grown into a great blaze now, like that other fire at Knocke when Mullett had died and he had lived. He heard the night train begin to drag itself towards the distant city.

Herbert Ruskin lifted the heavy revolver once again, pressed it firmly to his temple and fired.

Except for the glare of the flames around the church, darkness had fallen over the hills and the great Midland plain. The day was over and couples cycling homewards between the dark hedges looked up at the immense and brilliant wheel of stars turning across the sky. A perfect day! A day to remember!

On the station platform, hand in hand, the young boy and the man waited in silence, now and then peering along the track, watching for the train's lights to appear round the curve, looking at the glittering sky, wondering at the fire on the hill. But their minds already were at the end of their journey and at a new beginning, so that Peplow scarcely noticed their fellow travellers waiting uncomfortably a little beyond them: the young expert on school toilets and the woman he had met in the cafe. He could not know that for them, for Mrs. Loatley, Miss Prosser, Effie, the Rector, Thickness and Thickness's mother, this, too, had been a day of moment.

As the train drew squealing to a stop, he heard the noisy and persistent backfire of a car somewhere in the town but he thought nothing of it as they moved off, gathering speed into the night until, looking up from the sleeping boy still clutching his china pig, and seeing again the lonely farmhouse by its chestnut tree, he smiled and closed his eyes.

The Quince Tree Press, which remains a family affair, was established by J.L. Carr as the publishing house for a series of 'Pocket Books': small selections from the great poets (but exclusively those out of copyright), idiosyncratic Dictionaries, small Histories & volumes of Fabled Saying. Later a series of Wood Engravers, contemporary or near contemporary, were added. The hand-drawn, poster-sized historical County Maps completed the early productions that together funded the self-employment which, in part, enabled the novels to be written.

The first six novels were initially published by traditional publishing houses, but as they went out of print the rights were reacquired and *QTP* editions produced. The last two novels 'H&F' and 'Hetty' were produced entirely in-house. An author's desire to be independent of the frustrations and irritations of the regular publishing world was probably the incentive, but it developed into a positive pleasure in the design and production of a high quality volume complementary to the text - there is a degree of unconventionality about all the productions.

The Novels, Pocket Books and Maps continue to be published by us and are available directly from us or through good booksellers.

www.quincetreepress.co.uk

A Season in Sinji

This allegory of life set around a game of cricket is set on the wartime coasts of West Africa; and played out amongst the men of a flying-boat squadron.

"This whole business from start to end, was like a game of cricket, the issue never sure, who'd win, who'd lose, and who'd just watch… and go away!" - Flanders, an RAF photographer, whose idea of fair play is shattered by Turton, an officer but no gentleman. Turton sets out to take from people what they most want, self-esteem, success, the final on the dusty cricket square, even Caroline, the girl both Flanders and his friend Wakerley fall for. But all is not fair, even in love and war…

This is the best of the novels　　　　　　　　　　　　　　　　　　　　J.L. Carr

The best cricket based novel I have read, an analogy is drawn between the way one has to wait, both in life and in the game, for one's fortune to change…
　　　　　　　　　　　　　　　　　　　　　　　Matthew Engel, The Guardian

This is probably the most persuasive, humorous and knowledgeable account of cricket in existence. In so far as it is a cricket novel, it is the best I have read. But it is also a story of exile, and of unhappiness, nastiness and tragedy.
　　　　　　　　　　　　　　　　　　　Martin Seymour Smith, The Spectator

There is a blasting passion and, when the novel expands itself to receive the final notes of tragedy, it does so with a cunning that recalls the game at its best.
　　　　　　　　　　　　　　　　　　　　　　　William Trevor, The Guardian

The Harpole Report

George Harpole is in his first term as Acting Head of Tampling St Nicholas Primary School. Determined to climb the career ladder the way ahead seems clear to teaching success. Little does he imagine that he'll be hampered by his honesty, fair mindedness, and a genuine liking for the children in his care (and then there are his fellow teachers to consider). They all contribute to his downfall, or at least to the point where iron enters his soul…

"The idea was to write a sort of text book for teachers and to tell parents more about what goes on in primary schools. And there is just about everything here - free meals, hymn-singing, caretakers, the New Maths, school visits, log-books, etc. etc. But Emma Foxberrow got out of hand and perhaps not so many readers take it seriously as about education. But some do and it has been said that all teachers whilst training should read it …Any way it was all I wanted to say about a job I did for 9 years before the war and for 21 years after it." J.L. Carr

I was a teacher for fourteen years and am often wary of novels about teaching, especially if I'm assured that they are going to be funny. Because they often aren't. The Harpole Report, however, is not only the funniest book about teaching that I've ever read; it's also the funniest book - about anything - that I've read in a long time. Roddy Doyle

The funniest and perhaps the truest story about running a school that I have ever read. Frank Muir

Harpole remains quite the best book on the English School System. Brilliantly observed by a battle scarred veteran of the front line!
Kenneth Baker, Secretary of State for Education

How Steeple Sinderby Wanderers Won the FA Cup

More than just a book about football; this tale of the village team's ultimate success wryly observes the idiosyncrasies of rural life, the unique personalities therein and the power of ambition.

"Book-writing can be a tedious job needing some incentive to keep one at it. The impulse here was 'can this unbelievable feat be made to sound like the truth even though it didn't happen?' So I stacked the cards - a foreigner with remarkable theories, two young men with good reasons for having quit top-class football, a Chairman of Napoleonic ability.

Then I dredged up memories of 1930 when I was an unqualified teacher, 18 years old and playing that single season for South Milford White Rose when we won a final which never ended. (Pitch invasion and furious fights are not new things.) I learnt much of life during that long-gone autumn, winter and early spring… But is this story believable? Ah, it all depends upon whether you *want* to believe it." J.L. Carr

A strange and funny novel that, by not really being about football, gets to the heart of football's elegiac nature.
Jonathan Wilson, FSA Football Writer of the Year

This book is a truly wonderful curiosity, as real as it is fantastical. Most people would be satisfied with writing either a comic masterpiece or a dazzling social history. J.L.Carr did both at once. Brilliantly funny, heartrendingly wistful, and totally mad. Marina Hyde, Sports Journalist of the Year

One of the greatest football novels ever written. D.J. Taylor, The Guardian

A Month in the Country

A poignant tale of missed moments, love and discovery; set at the close of the Great War and enacted amongst a Yorkshire village community beneath the slowly unveiled mystery in the mediaeval wall-paintings of the church.

"During any prolonged activity one tends to forget original intentions. But I believe that, when making a start on *A Month in the Country*, my idea was to write an easy-going story, a rural idyll along the lines of Thomas Hardy's *Under the Greenwood Tree*. And, to establish the right tone of voice to tell such a story, I wanted its narrator to look back regretfully across forty or fifty years but, recalling a time irrecoverably lost, still feel a tug at the heart.

Novel-writing can be a cold-blooded business. One uses whatever happens to be lying around in memory, and employs it to suit one's ends. The visit to the dying girl, a first sermon, the Sunday-school treat, a day in a harvest field and much more happened between the Pennine Moors and the Yorkshire Wolds. But the church in the fields is in Northamptonshire, its churchyard in Norfolk, its vicarage London. All's grist that comes to the mill."
J.L.Carr

The book I keep coming back to, it's one of the best books I've ever read. I've never met anyone who didn't love it.
Richard Osman

Reading it I thought: this is just astonishing.
Miles Jupp

…as close to perfection as it is possible to get.
Benjamin Myers

Winner of the Guardian Fiction Prize
& Shortlisted for the Booker Prize 1980

THE BATTLE OF POLLOCKS CROSSING

The story is told by an Englishman who, fifty years earlier, had taught for a single year in drought ravaged Dakota. Like many an English lad, George Gidner had a deep infatuation with the Wild West, when at twenty-five the chance came to spend a year teaching High School in the middle of South Dakota he grabbed it.

Though he upset the establishment and lost his job, George had his fair share of admirers, from teenager Becky, to his landlord, Henry Farewell, manager of the Settler's Bank and hero of the Battle. The battle at the crossing forms the climax of this tale of pioneering spirit; underlying all, however, is a warning that, although we technically share a language, the Americans may be disturbingly different.

"In 1938 it took me seven days to reach the prairie town where I had contracted to teach in its high school for a twelvemonth. An eight year drought had not ended, there had been bank-crashes: deserted quarter-sections could be bought merely by paying off back taxes. I found folk unfailingly friendly, helpful and kind, yet, at the year's end the United States still seemed to me a very foreign land. Plainly there was something about the Americas which I had failed to fathom and, in this story, I have tried to hint at this unease."   J.L. Carr

It reconstructs a distant and dust-shrouded world, then sets it echoing with an outburst of violence.   Peter Kemp, Sunday Times

J.L.Carr is a wholly original writer and he has written a lovely book quite unlike any other.   Nina Bawden

Shortlisted for the Booker Prize 1985

WHAT HETTY DID

An eighteen year-old Sixth Form girl tells what happened to her when she left her Fenland home determined never to return.

Hetty is a spirited, intellectual girl, sustained by English literature in her struggles against a brutish home life (bullying fox-terrier of a father, timid and downtrodden mother, and nasty little brother eager for her downfall to spare his own hide). Apart from school friends her favoured companions are Keats and Browning.

When she discovers that she was in fact adopted, Hetty runs away from home, in search of her real parents. She finds shelter in Rose Gilpin-Jones' boarding house in Birmingham, where there are eccentric lodgers (including Emma Foxberrow from the Harpole Report). She experiences a wider world of ethics, music hall and mass demonstrations, and after many tribulations finds her root-stock (but maybe prefers to flower elsewhere).

His last novel brims with unusual optimism as well as his customary wit. For an author of 72 to have invented such a credible teenage girl is remarkable; What Hetty Did is like the first breath of spring. Amanda Craig, Sunday Express

This book, generally so witty, so vivacious and so original, is a gem.
Francis King, The Spectator

HARPOLE AND FOXBERROW GENERAL PUBLISHERS

J.L. Carr re-unites George Harpole with Emma Foxberrow (after their school-teaching confrontations in *The Harpole Report*) in a new venture to run a publishing business. With an inherited back-list of unpromising titles, their fortunes seemingly improve when they take on the pot-boiler romances of little known author Grace Pintle. Her nomination for the Big Britlit Prize, a shock in itself, sets off a train of surprises.

Himself a short-listed author for the Booker Prize in 1980 and 1985, J.L. Carr experienced the hype surrounding the novelist, the Big Lit prizes, and the daily round of the author-publisher.

The firm's beginning was accidental, its progress haphazard, its end hastened by spiritual ennui… This is a book about books and the business of books… the characters can be… moody, unreliable and bothersome, whereas books have body, and always will say what they said before. Or stay silent when you shut them up.

It is as accomplished, as entertaining and as funny as anything its author has done. D.J. Taylor, The Spectator